MW01102568

Contents

part one

Paul:
1958

1

Winnipeg, Manitoba, Canada
Saturday, June 21, 1958

It's morning. I've slept alone for the last time.

A cool breeze blows through the screen and the venetian blind taps against the window frame. I hear a metallic clicking sound: Dad must be outside, lopping off branches with his clippers. Or maybe he's levelling the quack grass around my brother's amateur-radio aerial tower. Why doesn't he take an axe to that tower, now that Greg doesn't live here anymore?

After today, I won't be living here anymore, either.

Catherine pops into my head: her long, dark brown hair, her blue eyes, her lips, her fragrance. Her body. I think of the chaste kiss I gave her last night at her door. I didn't linger. She wouldn't let me. It's bad luck to be together after midnight the night before the Big Day.

I swing my legs off the bed and sit up, facing my shelf of big-little-books. *Smokey Stover, the Foolish Foo Fighter* catches my eye. I've decided not to take my big-little-books with me, but can I leave *Smokey Stover* behind? Maybe I'll take this one, hide it in my suitcase—with the safes.

I stand and bend down to open the bottom drawer of my dresser. It contains a lot of clothing I never wear anymore: long underwear, scarves, draped trousers. This is the one drawer I'm sure my mother never opens. It's where I've stashed my gross of safes. Since the clinical side of life is never discussed in our house, except if someone gets sick, you have to tuck away items like this. I shove my hand under the underwear to be sure the package is still there. It is.

Buying the safes wasn't easy. The drug stores keep them behind the counter and I couldn't imagine myself walking up to the clerk and saying, "A gross of Sheiks, please." It'd be like saying: "Stick the

9

money in this bag and don't say a word." In either case, my voice would crack. So when the doctor who gave me my blood test asked if I wanted a birth control device, I said Yes, and he wrote out a prescription for me. I carried that piece of paper in a secret part of my wallet as if it was a pass to some exotic sex club.

For weeks, I sauntered past drug stores, hesitating at the door. I never considered the ones in my neighbourhood, where I might see someone I knew. I went to stores on downtown streets like Sherbrook and Sargent. But when I went in, I turned chicken. I couldn't make it to the prescription counter at the back. I ended up buying a magazine or a chocolate bar.

At last—this was two days ago and the pressure was on—I found the perfect place for my transaction: the pharmacy in the Medical Arts Building, where they sell only pharmaceutical products. The druggist was a man who wore a starched white smock, and he looked old and wise and inscrutable. I handed him my prescription without saying a word. He went away and came back with my package wrapped in plain brown paper, and he gave it to me without raising an eyebrow. Ahh, I thought as I paid him, the man's a professional.

Then there was the matter of trying one on. Here I was, twenty-three, a college graduate, and I'd never had reason to use one before. When I got home, my purchase hidden in my brief case, I locked myself in the bathroom. Just the thought of putting one on made me ready. I took off the outside wrapper and found a white box. Inside the box were rows of small grey boxes. I opened the lid of one and there were three little yellow envelopes. This process reminded me of those Russian dolls—you opened one up only to find another one inside. I took out one of the envelopes and felt the slight, circular bulk of its contents. I opened the flap. There was the "rubber", as my friend Steve calls them, all rolled up around itself.

After a few false starts, I had the safe half-unrolled and not on and impossible to roll up again. I hated to waste them this way. Why didn't they give you printed instructions? I tried another. This time, I got some skin twisted into the rubber. It hurt. No more success with a third. There were only one hundred and forty-one left.

Here it is, the morning of the Big Day, and I'm none too confident about the birth control end of things. I take an envelope out of the box, slip it into my pyjama pocket, and shut the dresser drawer.

"Paul!" my mother calls from the kitchen. "Ready for your breakfast?"

"Going to bath and shave first. About half an hour?"

"Better not be any more than that. We've all got lots to do."

I go into the bathroom and start the water. We have no shower and I like a deep tubful. I push down my pyjama bottoms and step out of them. Our bathroom has only one mirror, a small one on the medicine cabinet door, above the sink. Pretending to be the Don Juan I hope to be tonight, I hum a striptease tune and watch myself peel off my pyjama jacket. Artfully, I drop it to the floor. This puts me in the mood. The safe rolls on beautifully. I'm impressed. I step into the bathtub wearing it.

2

t w o

It's nearly two and a half years since Catherine Barber and I met. I'd seen her at school many times before that. She was a grade behind me, in the same classroom as my friend, The Shark. It was The Shark who first told me about her. He pointed her out at one of the dances— a radiant beauty gliding past in the arms of some suave guy who knew all the steps. The Shark talked about her all the time, but we both saw her as someone outside our circle, a classy girl who went out with older guys that drove their own cars. Later, I heard she went to university, but I never saw her there.

Along came the Winnipeg Little Theatre production of Noel Coward's one-act play, *Still Life*. My mother pointed out the audition ad in the *Tribune*. She knew my social life wasn't much—couple of nights drinking beer every week with The Shark and Steve, and sometimes Allan. I was a Bachelor of Commerce working in a trust company, but I had no girl friends. Over the years, I'd made Mom laugh with my recitations and my mimicking and she thought I should be an actor. To humour her, I went out on a blustery January night to the University of Manitoba Broadway campus classroom where the try-outs were taking place. Each of the hopefuls had to read a few lines on a sheet handed out by the director, a middle-aged dynamo named Mason Pilcer. The leads had already been cast, but there were five other parts for men and exactly five guys showed up. I got the role of Johnny, an English soldier who stumbles into a train station cafe with a pal and provides some comic relief after an intensive scene between the two main characters.

I didn't meet Catherine at the auditions. She didn't appear until the fourth rehearsal, held among the musty props backstage at the Dominion Theatre. The experienced actress originally playing Beryl Waters had been called out of town, and Pilcer replaced her with Catherine. Having got used to a short, impudent Beryl, I saw the tall, slender, dignified Catherine Barber as something of an impostor.

12

Beryl, a waitress in the cafe, needs to have an air of sassy servitude, a likeable working-class manner. She should dominate or fade into the woodwork as a scene requires. With her long brown hair, her blue eyes and her creamy complexion, Catherine seemed too regal. Besides, she hadn't memorized her lines. I found out later that she'd got the part because Pilcer knew her father.

Pilcer called for my soldier-partner and me to do our scene. We executed it perfectly, and Catherine laughed at every line. When we made our exit, she applauded. Before the end of the rehearsal, it struck me that I should ask her out for coffee. Normally, I wouldn't have had the nerve, but we were suddenly peers, and I wanted to approach her before someone else did.

"I'd love to," she said, "but Mr. Pilcer promised Daddy he'd see me home. Listen, I think your scene is really funny."

"Oh, thanks," I said. "Well, maybe after Sunday's rehearsal we could . . ."

"Sure, if I'm still in the play by then. Wasn't I *terrible?*"

By Sunday, she had memorized her lines, but Pilcer kept hounding her to move and speak more quickly. She could be animated enough when she wasn't acting, but when she played Beryl, she turned wooden. She was taller and lovelier than the woman who was playing Laura, the lead, and that seemed wrong.

"Do you think I'll ever be a Beryl?" she asked me in the coffee shop afterward.

"Of course," I lied. My last date had been five weeks before with a girl who thought the famous actor, Charles Laughton, was a wrestler. I was happy Catherine and I had something we could talk about. "You'll see. All of a sudden, the gestures will come naturally."

"I could be an actress if I put my heart into it. But Daddy wants me to finish my Arts degree and go into his business."

Her dad owned two medium-sized hotels, but I didn't learn any more about that at the time. We talked mostly about the play. I had my dad's car with me and she let me drive her home, but she jumped out of the car before I could offer to walk her to the door.

On dress rehearsal night, the two leads snapped at Catherine for missing cues. I tried to cheer her up on the way home, telling her I thought everyone was on edge. I told her bad dress rehearsals were a good omen. Perhaps out of gratitude, she lingered in the car outside her house and, when I moved close to her, she turned her face toward me. But this was winter, and I wore a heavy double-breasted overcoat with the wide lapels turned up. In our eagerness, we both kissed my right lapel.

The play went well. With continuous prodding from Pilcer, we actors showed pin-point timing. I paced up and down until my cue-line, and my partner and I barged onto the stage, singing *Roll Out the Barrel*, and there I was, facing the footlights for the first time, a soldier in an English railway station wanting a drink. What a relief, to be out there at last, being watched and appreciated, suddenly becoming real after a month of dreaming, hearing the lines rush out of my mouth as if I was thinking them up on the spot. After our scene, I watched the rest of the play from the wings. I loved the odd sensation of seeing both sides of an absolute dividing line, the back curtain. I could see the actors on stage and the actors and the technical crew backstage, two separate worlds transcended at precisely timed moments. I saw Catherine receiving last-minute instructions from Pilcer, then going out there and bringing Beryl to life as if she'd been performing the part for years.

"You were great!" Pilcer told her at the cast party.

"You *were* great," I said, in my dad's car much later.

Chuckling, she turned down my overcoat lapels. We were both a bit tipsy, but this time we made perfect contact. I've got to remember this, I thought, how it feels, the softness of her lips, so that I can describe it to The Shark.

He had come to see the play, the only one of my friends to do so. He stayed behind afterward, hoping to get to talk with Catherine, but she was too busy with her parents and friends, and, if she noticed The Shark, she didn't let on. I accepted his congratulations and then the cast was off to our party.

The next time I went to the beer parlour with Steve and The Shark, I sat back smugly and listened to them brag about their latest escapades. Steve talked about being with twins in a trailer at Clear Lake. The Shark, who was weirdly gifted with numbers and who had gone to work for an insurance company right after high school, talked about feeling up a secretary in the office vault. There was a pause and then I dropped my bombshell.

"I french-kissed Catherine Barber."

"B.S.," Steve scoffed.

The Shark looked shocked. "When?" he asked.

I told him when and where. By then, we'd drunk several beers, and I thought his scowl was a drunken leer. But he was angry.

"How could you?" he said.

"Yeah, Hodges," said Steve. "What is this, cutting The Shark's grass?"

"Wait a minute," I said. "Who says she's—"

"You know he's had the hots for her since high school."

"I wanted you to introduce me after the play," said The Shark, "let me renew acquaintances. You said she was too busy."

He stood up and his chair fell over. He looked like he might take a swing at me. A waiter came over quickly to step between us if he had to, but The Shark made a bee-line for the door. Steve went out after him, leaving me to pay our bill.

I didn't care. I was in the big leagues now. Let those guys suffer with their childish jealousy.

I phoned Catherine the next day and she told me Pilcer was thinking of putting the play on again. When we ran out of things to say, I asked her if she'd go out with me.

"Oh, I'd love to, Paul," she said, "but I'm going steady."

"I don't understand," I said.

"It's simple, isn't it? I'm going steady with this fellow at university."

"Where was he on the night of the play?"

"He had to miss it—he was writing a term paper."

"But . . . the way you . . . after the play…I—"

"You kissed me. Or rather, I kissed you. I was thanking you for all you did for me in the play— "

"But I thought—"

" —and the times you gave me a lift home. We can still be friends, can't we?"

I was stunned. After we'd said our goodbyes, I plunged into my work, phoning investment dealers to buy stocks and bonds for the pension funds under my control.

A few days later, I phoned The Shark and told him we'd been friends too long to let a girl come between us. I told him what had happened. He was glad I'd called and he suggested we get together with Allan and Steve for a few beers that night. He was amazingly cheerful when we met at the St. Vital Hotel. All three of them laughed long and loud at my misfortune.

"I'll bet you never kissed her at all," said Steve.

"Oh, come off it," I said.

"I'll bet you five bucks you didn't."

"How am I supposed to prove it?"

"You phone her. I'll listen in. If she says you did, I'll give you five bucks."

"Steve, grow up."

"Come on," said The Shark. "I'll give you five bucks too."

"You don't believe me either?"

We rolled out of the beer parlour and found a phone booth in the hotel. Allan and The Shark waited outside while Steve wedged in beside me. I dialled the number.

"Hello?"

"Catherine, hi," I said. "It's Paul Hodges."

"Oh, hi," she said.

"Catherine, this may sound strange but I've got this bet with some friends. If you vouch for the fact that I kissed you, they'll each pay me five dollars."

"Is that all you—"

"They're pretty cheap."

"I mean, is that the only reason you called?"

"No—well, yes, but—"

"I thought maybe you'd heard the news."

"What news?"

"Ray and I broke up."

"Really? Just a minute . . ."

I gave the phone to Steve and told him to keep her talking. I bolted out, past a bewildered Shark and out of the hotel and I drove my dad's car down St. Mary's Road to Kingston Row and down Kingston Row to her parents' house. Her father came to the door, a tall, solidly built man with thin brown hair, greying sideburns and a mustache.

"I think Catherine's on the phone," he said. "May I ask who you are?"

"Remember Johnny in the play that Catherine was in? That was me. Paul Hodges."

"Of course! I didn't recognize you without your English accent. We enjoyed you and your partner. Come in. I'll see if she's off the phone."

I stepped inside, out of the chilly April evening. Mr. Barber disappeared through an arch. All I could see was the vestibule and a hall, but the floor seemed carpeted everywhere. A minute later, Catherine came into the hall in a white blouse and a plaid skirt. My knees weakened at the sight of her.

"I thought you'd never get here," she said. "I was beginning to know your friend Steve better than you."

"Can you come out for coffee?"

"It's late. Why don't you come in and I'll make some. My mother wants to hear you do Johnny again."

I did some of the lines from the play for Mrs. Barber and she and Catherine laughed all over again. I parlayed that accent into a full-fledged date with Catherine (we went to see Ernest Borgnine in *Marty*) and then another. I helped her study for her exams, and she invited me to Convocation to see her receive her Bachelor of Arts degree. We both liked dancing and movies and just sitting around talking about everything from Plato and William Makepeace Thackeray to stocks and bonds. Her parents invited me for Sunday dinners (seldom did they let me get past dessert without delivering the line Catherine liked best, "We're soldiers, we are—willing to lay down our lives for you", in a Cockney dialect), and I played ping pong after dinner with Catherine's younger brothers, Wally and Gord.

Mr. Barber often had to go to check on one of his hotels in the evening, and sometimes he took Mrs. Barber with him. On those occasions, Catherine and I would sit in the basement room, watching TV or chatting in front of the fireplace, but Gord or Wally was usually around. Wally was a seventeen-year-old bookworm who read in the room we were in, while Gord at fifteen had a continuous stream of friends over. But, when we were left alone, we made the most of it. Catherine liked necking as much as I did. I'd get really heated up and she'd fetch a cool facecloth and gently dab my face.

Things really began to move fast. We swam at Winnipeg Beach, rode our bikes over to Assiniboine Park, went to a lot of movies. One August evening, Catherine and I drove out to Lockport, a town about twenty miles north of the city. We found a place to park in a row of steamed-up cars facing the Red River, an area below the locks where people fish. We necked until our windows turned opaque and she moved my hand onto the front of her sweater. I felt her breast for the first time. The sweater was a thin one and I could feel the shape of her bra.

17

"Will you go steady with me?" I whispered.

"Yes," she answered, pushing herself into my astonished palm.

There was a time when I would've reported this milestone to Allan, Steve and The Shark. But I hadn't seen them for a long while. I was sure they were mad at me, and who needed them anyway?

Catherine became manager in the coffee shop of one of her dad's hotels. Since that involved evenings, I enrolled in a night course in Sociology. Winter set in. I picked her up after work, we went out as often as we could, and we necked when we had the chance. I touched her bosom only occasionally, and it was always the same breast—the left one—as if I was saving the other for some magical future time.

Valentine's Day found us alone in the Barber house. The Barbers had driven down to Minneapolis and taken the boys with them. I was reading my Soc textbook on the basement room sofa while Catherine worked at the desk on some food orders.

"I've had it," she said, tossing her pencil down and stretching her arms above her head.

She came over and knelt beside me. She kissed me full on the mouth. Her face felt feverish. She sent one hand through my open collar down over the warm flesh of my back.

"We're all alone," she murmured.

"Yes."

"We could go all the way."

"Yes."

"But we won't."

"I love you, Cath."

"I love you."

I felt my control slipping a little. We started going to church together and I channelled some of my fervour into lusty hymn-singing. But once the snow was gone, I could no longer endure this cloistered existence. With the coming of the warm weather, the wide open spaces beckoned. I suggested to Catherine that we needed to get to know our province better. Every Saturday, we could pick a destination, drive there, have a picnic and come home. She liked the idea, and the look in her eyes told me she knew exactly what I was talking about. In the process of exploring Manitoba, we were going to explore each other.

The first week, we took the Austin I'd bought from my brother and went to Carman, only fifty miles from Winnipeg. We found a tree-lined park beside the fair grounds and ate the lunch Catherine had packed. I took some photographs of Catherine and then we tumbled into the back seat of the Austin and necked in broad daylight. The pink cotton T-shirt Catherine was wearing rode half-way up her solar plexis. I kissed the exposed flesh. As her fingers played in my hair, I laid my cheek against her chest. She hugged my head.

"You're burning," she said.

"I love you," I said.

I slid my hand under her T-shirt and felt the lacy detail of her bra as I cupped my pal, the left one.

On the way home, the fan belt broke and the car engine overheated. Machine mimics man, I thought. The engine did allow us to limp home, never quite boiling over, just as I never quite lost my control despite the bubbling disturbances inside me.

The following week, we went a lot further—to the town of Ninette.

The approach to Ninette was a surprise to us; we had always thought Manitoba was endlessly flat, only starting to roll as you reached the Saskatchewan border. We were driving along through the grain fields when, abruptly, we came to a point where the road seemed to stop on the edge of a cliff. Far below was the town and a shimmering lake. What a pleasant shock! But not equal to the sensation later when, on a blanket spread in a wheat field near Wawanesa, I ventured under Catherine's T-shirt and into her bra to discover the warmth and the smooth texture of the hillock I'd been fondling from outside her clothing for so long.

And so the summer of 1957 progressed:

In the sandhills of Grand Beach, early in the morning before the brats arrived with their sandpails and their parents and before the teen-agers arrived to bury each other, splash each other and chase each other, I approached her left breast from the top, reaching into her bathing suit and marvelling at the pliable stiffness of an erect nipple.

At twilight on a back road near Gretna and the American border, with a wind blowing topsoil and tumbleweed at the car, I ran my hand over the taut cotton fabric that covered her fine, firm buttocks.

On a bed of pine needles between McCreary and Riding Mountain National Park, where we could see a peak that in our minds rivalled the Rockies, I gently pushed up one side of her bra and touched my lips to the lovely pink tip of Mount Left One.

Between swatting horseflies and running from a garter snake near

Moose Lake, I loosened the waistband of her chinos enough to allow my hand onto the incredible curve of her bare behind.

One evening, after a day of hiking over the rocky terrain of that part of the Canadian Shield known as The Whiteshell, we ate sandwiches and drank Cokes and dangled our feet over the side of a secluded dock on West Hawk Lake, and I slid my fingers down the front of her chinos, a couple of inches below her navel.

In an uninhabited clearing overlooking the mouth of the mighty Winnipeg River, source of so much of our hydro-electric power, I folded back the skirt she wore for this occasion and felt the unbelievably smooth softness of her inner thighs.

Parked precariously on dry reeds by the Delta marsh, I reached far enough into her chinos to touch the edge of the soft tangled brush on *her* delta.

Now, whenever I thought of the map of Manitoba, it took on the shape of a woman's torso in semi-profile, from neck to upper thigh, with the jut of the north-eastern border forming the outline of her left breast and Winnipeg situated roughly where her private parts would be.

Through all the heated explorations, Catherine remained fairly passive, but, at last, in a schoolyard in Moosehorn, long after sundown, when we should've been headed home, she unzipped me and did several weeks of exploring in a few minutes.

"It must be terribly crowded in there," she said.

"It is."

"Let's let it get a bit of fresh air, for a change."

"Cath—I love you."

"It seems incredible that all of that could fit inside of me. It hurts me just to look at it."

"It's not *that* big—"

"Paul?"

"Yes?"

"It's important to you that we don't . . . isn't it?"

"Of course."

"Good."

"But, Cath?"

"Mmm?"

"Would you marry me?"

"Oh, yes, Paul."

"*Soon?*"

Soon! I think, as I dry myself and flush the safe down the toilet. It is now ten months later. Catherine agreed to "soon", but our ideas of what soon meant differed wildly. I had in mind a fall wedding, but Catherine laughed at that. Didn't I know how much planning went into a wedding? We'd have to wait at least ten months, she said, to prove we were getting married because we wanted to, not because we had to. Her mother would want a year to make all the preparations—after all, Catherine was her only daughter. But Catherine had always wanted a June wedding, so she was confident she could talk her mother into the next June, which was ten months away—June, 1958.

Sometimes it seemed as if June would never come. Some nights, after a party, when we kicked off our shoes in the rec room and lay together on the sofa, I wondered if I could wait that long. We'd vowed that we *would* wait, and this pact seemed to make Catherine more reckless instead of less. Sometimes I thought she was deliberately testing my resolve. She'd lie back in her white or blue or pink sheath dress and pull up the hem. I'd bend to kiss the twin bands of bare flesh between nylon stocking and pantie girdle, and I'd discover that she'd dabbed herself there with Chanel No. 5, and the scent mingled with her heat to produce a dizzying aphrodisiac. My mouth and hands would swarm over her (always avoiding the right breast); I'd even give the elastic of her panties a downward tug, knowing she knew I was only kidding, maddened by the knowledge that she trusted me so much, wishing I had the nerve to surprise her by violating that trust, but confident that I—

"Paul! Paul!" This is accompanied by a thump thump on the bathroom door.

"Yes, Mom?"

"Steve's here. He can't believe you're still in the bath."

21

3

I wrap a towel around my waist and hold the ends together at my hip. I open the door.

"You're out," says my mother. She's standing there in her apron with her upright vacuum cleaner beside her.

"I have to shave yet," I say.

I pad through the hall, the living room and the kitchen to the room we call The Back Shed.

"Hi, Evets, old man," I say. I've been saying his name backwards since high school. We used to do that with a lot of kids' names. Our favourite is Nodrog Notsnhoj.

"Luap, you're taking a leisurely bath while some of us are breaking our necks running errands," says Steve. He's a dark, good-looking guy with a brush cut and he's wearing his army-surplus clothes, the back of the jacket covered with people's autographs. "Say, good party last night."

"You were certainly cozying up to Shelagh."

"You know that stuff about her wearing falsies?"

"Steve, for crying out loud—"

"It's B.S. That was all her."

"Shhh—"

"Is the car stashed away?"

"Greg's got it. He's changing the oil and checking everything and then he'll bring it over and hide it in the Yetmans' garage."

"You trust him?"

"He's my brother!"

"I'll bet you five bucks Allan or The Shark is going to do something."

"You didn't tell them where the car—"

"No. I made it quite clear to them that, as ushers, all they get to do is ush."

"Good."

"Well, I'm off to find someone to pick up the aunts, check on the boutonnieres, slide by the hotel—"

"Evets, I really appreciate this."

"See you at quarter to three."

He gives me a reassuring pat on the arm and leaves. I walk back to the bathroom, past Mom, who is sitting at the kitchen table smoking her morning cigarette while she sews a button on Dad's good trousers. Such is the extent of wedding preparations for parents of the groom.

Back in the bathroom, I open the medicine cabinet. I glance at the shelves that hold corn plasters, pills, lotions and other mysteries of my parents' middle age. I take out the little blue box of razor blades, my safety razor and my shaving brush. After mixing up some lather and placing a new blade in the razor, I run hot water into the sink, dip a facecloth into it and apply the cloth to my cheeks and jaw. I recall the day my father did this, holding the hot cloth to my face as part of his lesson in how to shave. "It opens up the pores," he said. I assumed he meant the whiskers would be easier to cut. Now, here I am, some years later, still using my dad's method long after he has switched to an electric razor. Shaving with hot water and lather seems cleaner and more thorough. It *feels* better. I take away the cloth and give myself a rich beard of lather.

I run the razor up one side of my upper lip—and cut myself.

Whether I've cut off the top of a pimple or gouged my flesh, I'm not sure. There's a blotch of blood fouling my white jaw like the trace of a wounded animal on a snow-covered field. I wanted my face to be as smooth as a baby's bum for Catherine, but now it'll be marred. I have to be more careful. I dab at the cut with toilet paper, then touch a styptic pencil to it. It stings but it stops the blood. I run the razor over my skin more slowly—that's better. Someday, I might try a mustache.

On the night I went over to ask Catherine's father for her hand in marriage, I noticed how orange his mustache was. I'd never looked that closely before, but now I could see it was distinctly orange—was it a stain from smoking or from tomato soup?

"May I speak with you alone, sir?" I asked.

"Of course," he said. "How about a drink?"

"Yes, that'd be great. I'll have rum and Coke, please." This was a time when all the young men I knew drank dark rum and all the girls drank lemon gin. Our fathers drank rye or scotch and our mothers pretended not to drink.

We took our drinks to Mr. Barber's basement den and sat in easy chairs. With the door shut, I could hear him breathing and my heart thumping and water flowing somewhere.

"You called this meeting, Paul," he reminded me.

"Mr. Barber, Catherine and I have been going out for a while now, and I . . ."

"Yes?"

"I'd very much like to marry Catherine."

He pulled out a pipe and unfolded a leather tobacco pouch. He dipped the bowl of the pipe into the tobacco. The aroma nearly made me swoon. "You're the best-mannered fellow that ever came calling for her," he said. "A Commerce grad, too, aren't you?"

"Yes, sir."

He lit a match, waited until the flame was just right, and then drew the fire into the pipe. "You know what I've been wondering when you come here and I watch the two of you drive away?"

"I don't know—"

"I've been wondering if you'd ever take a risk."

"Sir, Catherine and I—"

"Up to now, you've been playing it safe. The trust company is pretty dull, isn't it? How'd you like to jump into a dynamic business? At least try it out." He pointed the stem of his pipe at me. "You'd make a hell of a fine hotelman."

A few minutes later, when we went upstairs, Mr. Barber announced that I was going to be his new executive trainee. Mrs. Barber, a stately woman with her grey-brown hair in a beehive style, came to me and embraced me. Catherine looked surprised. We all talked about the need for new front desk procedures at the Barber hotels.

But the real purpose of the evening wasn't forgotten, and, at the right moment, I went out to the glove compartment of my Austin and fetched the little Birks box. In the low-lit seclusion of the rec room (both Barber boys having been assigned errands), Catherine accepted the diamond ring. She kissed me passionately and opened her legs to my hand and I discovered she wasn't wearing a girdle as she normally did and the soft cotton barrier there was torrid—and she pulled away and ran upstairs to show her parents the ring, leaving me gasping.

It was several weeks before I left the trust company. Catherine kept working evenings and I took another Sociology course—actually, two half courses, one on Crime and the other on Modern Marriage. I wasn't sure if there was a connection. In my room (an addition to the house that was nearly as old as I but was still referred to by the family as The New Room), I tried reading the Crime textbook. It was so dull that I soon turned to the Modern Marriage reading list. One book was a study of engaged couples.

"*Engagement is the last trial period before marriage*," I read. "*Couple members should use it for testing their temperamental compatibility, the mutual satisfaction of their personality needs, and the binding character of their common interests . . .*

"*Couples are most likely to have sex relations before marriage if:*
a) the couple members have had sexual experience with some other persons;
b) the engagement period is sixteen months or longer;
c) the couples have different religious affiliations (or none at all).
Couples are least likely to have premarital intercourse if:
a) neither couple member had sex relations with some other person;
b) the engagement period is eight months or less;
c) couple members are both Catholic;
d) the woman has had some college education and the man has not.

"*By far the strongest deterrent to sex relations on the part of the engaged persons is their belief that it is not right. . . . Other reasons: fear of pregnancy, fear of hurting parents' feelings, fear of social disapproval.*

"*Sometimes the first instance of sexual intercourse is reported to have 'just happened'. More often it has been discussed and decided upon. But, once begun, it is likely to continue despite the fact that in certain cases reported one or both parties feel it is not right.*"

My eyes drifted from the page. I looked at my photos of Catherine: giving a come-hither look in the Delta marsh; standing on a dirt road near Carman with chest out, legs wide apart and hands on hips; showing cleavage at Moose Lake. Silently, I said to her, "We've decided we won't have sex before marriage. We've decided we won't have sex before marriage. We've . . ."

I went back to reading.

"*The social mores that dictate virginity before marriage are still upheld*

25

by church, school and parental precept. Yet these mores are being challenged by increasing practice of sex relations in engagement. This perhaps results from the increased freedom of association of young people and of the prevalence of physical intimacies popularly termed 'necking' and 'petting', permissible in dating. . . . However, fewer than one of seven of the couples studied state premarital intercourse took place 'frequently' (13%). A total of 53.7% answered 'never', 4.8% 'once', and 18.6% 'occasionally'."

Let me be one of that thirteen per cent! my heart cried out. The next time Catherine and I were alone, I talked about my Soc course and asked her if we shouldn't reconsider our decision.

"Please don't burden me with that," Catherine said. "I've got a million little wedding details to think about. We haven't picked out the bridesmaids' dresses yet. Your mother hasn't given me her guest list. There's the silverware pattern my mother and I are arguing about. But don't accuse me of standing in your way. If you want us to sleep together, say the word."

On Wednesday evenings, we met with the minister at our church, Reverend Westlake. He was a handsome man, with short, curly black hair, greying temples, and eyes that you liked to look into. When we sat in his vestry office, we felt we were in the presence of a grand but gentle power and all my carnal thoughts evaporated.

We sat in a semi-circle, with him in the middle in his grey suit, white dog-collar and black shirt. He said he was glad we were the same religion—worshipping together increased the potential for happiness. He told us, when things got rough, as they surely would from time to time, each of us must try hard to understand how the other thought and felt. One night, he gave us a pamphlet and pointed to a particular paragraph:

"A woman's emotions, as a rule, are more quickly stirred than a man's. She reacts more promptly to her immediate surroundings. She is more easily moved to laughter or tears. A man tends to be absorbed in a few main interests, often outside the home; and where those are not concerned, he is apt to be bored. A woman lives more in the home and more in the present. She finds in the passing moment entertainment and pleasure, as well as cause for apparently needless depression. This, and her keener sensitiveness, may make the process of settling down, in the first few months of marriage, more trying to the wife than to the husband, whose outside interests take his mind from the problems that ought to be faced by both of them. A man has, on the whole, smaller reserves of energy than a

woman. *She can miss a meal, or a proper night's rest, with less discomfort than he."*

While Catherine asked about some detail concerning the wedding ceremony, I turned the page and saw the bold heading, *Married Intercourse.* In a church pamphlet! A few lines caught my eye:

"At the beginning, when they are thrown together for the first time in close and continuous intimacy, it is hardly likely that husband and wife will reach the full happiness of marriage all at once. This is true of the sexual relationship as of other things. If intercourse is not quite as delightful and satisfying as they had both expected, they must accept their disappointment with good humour."

"May we take this pamphlet home?" I asked.

"Certainly, Paul," Mr. Westlake said. "Read it thoroughly, and, if you have any questions about it, please call me."

I read it as soon as I got home. It stressed the twin purposes of married intercourse:

"It is the act which leads to conception, and so to the birth of children. It is also the special way by which husband and wife express their love for each other."

The pamphlet briefly explained conception, with words like "ovaries" and "vagina" and "testes" and "scrotum" italicized. It explained the menstrual cycle. Under the heading, *Love's Sacrament,* I was astonished to read:

"Once intercourse has begun, it should reach its natural climax in both husband and wife; otherwise they will feel strained and dissatisfied. For the man the completion of the act is clearly marked, and is followed at once by relief and contentment. It should bring the same happiness to the wife, though she reaches her climax, as a rule, more slowly than her husband. He should therefore try to delay the climax in order to give her time. If he reaches it first, he should continue union as long as it is necessary for her to reach hers too. Experience will probably enable them in the end to reach their climax together."

This in a church pamphlet!

I read on through *The Honeymoon,* which emphasized the presence of the hymen in *"most unmarried women"* and, because this membrane had to be stretched or broken, *"it may be several days before complete union is possible".*

After a discussion of "How Often" and "Pregnancy", the pamphlet went on to discuss children, the spacing of children, and relationships with in-laws. Then there was a section on birth control, which was considered the man's responsibility.

I turned back to the section on sexual fulfilment. Sometimes I thought these matters were not very important to Catherine; she seemed preoccupied with the spectacle of the wedding. Yet here was the church putting emphasis on the physical and the emotional: "*The ideal is that intercourse should always be as welcome and as satisfying to the wife as to the husband.*"

I had to discuss this with Catherine. But, before I could broach the subject intelligently, I had to get a better idea of a woman's anatomy. All I knew about a woman's body was what I'd touched. I'd seen breasts—my mother's, inadvertently; a stripper's, in a Wallace Brothers carnival sideshow tent; Catherine's, fleetingly, and only the left one for a few heated moments after I'd pushed up her sweater and bra. I'd seen Becky's—she was a girl I dated in university for a while and on Grad night she got drunk and took off some of her clothes. But I knew nothing about women below the waist, except what I had managed to touch, which was laughably little—a few silky curls here, a warm bit of panty there.

I went to the university library and found a musty volume devoted to the human body. In a study carrel, I skipped past the chapters on the cardiovascular system, the blood and the lymph, the respiratory system, the alimentary system, the liver, the urinary system, metabolism and the endocrine system—though I knew precious little about any of those parts, either—and I found the chapters entitled *The Male Reproductive System* and *The Female Reproductive System*. I found a line drawing of the woman's reproductive system—an "anterior-posterior view", whatever that was. I stared at it. I couldn't make head nor tail of it. The vagina appeared to be below and behind where I thought it was. The labyrinth of tubes and tunnels seemed completely unrelated to sex. This book, I decided, was too clinical. I looked for marriage manuals, but the only one I could find had the pertinent illustrations ripped out.

I went through the next few weeks in a bewildered state. In church, I felt the eyes of Mr. Westlake upon me as I stewed about Catherine's reproductive system. Catherine seemed oblivious to my turmoil.

One night, I couldn't stand it any longer. Catherine was going on and on about her mother's suggestions for numbers of attendants and what the possible candidates would look best in. We were in the rec room and her brothers weren't there. I threw my arms around her, catching her in mid-sentence, kissed her lips—so dry after all the talking—and pushed my hand down the front of her slacks.

"What are you doing?" she snapped, yanking my hand out.

"Cath, I'm sorry, but I'm dying to know what you feel like down there."

She surprised me by smiling. "You sure have a funny way of going about things."

"Don't you think we—"

"No, it takes all the fun out of it if we talk about it. Let's wait till we're both in the mood and see what we want to do then. I know it won't be this week, darling, because I happen to have my monthly visitor."

None of this would've been so unsettling if the other parts of my life had remained stable, but they hadn't. While Catherine worked at her father's hotel, The Royal Coach, I became Food and Beverage Manager at his other one, The Barbary. The liquor laws were changing; going were the days of Men-Only beer parlours. The power of the Women's Christian Temperance Union had vanished and the provincial government had made into law all the recommendations of the Bracken Commission to allow wine, beer and spirits to be more readily available. Women could now have a drink with men. People could drink liquor at a place other than their homes. They could even have something to eat with their booze. It was a historic time to be working in the hotel industry in Manitoba, and I was so busy, I had to quit my Sociology course.

My meetings with Catherine became more and more business-like as we concentrated on wedding plans. We had a fight over who should be my attendants; she thought I should ask our three brothers, I wanted my friends.

"What friends?" she asked.

"Shark, Steve and Allan."

"You haven't seen any one of them in weeks."

"I've been seeing you or working every night. They're still expecting me to ask them."

"My parents expect you to ask my brothers."

"Aren't you having friends for your attendants?"

"Because we don't have any sisters."

"Who are you having, by the way?"

"Shelagh and Frances and Charleen."

"Who's Charleen?"

"You don't know her. She's a daughter of the Boltons, good friends of my parents. Don't you dare comment—I've already argued about Charleen with Mother and lost."

"Is your mother trying to dictate who stands up for me?"

"Leave my mother out of this. I want my brothers and your brother. You told me you hate The Shark."

"I don't hate him. I think he's been pretty childish lately, but he'll come around."

"You'd better go home and think about these choices of yours. And think about the people you're going to hurt if you keep being so stubborn. If you don't change your mind, *you* can announce your choices to my parents."

"I noticed your parents weren't talking to each other. What's that about?"

"Mother booked the Fort Garry for the reception instead of one of Dad's hotels."

"I thought that was your dad's idea—"

"Look, forget about my parents, all right?"

"Isn't your mother being a little bit domineering—"

"Paul—"

" —and pretentious?"

Catherine pulled the ring off her finger and held it in front of me.

"I think you'd better leave before I throw this at you."

"You wouldn't—"

"Leave. And don't call me tomorrow. I need some time to think."

I left. I wondered what was happening to our good feeling. I went home to find that Greg had dropped off a package for me. There was a note with it: "Paul. You may find this helpful. I know I did. All the best, Greg." Inside was his copy of a book called *Successful Marriage*. I wanted to throw it into the garbage. Instead, I climbed into bed and read:

"*. . . On the inner aspects of the larger labia, on each side of the archway, the inner or lesser lips or labia converge above as hanging skin folds. They vary markedly at times in size and shape and surface and projection. They meet over the top of the clitoris to form its cover, called, as in the male, the foreskin or prepuce. The clitoris, not unlike a miniature* *penis without its water passage, is the external center of erotic sensation. Its rounded end, the glans, is endowed with closely packed nerve ends. . . . The vagina is not furnished with glands to provide secretion, yet is moist. This is due to the mucus coming down from the inch-long canal of the cervix with its generous equipment of glands, especially active during sexual excitement."*

I closed the book. I had safaried so near to this exotic and mysterious territory, but now it seemed a million miles away.

4

"Your breakfast is ready!" my mother calls.

Clean shaven, the wound sealed with styptic, I don a dressing gown, go into the kitchen and sit down at the table. It's one of those old-fashioned porcelain-top tables with wooden legs and a drawer for cutlery. Our kitchen is so small that one side of the table runs flush with the wall—you have to move the table every time you want to take the ironing board out of its cupboard. When I'm sitting at my end, I block the door to the back shed.

My mother serves me two fried eggs sunny side up, bacon, toast, honey, orange juice and coffee. As I eat, she stands at the sink, washing and drying dishes. The only woman in a house of men, she's always performed the domestic chores, and the word among us men is that she likes doing them. She turns to me, her face red from working over the hot stove and the sink of hot water.

"I don't care what you say," she says, "you're too young to get married."

She's been saying things like this all week. Do you know how to change a light bulb? Can you fix a leaky faucet? Can you hang a curtain? Do you know where to find the raisin bread in the grocery store? She said I hadn't brought many girls home before Catherine and she was right: two, to be exact—Irene Norby, my high school graduation date, and Becky Wyatt, my university graduation date. I'd brought them home so that Mom could take pictures of us, milestone photographs for the family album.

"Mom, I'm twenty-three," I say.

"Your brother didn't get married till he was twenty-eight."

"Greg was a late bloomer."

"Speaking of Gregory—" She points to the kitchen window.

"Hello, folks," Greg says through the screen, and I hear him open the door into the back shed. An instant later, he bangs the kitchen

32

door against the back of my chair. "Oops, sorry."

I pull my chair in to let him squeeze into the room. He comes in wearing the same leather windbreaker he's been wearing his whole adult life. He pushes back the hair that's always falling across his forehead and his left eye.

"The car's oiled and greased," he says. "I even washed it for you." Greg's a math teacher at Glenlawn Collegiate but his passion is servicing cars. My Austin used to be his and he keeps it ticking like a fine watch. "The carburetor was a little loose so I tightened it. You're all set. So what do you say to a quick nine holes?"

"Gregory!" Mom cries. "Paul isn't even packed yet and he's going away for two weeks and besides, he can't just— "

"Mom, I think it's a great idea," I say. "You'll help me pack, won't you?" I wolf down the rest of my breakfast.

"I knew you'd want me to pack for you. You can't fold a newspaper, never mind a shirt."

She smiles and I know we're going golfing.

"What will Catherine say when she finds out?" says Mom.

"We won't tell her!"

When I leave the house dressed in a golf shirt and cotton slacks, our next-door neighbour, Mrs. Jarvis, is standing at her back door shaking a mat. Her back door faces ours and she has the knack of being there whenever there's something worth watching at our place. She was there the day Catherine and I argued on our back steps about who should take the wedding photographs. She was there the night I tried to sneak Becky Wyatt into the house when my parents weren't home. She was there the day my dad got mad at us and slammed out of the house, yelling, "This time I won't be back!"

"Nice day for the wedding, Paul," Mrs. Jarvis calls to me.

"A better one for golf, Mrs. J," I answer, and, hoisting my bag of clubs onto my shoulder, I head for the garage.

My father's there, smoking a cigarette, but, as soon as he sees me, he pretends to look for something.

"Have you seen my trowel?" he says. He hates to be caught doing nothing.

"No, I haven't. Dad, we're going golfing. You, me and Greg. He's getting his old clubs and your new ones out of the basement."

"What does your mother say?"

"She's being a good sport about it."

A few minutes later, we're off, me sitting between Dad and Greg in Dad's '57 Chevy. It feels good, this last little bit of camaraderie before I leave home.

Dad drives over to the B.A. station at the corner of Harrowby and St. Mary's to get gas. The three of us stand around chatting with Bert the proprietor when I notice a familiar car going by on the river side of St. Mary's.

"Oh, no!" I cry, and I duck down behind Dad's car.

"What's the matter?" says Greg.

"That Oldsmobile 98. That's Catherine's dad's car and that's Catherine driving."

"It's gone now."

"I think the bridesmaids were with her. Probably going to the hairdresser's."

"Did Catherine see you?"

"No. No, I don't think she did."

"It's still bad luck if you see her, though, isn't it?"

I wish we'd never come golfing. The first tee's jammed with people—at least thirty ahead of us. The guy keeping track of who goes next sits up on a tower, something like the kind lifeguards sit on at beaches. He has to have a high perch because there's a little valley between here and the green and once the golfers get down there you can't see how far away they are.

"Numbers 246, 247, 248 and 249," the guy says. My tag is 282.

All the things I should be doing! Shining my black oxfords, packing, checking the maps . . . well, at least I can go over my notes. While Dad and Greg practise their putting, I lean against a tree and pull out two folded sheets of paper. One is my speech outline:

"Ref to toast
Agree (?) w. Dr.
Cath terrif
Boss's daughter
Cath's mom & dad terrif
Tea & toast
Invite folks
Not all at same time"

The double reference to "toast" bothers me. What if I mix up

Mrs. Barber's raisin toast with Dr. Bolton's Toast to the Bride?

I hold the notes inside an open scorecard—if anyone's watching me, he'll think I'm studying the length of each hole. I turn to the other page, an outline of all the wedding-night advice I've been accumulating:

"Wed nite no big deal
(but could be!)
Be gentle
Don't rush
Don't dawdle
Don't smother
Be considerate—exhausting day for bride
Hymen more likely to stretch than pop
Shave first?
Lights on or off?
Pyjamas on or off?"

I look up into the trees. There were times over the past year when I wondered if this day would ever come. We couldn't agree on anything—we fought over Mrs. Barber's decree that the reception would be an afternoon tea, not a dinner and dance; Catherine told her mother Charleen was too fat to be a bridesmaid; there was trouble over the dresses; we disagreed on where the photographer should take pictures; I gave in on the issue of her young brothers being ushers only to have her tell me she hated them, they were being such idiots, and we argued about that, with me fighting for Wally and Gord this time. By then, I'd been trying to talk to The Shark and he was ignoring me, so what was the point? Catherine and I hardly saw each other, and, when we did, we didn't touch. But all that changed one Sunday, two weeks ago.

We'd been to church, where Mr. Westlake read the banns: "I publish the Banns of Marriage between Paul Henry Hodges of this Parish and Catherine Anne Barber of this Parish. If any of you know cause or just impediment why these two persons should not be joined in holy Matrimony, ye are to declare it. This is the second time of asking." Catherine reached over and squeezed my hand. It was her first affectionate gesture in weeks. We went to Greg's house for lunch with Greg and his wife Helen and my parents, and everyone was in a good mood. When we left in mid-afternoon, Catherine suggested we go for a drive, and we ended up walking hand-in-hand in Assiniboine

Park, as if we needed this time alone to get re-acquainted. After going home to change to more casual clothes, we went to my parents' place for dinner. We then went to our apartment to build a brick-and-board bookshelf.

The apartment was on the third floor of a two-storey building in the suburb of St. James. We had to rent it for the whole month of June in order to get the one we wanted. It gave us a place to take shower gifts and early wedding presents and the chesterfield suite we bought for ourselves. Our living room and bedroom windows looked out on busy Portage Avenue, just three blocks from The Barbary. There we were, sitting on the chesterfield, drinking beer and admiring our building job. It was getting dark, but we were too lazy or too contented to turn on the lights. The streetlamp outside was enough. We didn't yet have drapes on the windows.

"What do you say we invest in an original oil and hang it over the shelves?" I said.

"Let's," said Catherine.

"You mean it?"

"Yes. I'd like an original oil."

"Wow, that didn't hurt a bit."

"What?"

"Agreeing on something right away."

"It's this apartment. It's so cozy."

We didn't talk for a minute or two. A semi-trailer slowed down as it went by and the noise of its gears and its brakes filled the room. We snickered. Catherine moved closer to me and we kissed. And we kissed. It was the longest, deepest kiss we'd permitted ourselves in months. She'd had five showers, all supposedly surprises, and I'd had to tell the most ridiculous lies to get her to her friends' houses each time, sometimes on a day when we weren't speaking, and she'd been properly grateful and emotional for the parties, but unwilling to warm up to me. Now we were embracing and it felt so good. I took her further into my arms, attempting my best combination of strength and tenderness. She responded by pushing her bosom into my chest and through my T-shirt I could feel the points of her bra flatten against me. I was listing sideways against a cushion and one upholstered arm. Catherine moved her legs up onto the chesterfield. I ran one hand around and around on her back as her hands played in my hair, and I sent both my hands up under her blouse and, using the technique she'd taught me so many months ago on our Manitoba tour, I unhooked her bra. She kissed my face, her mouth open and hot and wet, and I fondled my old buddy. It was marvellous to be kissing like that again, to be squeezing that familiar handful again, after so many barren weeks, and I would've been content with that, now that the wedding was only two weeks away. But Catherine was kissing my face and neck so earnestly, I began to think, What am I saving it for?

I moved in on the *right breast.*

It was every bit as smooth and round and warm as its twin—no. It was smoother and rounder and warmer and even a little fuller, I swear it!

Catherine gasped. She breathed more heavily. My venturing onto a new frontier semed to make her more aggressive. She ran her fingers through my chest hair and teased my nipples. She got so passionate, I found myself sending one hand on a jaunt to her hip, where it encountered the side-zipper of her shorts and slowly slid it open. Now we were both lying down on that brand new chesterfield that I hadn't liked that much at all when I first saw it at Eaton's (I'd argued that brown would be better, something with more delicate arms, but now I thought the green was fine and the cushions and arms firm and supportive), and Catherine rotated her hips a few degrees to allow better access to her abdomen and she took my hand and moved it to the silky soft pelt that had been so coyly withheld from me. She was warm all over and especially warm there and she was still lurching around and now she was practically under me, frenzied in her licking, biting, caressing and massaging. With my one hand still enjoying the spongy, wobbly heft of the right breast, I tried to clear my mind enough to recall the diagrams of a woman's nether region as I inched my fingers lower and lower, moving them ever so slowly in a single direction . . . further, further, until I felt the beginning of a furrow.

"Paul," she whispered. "Paul, I want you. Now."

She unzipped my trousers.

"I mean it, Paul. Come on."

I thought of all the feverish nights I'd spent perusing the manuals and the pamphlets and wondering if Catherine would ever crave physical pleasure the way I thought I did, and now here she was writhing against me and *begging for it* and what popped into my head?

The smiling, handsome, beatific face of Reverend Westlake.

"We can't," I said, the words sounding stupid as I uttered them.

"Come on," she urged. "Everything's okay, and I want you very badly."

"We made a promise. We've got this far. Let's not spoil things. It wouldn't be fair."

"*Fair?*"

"Yes, to our parents, to Mr. Westlake—"

"But what about *me?*"

She pushed me away and flipped onto the floor. She sat with her back to me and wept for a minute or two. I reached out to pat her shoulder in a dumb sort of "There, there" gesture, but she shrugged me off. She did up her bra under her blouse and she pulled up her shorts, all the while keeping her back to me. I thought for a terrible moment that she was going to get up and march right out of the apartment and call off the wedding.

Instead, she suddenly turned and kissed my cheek.

"Thank God for your cool head," she said.

I felt as if I might cry.

"I almost spoiled everything," she said. "Thanks to you, the wedding is going to be just as perfect as we planned."

My ball soars high, seems to hang for a moment in the deep blue Manitoba sky, and descends swiftly to a spot over the hill and off to the right. Greg drives his ball further, but off to the left, near the wire fence that separates the golf course from a row of suburban backyards. Dad puffs and grunts as he takes a couple of practice swings—he's overweight and he smokes too much—but as usual he hits his ball straight toward the pin. He'll be an easy seven-iron shot away. The golfers waiting behind us give Dad a smattering of applause.

Head down, Greg hurries off after his ball. Dad saunters along beside me into the gully.

"Catherine's got a lot of spunk," he says. "It might take all your wits to keep her happy. The two of you working for her father—I don't know about that."

"We're going to be fine, Dad."

He helps me look for my ball in the rough. We can't find it but we don't want to wave the next group through because it will only delay us more.

"Here it is!" Dad calls from a location that's further than I think it could've gone.

I walk over to him and, though it's still in the rough, there's a clear path through the trees to the green. I suspect Dad hasn't found my ball at all but, to save time, has dropped one of his onto the long grass. Or maybe he isn't thinking about time at all; maybe this is one of those paternal gestures meant to make things a little easier for a son. I don't bother to check if the ball really is mine. For a moment I consider which club I should use.

"You're all right as far as tonight is concerned?" Dad says.

The question startles me. I expected a suggestion on how to hit the ball out of the rough, not a bashful attempt at some eleventh-hour sex advice.

"Dad, everything's fine," I say, "I know more than you think," and I laugh, trying to let him believe he's been a good father even if he hasn't ever talked to me about personal things.

I blast the ball out of the rough with my five-iron. The ball hits the thick grass of the apron and hops onto the green.

"Paul," Dad says, persisting in his man-to-man tone, "don't expect the first time to be a picnic."

"Don't worry, Dad."

We head toward his ball in the middle of the fairway.

"FORE!"

I look around—thunk!—I'm hit! On the forehead!

"Damn fool didn't wait!" Dad says. He shakes his fist at the person back on the tee—we can see his head over the crest of the hill. "Are you all right?"

"Oh sure. The ball must've bounced before it got to me. I'm okay."

"Let's see. There's a mark. You may develop a bump."

Greg comes running over.

"I waved them on," he says. "Gosh, I'm sorry. I thought you were lost. Are you all right?"

"I'm okay. Honest, it's nothing. Let's get moving."

"We'll finish this hole and that'll be it," says Dad.

We walk along together, pausing while Dad hits a chip shot that bites into the green. I run my fingers lightly over the sore spot and think, This is my bad luck for seeing Catherine before I'm supposed to.

Greg muffs his second and third; his fourth is a "grass-cutter" that makes it onto the green and rolls to within a foot of the hole. We walk to the green together and Greg pulls the flag.

I squat to size up my long putt. The shaft of my putter feels phallic as I stare at the hole. *Don't expect the first time to be a picnic.* With hands turning clammy and the bump on my head throbbing, I putt. The shot seems hard and accurate enough, but the ball rims the cup and stops a few inches away. I hope this isn't an omen.

Dad sinks his for a birdie; Greg sinks his for a bogey; I tap mine in for a par. Greg and I each give Dad a quarter and we hurry to the bridge over the creek they call the Seine River. We cross it, cut around behind the golfers just leaving the second tee and hurry over toward the bush by the ninth hole. Sticking close to the trees and well away from anyone's shots, we head for the parking lot. There's nothing about our outward appearances that would tell anyone we're members of a wedding party. As we chatter about the shots we made and the shots we missed, we're a trio of golfing buddies heading home.

5

When we walk into the house, Mom scolds us, even after I show her the bump on my forehead.

"It wouldn't have happened if you'd stayed home," she says.

She takes a closer look, puts some cream on it and says I'll be lucky if I don't have a shiner. It's 12:30. Time for me to have a quick bath and then Mom's going to wash my hair. I hurry to my bedroom, where my suitcase is open on the bed. Good old Mom has started to pack for me.

I close the bedroom door. Now's a good time to transfer my box of french safes from their hiding place to the suitcase. I kneel beside my dresser and open the bottom drawer. I look under the clothes.

I don't see the box.

I pull out a couple of old cardigans, lift the sleeveless sweater that Mom knit, push aside a pile of undershirts.

Nothing.

I throw everything out of the drawer.

The box isn't there.

I panic. I look into other drawers, knowing it can't possibly be in them. It isn't.

I consider trying to get hold of Steve—is this his idea of a joke? Oh, he couldn't have taken them; he hasn't been in my room. Maybe I can ask him to get me more—but he'll only say, "Why do you need safes? You don't wear a raincoat in the shower, do you?" and I don't want to get into a discussion of birth control with him. I have no idea where he is, anyway.

Something makes me check the suitcase. My new pyjamas are there, and so are my socks, my new underwear, my sport shirts, my trousers . . .

The safes. Mom packed the safes.

I'm so embarrassed, I stay in the bathtub until the water is cold.

41

There's a loud knock on the door.

"Paul, hurry up," says Dad. "I have to have a bath, too, you know."

"Okay, Dad." My bump is really pounding.

Eventually, in my dressing gown, I venture into the kitchen. Mom's at the sink, waiting for me. Avoiding her eyes, I sit on a chair facing the sink. I bend forward—it's awkward, hard to get close because the cabinet Dad built under the sink gives you no place to put your legs, but we've done this for years. She wets my hair under the tap; is it my imagination or is she holding my head there longer than usual? She works up a good lather, scrubs my hair, massages my scalp. I keep my eyes squeezed shut. While she has me at her mercy, she grumbles about my lack of maturity—and who's going to wash my hair from now on? She seems to be rubbing my head a lot harder than usual.

She rinses my hair and dries it with a towel. I sort of wish she'd mention the safes—maybe laugh about them or compliment me on the decision not to have kids for a while. She doesn't. "There," she says.

"Thank you," I say, still avoiding her eyes as I get up from the sink.

The time is 1:35.

The telephone rings. It's in the hall that leads to my bedroom so I answer it.

"Hi—Paul?"

"Yes?"

"How are you?"

"Great. Who is this?"

"You don't remember me?" It's a female voice.

"Gosh, I don't—"

"Paul, it isn't *that* long ago."

"Sorry, I—"

"It's Becky."

"Becky! How are you?"

"Fine. Really fine."

"I hear you're engaged to—"

"We broke up."

"I'm sorry to hear that."

"I'm not sorry at all."

"Well, that's good."

"I just heard a rumour that you're getting married. Is it true?"

"Yes, it is."

"When?"

"In a little less than two hours from now."

"*Today?*"

"That's right."

"Holy . . . Who to?"

"Her name is Catherine Barber."

"I don't know her, do I?"

"I guess not. She was behind us in university. Remember that Little Theatre production I had a bit part in? She was in it, too. That's how we met."

"Holy cow. Today."

Dad comes out of the bathroom in a towel, looking clean and red as a royal flush. He gives me the throat-slitting sign: time to get off the phone.

"Becky, I have to—what is it you—"

"You were always such a good listener, and I wanted to talk with you about something, but I guess it's too late."

"Well, maybe we—"

"It was nice knowing you, Paul."

"Gosh, Becky, we could still—"

"You're getting *married*."

"But . . . look, Becky, I have to go—"

"Okay. Well . . . best of luck, eh?"

"Thank you."

"Bye."

"Bye, Becky."

She doesn't hang up right away. I can hear her breathing. I remember the night she got drunk and took off her sweater and her bra. I think she expected me to do something but I didn't want to get into trouble. We stopped seeing each other after that.

I carefully set the receiver in its cradle.

I get dressed: white Arrow shirt, cuff links, plain black socks, dark blue suit trousers, black belt, black oxfords, blue and red silk tie.

The time is 2:40. Allan and The Shark will be at the church by now. My stomach growls but I daren't eat. I check my wallet to make sure I have my money and my travellers' cheques.

The doorbell rings. I peek through my venetian blinds. There's a silver-grey limousine parked outside. I run to the front door. Dad and Steve are standing there all dressed up and looking mighty pleased with themselves.

"Where did you—"

"Your dad arranged it," Steve says.

"Why didn't you tell me, Dad?"

"There have to be *some* surprises."

A two-door Studebaker drives up behind the limousine and out steps a fellow carrying a camera and a flash unit. As he scurries up the sidewalk, another car arrives—Dad's Chevy—carrying Greg and his wife, Helen. Mrs. Jarvis is outside in a blue floral dress and a fox fur piece, watching this sudden flurry of traffic, a gloved hand shielding her eyes from the sun.

"Here's your boutonniere, Luap," Steve says. On my lapel he pins a carnation, a white one like his.

"Do that again and smile," says the photographer.

"Cheese," says Steve, and the guy takes a couple of shots of us and dashes off.

Steve and I go to my room to finish packing. I give Steve the ring and he tucks it into one of his pockets.

"The money for the minister?" Steve says.

"My speech! I just about forgot my speech." I grab my notes out of my golf slacks.

"The money for the minister?" Steve repeats.

I pull open the top drawer of my desk, take out an envelope and hand it to him. He helps me on with my suit jacket, removes a bit of lint from one shoulder, does up one of the front buttons.

"Got everything?" he asks.

"I hope so."

"Watch?"

"Yup."

"Wallet?"

"Yup."

"Spectacles?"

"Uh huh."

"Testicles?"

"Roger."

He closes the suitcase; I have to sit on one side of it to make the latches click into place. As we leave the bedroom, I give it a fond backward glance. The phone rings and Dad answers it. He tells whoever it is what church to go to. Mom's dressed in her finest and looking in the oddest places—the buffet, the pantry—for one of her white gloves.

It's 3:05.

"Time to go," says Steve.

The ride to St. Timothy's Church should take about ten minutes. Steve and I wave to my family and to Mrs. Jarvis. Sid, the limousine driver, pulls away as Steve and I slouch in our seat, stretching our legs way out in front of us.

"What do you think, Luap?"

"This is the only way to go."

"Sure beats going in your little puddle-jumper."

"You're not kidding."

"Well, Luap, this is one clootch I didn't line you up with. Didn't I get you your grad date in high school?"

"Irene Norby, yes."

"She used to like to pull my wire. Did she pull yours?"

"No."

"But you knew she pulled mine."

"That's why I never held hands with her."

He punches my shoulder. "I've got to give you credit. You found Catherine all by yourself. Who'd have thought you'd get hitched before me? You're only minutes away from losing your freedom."

We chatter on about the ball and chain that The Shark locked onto my leg at my stag party, how Allan got falling-down drunk and how Pete Warwick sat sideways at a piano and snapped out one raunchy vaudeville song after another.

"Say," says Steve, "there's this guy at work who knows Catherine's old boyfriend, Ray. Ray claims he put the blocks to her. You don't suppose—"

"Are you kidding?"

"I told him he was full of B.S."

"That's for sure."

Sid turns into St. Timothy's Place, a short street with shallow ditches on both sides. Parked cars line the road, all of them probably belonging to wedding guests. One of the people I see walking toward the church is Becky Wyatt in a wide-brimmed hat. I give her a lazy wave, the kind the Queen gives from a moving vehicle. *Ray couldn't have slept with Catherine.* Why would Steve suggest such a thing?

Sid pulls up to the door of the church hall. It's 3:22. Sid opens the car door and Steve gives me a little shove. I step out, feeling suddenly exhilarated. *He's just jealous, that's what it is.*

After the bright outdoors, the hall seems dark. We head for the vestry. I hear the organ playing. My eyes adjust and see Mr. Westlake in wedding-service regalia, coming toward us with hands extended.

"Good afternoon, Paul," he says, his face beaming. He shakes my hand. "Good afternoon, Allan."

"Steve," my best man and I say in unison.

"Steve, of course." He shakes Steve's hand.

"The bride's name is Catherine," says Steve in his reckless way. The three of us laugh.

I touch my forehead; the bump feels huge. I straighten my tie. We're in the vestry, Steve and I unable to stand still, when a buzzer sounds.

"The bride is here," says Mr. Westlake.

It's 3:32.

6

Mr. Westlake picks up his *Book of Common Prayer* and leads Steve and me down a corridor into the sacristy, where he gives us a quick glance over his shoulder to make sure we're still with him. He opens the door and we follow him in. Fighting off the urge to look down at my feet, I try to look confident and happy without seeming smug. I glance out at the blur of people, all facing us. There's Greg's wife, Helen; when I focus on her, she mouths the word, "*Golf.*" There's Mom, dabbing at her eyes with a hankie. Dad's got this broad grin on his face, and so have a lot of other folks. Good old St. Timothy's is full.

Mr. Westlake stops at the head of the centre aisle and faces the congregation. I take up my position in front of him, half-turned so that I can look down the aisle. The ushers and the bridesmaids are sorting themselves out in the vestibule—The Shark looks like he's doing something with Charleen's bouquet and Allan's tying his shoelace—and behind them I can see crescents of white—the hoop skirt of my bride's dress.

There's a pause. No music, no voices, only a cough and some shuffling of feet.

The organ breaks into *Here Comes the Bride*.

Here instead come the ushers, two abreast: Allan and The Shark. Both of them look self-conscious and even a little ridiculous in their dark blue suits. Allan seems to be in agony. (He isn't used to all this fuss; he and Pris didn't have a church wedding because she was six months gone.) Beside him, The Shark stands tall, looking down that long nose of his. His mouth is open and I can see the points of his oversized eye-teeth. (The Shark's called The Shark not because of any special prowess at cards or snooker but because he looks – in a mean, handsome sort of way — like a shark.) With his head held high, he isn't a good partner for Allan, whose married eyebrows dip in a frown

47

as he stares at the floor, his shoulders hunched. Yet Allan and The Shark manage to do the hesitation step in unison.

Four paces behind them come the bridesmaids. One is Charleen Bolton, who's done a fine job of losing weight, enough at least to allow room beside her for Frances Drake. Charleen's the daughter of the Barbers' oldest friends—it's her dad who's going to give the Toast to the Bride. The tall and willowy Frances (who used to be called "Spanish Armada" at school) is a neighbour of Catherine's. As Allan and The Shark reach Mr. Westlake and move off alongside Steve, I get a good look at Frances and Charleen—our own Laurel and Hardy. Both seem delighted to be bridesmaids—their pale green outfits suit their rosy complexions and their genuine smiles. They take their places on the bride's side.

Shelagh Swainson, our maid of honour, is wearing a deeper shade of green. Her blond hair glistens, her eyes glow. She's one of those beautiful girls who laugh on cue, never say much and wouldn't be caught dead with their hair messed. She and Catherine met at university when they were both asked to run for Freshie Queen.

Shelagh steps off to the side and there at last is The Bride.

In white, virginal white.

She never would've let Ray near her, I know she wouldn't.

For all Shelagh's serene good looks, she's no match for Catherine, who radiates—I don't know—confidence, verve. And that's just in the way she carries herself, because I can't really see her face; it's covered by a veil, her mother's, the "something old" that every bride has to have in her wardrobe. I feel a rush of warmth: this beautiful young woman is my bride.

Beside her, Mr. Barber—my boss—is tall and tanned and looking distinguished, but he seems just a bit bewildered as if, after years of catering weddings, he's discovered that being the father of the bride is more demanding than he thought. (Or maybe he's still mad at Mrs. Barber.) He escorts Catherine to her place in front of Mr. Westlake.

"Dearly beloved," our minister begins, "we are gathered here, in the sight of God and in the face of this congregation, to join this man and this woman in holy matrimony . . ."

My heart pounds. My hands sweat. I'm facing the altar now and my eyes drift up to the choir pews where Gail Hetherington, Charleen's married sister, sits waiting to sing the two solos. I look back at Mr.

Westlake as he half-reads, half-recites, but I don't really hear the words until he asks if any man can show just cause why Catherine and I shouldn't marry.

There's dead silence. No old beaus come out of the woodwork. No Ray, no childhood sweetheart. Not a peep out of The Shark.

We go into the questions: "Paul Henry, wilt thou have this woman to thy wedded wife, to live together . . ."

Etc., etc. Dry as my throat is, I answer clearly: "I will."

"Catherine Anne, wilt thou have this man to thy wedded husband, to live together . . . ? Wilt thou obey him, and serve him, love, honour and keep him . . . ?"

I look at Catherine as she says in a soft voice, "I will."

"Who giveth this woman to be married to this man?"

"I do," says Mr. Barber. He steps into the pew beside Mrs. Barber.

Catherine moves closer to me, sending a shiver up my side, as Mr. Westlake places her right hand in mine and asks me to repeat after him. As we go through the rest of the formalities, I feel like a million bucks. I slip the ring onto her finger, we kneel, Mr. Westlake leads us in prayer— "Those whom God hath joined together let no man put asunder!"—and Gail sings the Twenty-third Psalm. The time comes for us to stand and kiss. I lift Catherine's veil and ignore her breath (all the books told me, Remember this day is a trying one for the bride).

Someone coughs—I think it's The Shark, who seldom goes this long without a cigarette. I hear a nose being blown, a throat being cleared. We're married!

All of us—Allan, The Shark, Steve, Charleen, Frances, Shelagh, Catherine and I—follow Mr. Westlake into the vestry for the signing of the marriage certificate. We jam into the little room while the organ introduces Gail's second solo, The Lord's Prayer.

"You did it, Luap, congratulations," says Steve, shaking my hand.

"Did you see me coming up the aisle?" says The Shark. "I stepped on some gum or something and my shoe nearly came off."

Catherine says, "My shoe nearly—Paul. What did you do to your forehead? And your lip?"

"Last night," Steve says, before I can answer, "after the rehearsal party, he dropped by the hotel and got into a little rumble—"

"Paul!" says Charleen.

"He's kidding," I say. "I was hit by a golf ball—"

"Steve said you were lying around in bed all morning," says Allan. "I suppose some stray golf ball just happened to come flying through your window."

"Uh, Catherine," Mr. Westlake says, "Could I have you sit here first and sign right—uh—there, please."

"Of course, yes," says Catherine, and she sits at Mr. Westlake's desk.

"Got any mints?" I whisper in Steve's ear.

"Presto!" he says, producing a package of mint-flavoured LifeSavers.

"Give the first one to the new Mrs. Hodges," I say, and Charleen and Frances chuckle at the bride's new name.

"Okay if I smoke?" says The Shark. "I'm dying."

"Better wait till we're outside," says Steve. "Have a mint."

When it's my turn to sign, Steve dictates: "L-U-A-P—"

And everyone laughs. Shelagh goes next, signing in a clear, child-like hand. Steve flourishes his pen-hand over the paper in ever-diminishing circles that end up in an unreadable scrawl.

Allan and The Shark joke about using Mr. Westlake's phone to cancel the date I have for tonight. Frances adjusts Charleen's bustle. Mr. Westlake signals to the organist before I get a chance to explain the bump.

Up comes the recessional music and I'm out in front of the congregation again, walking toward the centre aisle arm-in-arm with Catherine, believing that everyone is staring at the bump. There's Mr. Barber, looking worldly and affluent and staring at the bump; his little mother nodding beside him and staring at the bump; Mrs. Barber, chic and comely—except for a nerve pulsing down her long, well-bred neck—and staring at the bump; Catherine's brother Wally scowling (he wanted to be an usher) and staring at the bump; Catherine's three old aunties clutching hankies and staring at the bump; and Catherine's brother Gord whispering to one of the aunts and pointing to the bump.

As we head down the aisle, I try to forget the bump and acknowledge as many nods and smiles as I can: Doctor and Mrs. Bolton, Sam Pearson, Mrs. Jarvis, a couple I don't recognize—he's in a madras jacket and an open shirt and she's wearing a white summer dress—who are they? Catherine's arm presses mine and I see she wants me to acknowledge her favourite English prof, "Polonius" Martin, so-called because of the energetic way he rattles off the

"Neither a borrower nor a lender be" speech in *Hamlet* class. I give him a little salute. A few other faces register: Sally and Michael Short, who want us to help them run the St. Tim's Young People's group; John Proctor, manager of the hotel I work in, The Barbary; Len Pinkus, a distant cousin of mine who fought in Korea and put a notch in his rifle for every woman he seduced over there; and Max Godfrey, The Shark's practical joker of a dad—he's not invited to the wedding but he's come to the church to show off his new tie that lights up and reads "Hiya, Cutie!" as we pass.

The eight of us cluster in the vestibule while the people file out into the warm summer air. The Shark takes out a cigarette with the slightly shaky hand of an addict and holds it up to his nose for a sniff of the tobacco. Frances says, "Is it still there?" meaning the English sixpence Catherine put in her shoe for good luck.

Catherine says, "I think that's what's making my foot hurt." We laugh and exaggerate the discomfort of being squeezed into this small space.

"Let's smash the first person who throws something at us," says Allan.

"Okay, you two," says Steve, "you go first."

Catherine and I go outside and pause on the top step. Everyone applauds and a lot of people take photos. The sun's broken through the clouds. As we start down the steps, careful not to trip on Catherine's skirt, the women rip open bags of confetti and rice and throw handfuls at us. I try to keep smiling as the bits hit my eyes and mouth. I squint past the crowd and see the limousine parked at the end of the sidewalk.

"'Scuse us," I say, "'scuse us, please." I gently tug Catherine's hand and plunge ahead like a fullback.

Catherine takes a couple of moments to hug her mother and my mother. The crowd parts to let us through. More confetti. "Oh, Paul, not so fast," says Catherine, but she's laughing.

Sid has the limousine door open. The back is roomy enough for Catherine to step inside and turn around, and I help her with the hoop skirt. Someone tosses a ton of confetti in after us just before Sid closes the door. Faces appear at the windows—folks trying to get another look at the bride and my bump.

Mrs. Bolton wants to say something to us, so I wind down the window. "You look divine, dear. How are the combs?"

"Terrific, Aunt Hazel, terrific!" (The combs are Mrs. Bolton's, the "something borrowed" that every bride has to have. They're somewhere in Catherine's hair, I think, holding the veil in place.)

Sid inches the car away. Steve comes running over to Sid's window.

"Don't go any faster than this," he says, "and we'll fall in line behind you."

"Who was the man in the madras jacket?" Catherine asks me.

"I don't know. Don't you know?"

"No. I thought they were your mom's guests."

"No. Maybe they came to the wrong wedding and were too embarrassed to leave."

"Mom'll have a fit if they come to the reception—unless they're friends of the Boltons or something. They didn't seem to be talking to anyone."

There's a loud honk from the car behind us. I look back and see Steve and The Shark waving madly. They want me to tell Sid to start honking, so I do and he does. We're on Main Street now, Sid's rhythmic blasts proclaiming to Greater Winnipeg that Catherine Barber and Paul Hodges are married.

"Well?" says Catherine. "Aren't you going to tell me the story of the bump? Were you really hit by a golfball?"

"Yes. Greg and Dad and I went golfing. Just one hole, around noon."

"You didn't."

"Honest, we did. I'm sorry I didn't tell you; it was a silly spur-of-the-moment thing—"

"Silly? I think it was a great idea. I wish I'd done something like that. So somebody hit you. Is it sore?"

"It's okay. Does it look awful?"

"Makes you look rugged. Now, what about the cut?"

We both laugh and Catherine snuggles up to me—as much as you can snuggle when you're wearing a hoop skirt. This brings a new round of honks from the guys behind us. We kiss. Catherine's mouth tastes minty-fresh.

7

At the stately Fort Garry Hotel, we assemble on the mezzanine for photographs. Dad's making Mrs. Barber laugh—a good sign—while Mr. Barber talks to Shelagh about hotel decor. Charleen's found a wet cloth somewhere and she's trying to get a spot off Allan's lapel. The Shark is smoking furiously. Frances is telling Mom and Catherine how nervous she was in church, while Steve discusses angles and backgrounds with the photographer.

"Could we have the parents first?" the photographer calls out. "With the bride and groom, of course."

We move over to a spot in front of some maroon drapes.

The photographer says, "You're the groom's father, aren't you?"

"Yes?" says Dad.

"You should be on the groom's side, with your wife. And Mrs. Hodges—I mean Mrs. Hodges Senior. Your hat's a bit off centre . . . good. All right, *cheese.*"

Next up are the attendants. Mrs. Barber stands back with the photographer and looks at us with cocked head and critical eye. She says, "Straighten up, Allan, that's the boy. What's that on your face, Paul?"

"The famous Hodges nose," says Dad.

The photographer comes over to examine my upper lip.

"It's a cut," I say.

"We can retouch it out, if you like," says the photographer.

"That would be nice," says Mrs. Barber.

"While you're at it," says The Shark, "could you give me a chin?"

Steve tells us that the speeches will start in about two minutes. The receiving line went well, though Allan's wife Pris gave me a french kiss (Steve says she has a tongue like a stray cat—it'll go in anywhere) and Polonius Martin spent a little too long embracing Catherine.

Charleen's sister Gail cried when we told her how well she sang and
Rose Benson laughed too much for someone whose boyfriend, Wheels
McGarvey, is in the hospital recuperating from a serious accident.
(Wheels loves to play car tag.) Steve's girlfriend, Joy, came in with
Rose and she looked sad, as if she figures Steve'll never marry her.

The guests have eaten their chicken salad and ice cream and I've
drunk three glasses of punch. Steve stands and clinks his glass.

"Ladies and gentlemen, I'm Steve Bristow and I'm honoured to
be the groomsman this afternoon. I use that term because Paul and
Allan and The Shark and I are such good friends, we don't want to
say which of us is the *best* man."

At the parents' table, everyone looks a little worried about what
Steve might say next—everyone except Mr. Westlake, who nods and
chuckles. I look around the room and—there's the guy in the madras
jacket and the woman in white. Who are they and how did they get
past the receiving line?

" . . . and to give the Toast to the Bride, I'd like to call on Dr. John
Bolton. Doctor?"

The Doctor rises from his seat at the parents' table, looking relaxed.
He isn't holding any notes.

"Ladies and gentlemen. Any time I'm asked to speak, I regard it as
an honour. A few months ago, I was asked to speak to the Chamber
of Commerce and, before I got started, I was called away to deliver a
baby. Today, I *counted* on being called away. Since I haven't been, I'm
going to use the Chamber of Commerce speech."

There's a smattering of polite laughter until Steve breaks the ice
with a loud whoop.

"I've always thought that Winnipeg was the best of all possible
cities because of its four distinct seasons, its medium size, its access
to some of the finest fresh water lakes in the world—"

Everyone laughs—he *is* giving his Chamber of Commerce speech.
"But what makes Winnipeg the place I love is the citizens, and I've
known some of the best. Among them I count the Barbers." I try to
concentrate on what he's saying because I've got to answer him, but
my mind keeps wandering. Thank goodness I've prepared
something—I just hope I can relate it to what he's saying. How come
the books I read were full of the bride's fatigue and said nothing
about the groom's anxiety?

"You see this lovely, serene young bride? She might never have been so composed if it hadn't been for my wife, Hazel. Hazel gave Catherine her first blanket, which provided the best of satin-edged security for years. Catherine's mother, Marilyn, deserves a lot of credit, too, for taking the blanket away from her daughter at the right time . . . as a matter of fact, just yesterday." From a brown paper bag he takes a tattered fragment of pink cloth—about a square foot in size— with a pink satin border along two sides of it. He holds it up and everyone laughs. "Marilyn figures Catherine won't need it now that she has Paul."

He goes on to talk about Catherine's life at school and university, how supportive the family was of everything she did, including her little fling at theatre. He talks about how she met me and how I got into the family business, and he returns to a description of Catherine and me:

"Catherine we knew to be a beautiful, level-headed, personable young lady and we soon found out that Paul was hard-working, intelligent and sincere. Yet the families worried that the two of them might be incompatible. Well, I have done some extensive research and I can assure you that there will never be any problem as long as the groom has *income* and the bride is *patable*.

"Ladies and gentlemen, would you please join with me in wishing Catherine—well, Paul and Catherine—a lifetime of health and happiness . . . as we drink a toast . . . to the Bride."

Clothing rustles and chairs scrape as the people stand up, clink their glasses, say, "To the Bride!" and sip their drinks. A shiver runs through me. Everything I've eaten presses up against my heart and lungs. I feel dazed—did that golf ball give me a mild concussion?

"Thank you, Dr. Bolton," says Steve. "Now, with his reply, here's the co-star of our show, my old buddy, known to his closest friends as . . . Luap Segdoh."

Everyone applauds. Catherine squeezes my wrist. I shoot a hand into my jacket and take out a folded-up piece of paper. As I stand, I glance at my notes:

"Wed nite no big deal
(but could be!)
Be gentle
Don't rush
Don't dawdle
Don't smother

Be considerate—exhausting day for bride
Hymen more likely to stretch than pop
Shave first?
Lights on or off?
Pyjamas on or off?"

The wrong notes! I shove the paper back into my pocket. There's no other paper there. I look out at the crowd: my mother's smiling but Catherine's mother isn't. Len Pinkus looks ready to burst out laughing. Helen is holding her hand over her mouth and Pris is adjusting a bra strap. I have to speak.

"Um, hi, everybody."

I once read that "Hi" is disarming. A hush falls over the crowd. For a crazy moment I think of the lines from the play: *We're soldiers, we are, willing to lay down our lives for you—*

"From the very first time I saw —"

I pause for effect but I'm sure most people think I've forgotten the bride's name. "—Catherine, that was a few years before I, you know, actually met her . . . . From the first day, I *knew* . . . well, I mean, it didn't take any great powers of perception or anything . . . but I knew what a lovely girl Catherine was—is—and now we've all had it confirmed by—by a doctor, who's a specialist in these things."

There's a collective sigh from the sentimental folks and a nervous laugh from a few others.

"I agree with everything he said, not only about Catherine but also about her parents. They are two of the liveliest, most industrious people you'd ever want to meet. Uh . . . It was difficult at first to convince Catherine's dad that I'd rather take out his daughter than discuss the Bracken Commission and the effects of the new liquor laws. And her mom couldn't quite understand my great passion for—for tea and toast. But you sure can't beat marrying the boss's daughter, can you?"

My notes are coming back to me and I'm in the home stretch.

"It's so good to see all of you today, and we thank you for all you've done for us. As you know, Catherine and I are going away for two weeks, but when we come back, we want each of you to come and visit us in our new home at Suite 15 in the Falcon Apartments. Not all of you at once, of course. And when you come, all we ask is that you bring a little house-warming gift, like a chesterfield, a chair or a dining room suite. Um, thank you."

Applause. My knees weaken. I did it. I sit down.

"Thanks, Luap," says Steve. "Now, if you'll all rise once again and lift your glasses, it's my pleasure to draw your attention to the lovely bridesmaids—as if you haven't noticed them already. Ladies and gentlemen, here's to the Maid of Honour and the Bridesmaids."

We all stand and toast them.

"Now I have some telegrams to read," says Steve. "The first says, 'To Mr. and Mrs Paul Hodges. You met in *Still Life*. You're now indulging in a little *Pomp and Circumstance*. May you progress onward to *This Happy Breed*. Love, Carole and Ian Hodges, Los Angeles.' Here's another: 'Dear Paul. Hear you have a new apartment. Am coming to Winnipeg and hope to be able to stay with you until I get settled. Love, Fifi.' "

Laughter and a belated shriek.

"Here's another. 'Catherine and Paul: All the best to you as you set off down Life's highway together. Much love from Aunt Allison in Halifax.' And one more. 'Remember: Once a king, always a king, but once a knight's enough.' Oops! How did that one get in there?"

Some laughter, most of it embarrassed. Mr. Westlake laughs loudest—I think he's had a good quantity of punch.

Before we know it, Catherine and I have cut the cake and we're circulating, handing out souvenir pieces. Mr. Barber shakes my hand, Mr. Westlake pats my shoulder, and Mrs. Barber touches her cheek against mine as she says, "I thought the off-colour telegram was a little unnecessary." Helen hugs Catherine; I chat with Joy and Pris. Catherine talks with Polonius Martin and his red-haired wife while I move on to Harriet and Phil Dutchuk. (When Catherine and I visited the Dutchuks last, we couldn't sit in the living room because it was filled with the half-finished hull of a sailboat. We spent the evening in their kitchen drinking home brew.)

I take a swig of punch. Harriet is about to speak to me when Mrs. Jarvis steps between us and says, "Mind you have a happy life, now, Paul!"

While Catherine's off in a room changing to her going-away suit, The Shark and I go to another room we've reserved for relaxing. Steve's stocked it with booze and mix and ice and glasses. I make myself a rye and Seven-up and sink into an armchair. The Shark lights up a cigarette and goes into the bathroom.

My mind flips back to that time two and a half years earlier, during my one and only stage performance, when I stood in the wings and saw what the audience could see on one side of the curtain and what they couldn't see on the other. I gaze at the bed and think, A wedding's like that, with its public ritual—the ceremony and the reception—and its private ritual—

"Hey," says The Shark, coming out of the bathroom and flinging his suit jacket onto the bed, "enough of this wedding caper. What do you say we drive out to Grand Beach and see what we can pick up?"

"Those days are over."

"For you, maybe. What about your poor old buddy here?"

"Shark. This could just as easily have been you as me who's just tied the knot."

"But it isn't, is it?"

"I'm just saying—"

"Well, don't say. It's your toothbrush that's going to be sitting beside Catherine Barber's. Not mine."

"Look, I know how you feel."

"No, you don't. You don't have a clue how I feel."

"All right."

He sits down on the bed, facing me. "Paul, will you promise me one thing?"

I'm a little taken aback by his serious, almost grim expression. "What's that?"

"That you'll look after her. I mean, really look after her. She is so outstanding."

"I'll look after her, Shark. I promise."

There's a knock on the door and The Shark is quick to answer it. In come Mom and Dad and Greg. I jump up.

"How about a drink, Dad? Greg?"

"No, thanks," says Dad. "We just came by to wish you a safe trip."

"You'll send us a postcard, won't you?" says Mom.

"When you're golfing in Banff," says Greg, "think of the peasants back home."

"Take care, my boy," Dad says, in the same tone he used on the golf course.

He hugs me. In the face of all this family stuff, The Shark turns away, pretending to be busy at the bar. I think it's the first time Dad ever hugged me. He just isn't the kind of man who hugs. It's funny how a hug from your dad can bring tears to your eyes.

8

Catherine, in stylish blue suit with mink trim, leans over the mezzanine railing and holds her bouquet high above her head. In the hotel lobby below stand the single girls, bracing themselves for the moment. Steve turns Catherine around so that her back is to the railing.

He says, "One, two, three—throw!"

Catherine tosses the flowers up and they brush the ceiling before dropping into the cluster of girls. "Grab 'em, Rose!" someone yells. "Jump for it, Charleen!" cries someone else. The crowd cheers when one person emerges with the bouquet clutched in her two hands: Frances Drake.

"Now it's the men's turn," says Steve.

Catherine gives me the garter she wore under her wedding dress— the "something blue"—and the single guys assemble in the area where the girls were. I turn my back to them and fling the garter over my head and down into the lobby. Len Pinkus, the tallest, makes a good try, but The Shark leaps high, tosses a pretty serious elbow, and plucks the thing out of the air.

"Okay, you two," says Steve, "we're off."

He leads the way down the stairs. Catherine and I say our last-minute goodbyes to the folks as we move to the door. The Shark swoops into our midst and gives Catherine a quick, hard kiss.

"So long," he says.

"Ask Fran out," says Catherine. "She'd like that."

"Bye, Shark," I say, and I shake his hand.

Outside, Steve has the Barber Oldsmobile running. He tips the doorman for watching it for him. The plan is that he'll drive us and Catherine's suitcases to my car and the Barbers will catch a ride home with the Boltons.

Once we're on our way, Catherine says, "Everything went perfectly." She puts her hand on Steve's shoulder. "You were fabulous."

We talk about the wedding as Steve drives over the Main Street Bridge and the Norwood Bridge and through the Norwood Flats. I sit back, my arm around my bride.

"I wonder if anyone got to the getaway car," I say. "Allan was gone for a while. Do you think he might've?"

"Naww," says Steve. "He doesn't know where the car is."

"Greg knows. He could've told Allan. Some guys just love to fill the air vents with confetti, steal the battery, flatten the tires . . ."

We talk about these possibilities. The last thing I want is tin cans tied to the axle or "Just Married" scrawled across the trunk. I want to drive to the motel inconspicuously and park the car inconspicuously.

Steve drives slowly down the back alley, past garbage cans and garages and hollyhocks and fences. A man dumps his grass-cuttings into a heap by the lane. A kid runs to a telephone pole ahead of us crying, "One two three on Jeffrey."

We reach the garage and Steve stops the car. I jump out and follow him to the side door. This garage belongs to a widow, Mrs. Yetman, who doesn't have a car. She doesn't have a lock for the garage, either, so we had to buy a padlock especially for this occasion. Steve unlocks it and we enter the leaning old structure. The earth floor looks damp and the whole place stinks, but the car is untouched.

"*Voila*," says Steve.

There's a two-by-four across the double doors. Steve lifts it out of its slots and pushes the doors open. They creak. Steve fetches Catherine's matched set of luggage from the Olds.

Catherine gets out of her dad's car and comes over to look at the Austin. "It looks okay," she says slowly, sounding disappointed.

Steve puts two of her suitcases into the Austin trunk and the third with my one and the golf clubs in the back seat. He hands me the car key.

"Have a five-star honeymoon, Luap," he says.

"I can't thank you enough," I say, shaking his hand.

"Then don't. Look after the lad, Enirehtac." He takes Catherine into his arms and squeezes her. "Now get lost."

We get into the Austin. I turn the key. There are some anxious seconds of ignition noise. The engine catches. My heart leaps.

Steve backs the Olds out of the way.

We drive out of the garage and down the lane, past Mrs. Jarvis's, past the Hogans', past our house with its profusion of lilac bushes.

I drive just as slowly as Steve did, in case some kid darts out of a yard. As we reach the end of the alley and turn into the street, we wave to Steve. He waves back and drives off in the opposite direction.

"We're alone!" I cry. "I can't believe it!"

"Free!"

We cackle like children. I run my hand up her thigh; she runs hers up mine.

"Careful," she says.

"Sorry," I say, and I take my hand away.

"I don't mean *that*. I mean, watch where you're going."

"Right. But I'd better keep both hands on the wheel, too."

I try to concentrate on my driving but fragments of advice from the books I've read keep floating through my head: *It is often supposed that marriage must be consummated by a complete union on the first night of the honeymoon. . . . However much it is desired, it may be several days before complete union is possible. . . . It is certainly not too much to ask that the bridegroom be the personification of tenderness. . . . The first embrace to be completed will depend on the bride's being fit for response after recovering from the fatigue of the wedding . . .*

"How do you feel?" I ask.

"Gloriously tired."

My heart sinks. "Really?"

"Don't you?"

"I guess a little."

"Well, don't drop off there at the wheel."

"I won't."

We're heading through town to the Number 1 Highway and fifty miles west to Portage la Prairie, where we've booked a motel room. Who'd ever think of looking for us in Portage?

Catherine leans her head on the back of the seat. Is she going to sleep?

"Wasn't the doctor a riot?" she says.

"He sure was. But we knew he'd be good."

"How did you think Pris looked?"

"Dowdy."

"I mean, do you think she looked pregnant?"

"I'd say so. It affects her eyes somehow."

"I thought so, too."

We're stopped for a traffic light. A woman in a light summer dress crosses in front of us pushing a baby carriage.

"That'll be me a year from now," says Catherine.

"I thought we decided not to—"

"Just fooling! Gosh, you're jumpy."

The light changes. I accelerate too quickly.

"Heyy!"

"Sorry."

"The last thing we want is an accident."

"You're not kidding."

"Say, did you ever find out who the man in the madras jacket was?"

"No, I didn't. Did you?"

"No."

"Your mother'll know."

"Let's hope so."

Over the bridges we go, up Main Street, past the CNR station. And in my head: . . . *The ducts of these glands open just outside the hymen and furnish abundant lubrication during sexual excitement in order to facilitate entry. . . . The physical side of married life is as truly a part of God's purpose as any other. . . .*

"I can't get over how beautifully Gail sang," I say.

"Mmn."

"Are you going to sleep?"

"Of course not."

"Good."

"I'm just resting my eyes."

She drifts off before we reach the suburb of St. James. At first I'm disappointed, but then I figure this is the best thing, to let the bride snooze a little and get over the fatigue of the day so that later she'll be lively and responsive.

I glance at her. She's the loveliest girl I've ever seen, even lovelier in repose, if that's possible. I can't believe she's with me, and I can't believe she's delivered herself into my care this way. I'd better keep my eyes on the road.

You don't have a clue how I feel, The Shark said. Won't he ever let go of the notion that I stole the girl he idolizes?

When I finally sorted out with Catherine that I should have my

62

closest friends stand up for me, I had to practically beg them. Well, not Allan, he was the least of my worries. The one guy in our foursome who had to get married—I included him I guess because I've always sort of felt sorry for him. But I phoned Steve first, and, after giving me the gears about letting a girl dominate my life, he said he'd be the best man if I patched things up with The Shark. I phoned The Shark and he wouldn't talk to me.

The whole idea that I'd taken The Shark's dream girl away from him took on crazy proportions. Even Steve acted like he believed it. I finally went over to The Shark's house and told his dad it was nuts for The Shark and me to be mad at each other. His dad sat us down in their rec room with a few Carling Black Labels and told us not to come upstairs until we'd got over whatever it was that was bugging us. That's the kind of guy The Shark's dad is.

After just sitting there looking at his beer for what seemed like forever, The Shark said, "I never told you this. I used to follow Catherine home. From a distance. I saw her every day in class but I couldn't ever think of what to say. I did things that made her laugh, but I thought of her as being above me somehow, like a queen or something. When I started working and she went to university, I used to drive by her place. Sometimes, I'd park, hoping I'd catch a glimpse of her. I saw her leaving with a guy a few times over the years, always in a fancy car. Then you tell me you're in this play with her and I think, She's come down to earth. Maybe Paul can set something up so I can meet her, talk about our high school days."

I tried to hide my surprise. "Believe me, Shark, I thought she was out of my league, too. This was a very gradual thing—I never thought she'd—"

"What I'm trying to say to you is . . . it's hard for me to see her with you. I mean, no offence, Paul, but I keep asking myself, what does she see in that guy that she doesn't see in me?"

"Thanks a lot."

"But do you see what I mean?"

"Shark, you've got to get over this." All I could think was: I can't ask him to be an usher at my wedding; it'd be the supreme insult in his eyes.

But then he said, "You want to know what I think? I think you're here today because you want to ask me to be your best man and you have no idea how that would make me feel."

"I do *not* want you to be my best man."

"Thank God for that."

"I want you to be an usher."

He stared at me, looking me in the eye for the first time. He looked as if he might reach out and grab me by the collar. Instead, he started to laugh.

"You're beautiful, Pauly." He kept laughing. I sat there, wondering if his dad would let me go without resolving this. Then The Shark said: "You know what? I think it's the perfect role for me. I'll do it."

9

n i n e

In the motel office, I nearly gag on the words: "The name is Mr. and Mrs. Hodges. We have a reservation."

The proprietor, a woman wearing a dressing gown and curlers in her hair, seems to be trying hard not to laugh. She smirks as she looks past me, out to the car where Catherine is. Does she think we aren't married? Even though there's confetti falling out of my hair onto her counter?

My hand shakes. I can hardly write my name.

"Unit Number Six," the woman says.

"Thank you," I say, reaching for the key. I don't quite have hold of it and it falls to the floor. Avoiding the woman's eyes, I bend to pick it up.

"Number Six," I say as I get back into the car.

"Too bad you couldn't get Seven for good luck," says Catherine in a sleepy voice.

I drive past the first five units. They're painted pink and they all have picture windows with closed venetian blinds. I pull into the parking spot in front of "6", alongside a DeSoto sedan from Nebraska. I turn off the ignition.

Catherine says, "Are you going to carry me across the threshold?"

"Don't I do that when we move into our apartment?"

"Come on. I want to be carried."

We get out of the car and walk up to the motel door. I unlock it and swing it open. Embarrassed but eager to please, I put one arm behind Catherine's back and another behind her knees. She leaps and I catch her.

"Oof!" I gasp.

"I'm not *that* heavy."

"I'm out of shape."

"Don't trip—hey, you're doing fine."

I stagger into the room, carry her over to the bed and drop her.

65

"Oh!" She laughs.

"How is it?"

"Not too firm." She bounces twice. "Not too soft. Just right."

"And I'm Poppa Bear!" I growl.

"Save me! Please save me!"

"Shhh! Not so loud, Cath. The door's still open."

"Then close it."

"I'll get the suitcases."

"Hurry."

I scamper out, take the bags out of the car and lock up. It's twilight. The place seems full but nobody else is outside. I pick up all four cases, lug them inside and set them on the carpet. Catherine has turned on a lamp but she's still lying on the bed. I close the door. The click of the lock stirs my blood.

"Don't you want to change," I say, "or shower or—"

"Why don't you just ravish me quick before I fall asleep again."

"Cath!"

She laughs and swings her legs over the edge of the bed and sits up. "I can't wait till we get to Banff, can you?"

"Gosh, I hope we don't have to."

Chuckling, she lifts one of her suitcases onto the bed. "We'd better hang a few things up."

I'm overwhelmed by the sight of her just doing something like taking a dress out of her case. I put my arms around her waist from behind.

"I still can't believe this," I say. "Do you realize how many envious guys we left behind?"

"Uh—let me hang this up, okay?"

Don't expect the first time to be a picnic, I remind myself as she walks over to the closet with the dress. She opens the closet door.

"*Surprise!*"

Out pops The Shark.

Catherine shrieks.

"How're you doing, Poppa Bear?" says The Shark. He's wearing his wedding clothes, minus the jacket, tie and shoes.

"Shark, you could've given us both heart attacks!" says Catherine.

"Sorry."

"Did you hear what we—"

"Every word."

"How did you get in here?"

"My dad knows the owner."

"But how did you know we were coming *here*?" I demand. "It was a secret."

"I knew you had to come this way and my dad sells cleaning supplies to the motels around here. I got him to check some reservations."

"You really scared me," says Catherine, giggling. She hangs up the dress.

"Sorry, but somebody had to do something. We couldn't let you get off scot free."

"Did you put cracker crumbs—" Catherine grabs the bed covers and throws them back.

"No, no," says The Shark.

She rushes into the bathroom. "Glue on the toilet seat? Gum in the taps?"

"No, no, I didn't have time. I just got here a little ahead of you." He lights up a cigarette.

"I expected *some* pranks. When there were no messages scrawled on the car, I was disappointed."

"So you're glad I came?"

"We sure are. Aren't we, Paul?"

"Yeah, are we ever."

"How about a drink?" says Catherine.

"Oh, no!" I groan.

"What's wrong?"

"I meant to bring a bottle. I forgot." I have one in my suitcase but I want The Shark out of here. Now.

"Never fear," says The Shark, "I've got one." He drops to his knees and pulls a bottle out from under the bed. "Rye okay?"

"Terrific," says Catherine. "Paul, maybe you can get some ginger ale from the motel office."

"Got that, too," says The Shark, and he reaches under the bed and takes out a couple of bottles of Canada Dry. He gets up, goes over to the desk and opens a drawer. "And presto!" He takes out a bucket. "Ice!"

These conjuring tricks are beginning to get to me.

"Glasses?" I say.

"In here," says Catherine, doing a hippety-hop into the bathroom.

"Shark, you silly devil," I say. *Get out of here!*

"You aren't mad, are you?"

"Mad?" says Catherine, coming out with three glasses. "Of course we aren't mad. As a matter of fact, we were starting to get a little bored."

The Shark sees my startled look and busies himself with the drinks. He says, "The wedding sure went well, didn't it?"

"I thought so," says Catherine.

The Shark hands Catherine a drink. "This one for the beautiful bride . . ."

"Why, thank you, Shark. That's very sweet of you."

"And this one for the dashing groom."

"Thanks." I'm giving him the evil eye but he's ignoring it.

"And one for the lowly usher. Here's to both of you."

We clink glasses and take sips. Catherine gives The Shark a quick kiss on the cheek. I'm raging inside. Not one of those books said anything about this.

"So when is it going to be your turn to tie the knot?" she asks him.

"I have to find a girl first."

"You seemed to hit it off with Frances."

"I don't think she'd want anything to do with a lowly insurance clerk with a Grade Twelve education. She said something about her boyfriend being in Pre-Med—well, maybe it was her ex-boyfriend, I'm not sure. And she has her nursing degree—"

"Oh, come on, now," says Catherine, "you shouldn't sell yourself short. I've heard you're doing very well. And I happen to know Fran's anxious to dump the Pre-Med guy and she's just too nice a person to come right out and tell him. But she did take a shine to you at the rehearsal party. This morning, when we were getting our hair done, she wanted to know all about you, but I had to say I really didn't know a lot about your love life. I told her you were a good friend of Paul's and he was always saying what a lot of fun you were, but, as far as I knew, you were still dating Dar—"

"Excuse me," I say. Someone has to put a stop to this.

"Yes?" says Catherine.

"I was just wondering . . ."

"Yes?"

" . . . if maybe you'd like something to eat."

"Now that you mention it, I am pretty hungry. I hardly ate a thing at the reception. How about you, Shark?"

"I—uh . . ." He looks at me and I try to give him a signal by nodding toward the door without Catherine seeing me. "Well, I am pretty hungry . . ."

"I'm craving a nice greasy hamburger," says Catherine. "I saw an A & W on the way into town; let's all go over there."

"Why don't I go and get the burgers?" says The Shark. "You two can get settled—"

"You wouldn't leave us alone!" Catherine cries in mock horror.

The Shark gives a rather weak laugh.

"If he doesn't leave us alone soon," I say, "I might consider murder."

"Okay, okay! I can take a hint."

"A hint! I'm giving you a message in neon lights!"

"Pau-ul!"

"It's all right," says The Shark, "I really have stayed too long."

"You have not. At least finish your drink."

He downs it in two quick gulps.

"I'll be running along."

"You look so cute with no shoes on," says Catherine.

"They're in the car," he says.

"I wish Fran could see you right now," says Catherine. "You have that lost-little-boy look."

"Shark," I say. "Amscray."

"I'm going! So long, folks."

"Bye, Shark." Catherine gives him a little hug and kisses him on the cheek. "Thank you for everything. We'll always remember this."

"Goodbye, Catherine."

"Oh, don't forget your rye."

"No, no, you keep it. Bye, now. See you when you get back."

He gives me a quick apologetic grin, waves his hand and leaves. I get up and close the door behind him.

"Phew!" says Catherine. "I thought he'd never go."

"I guess I was a little abrupt."

"Are you kidding? You deserve a medal for tolerance."

"Quite an entrance he made."

"I've never had a scare as bad as that."

"Do you still want that hamburger?"

"Well yes, I'd love one."

"I'll go and get a couple."

"Let's both go."

"Before . . . ?"

"Uhh . . . no. After."

"Oh, Cath." I embrace her.

"I'll need a bath," she says.

"After?"

"No. Before."

"I should have one, too," I say.

"After," she says.

"Before," I say.

"No," she says, "I mean, after I have mine."

"Oh. Yes, okay, sure."

"Why don't I have mine right now?"

"Please do."

"I won't be long."

"Good."

"Is it warm in here or is it me?"

"I hope it's you."

She chuckles suggestively, takes the smallest of her suitcases and heads into the bathroom. She closes the door and locks it. I listen as she turns on a tap. I hear her open and shut her case, open and shut the medicine cabinet. I hear her start the shower. *She's naked in there right now.* Unbelievable as it may seem, I'm married to Catherine Barber. *I'm going to sleep with Catherine Barber.*

I take off my jacket, pull off my tie and undo the top button of my shirt. After I've hung up my jacket, I open my suitcase and take out my new pyjamas. I find the box of safes and take one out, leaving it in its envelope. Where should I put it? It won't be very discreet to have it sitting out on the night table when Catherine comes out of the bathroom. I pull back the bedclothes and slip the little envelope under one of the pillows, and then I remake the bed and put the rest of the safes back in my suitcase.

It *is* warm in here. I go over to the front window and find that it doesn't open. The one at the back does open but it won't stay. Do I really want it open? Won't our voices carry out into the street? Our cries of ecstasy? I decide to open it for a while and I prop it up with the Gideon Bible.

I hear a couple of thumps and some kids' laughter next door.

Sounds as if the Nebraskans are playing baseball in their room.

I sit down on the bed and untie my shoes. Something makes me check the pillows to be sure I know which one the safe is under. *The physical side of marriage is as truly a part of God's purpose as any other.*

The water stops running. It's quiet in there. I pull my shoes off and set them in the closet. Another thump: was it next door or in the bathroom? Is she all right?

The bathroom door opens. A pungent perfume precedes Catherine into the room.

"Hi," she says.

She poses in the doorway. Her dark brown hair's been brushed out and she's wearing a mauve negligee and matching peignoir. She's put on fresh lipstick.

"That was heaven," she says.

"You're beautiful," I say.

She comes to me and I take her into my arms. Her body feels so warm, the lingerie so soft. Her hair smells of the outdoors, fragrant fields, sunlit flowers.

"I'm glad we waited," she says.

"Oh, so am I!"

"And now the time has come."

"The time has come."

"D-Day."

"D-Day."

"Do you *have* to have a bath?"

"I should."

"Aww—"

"I'll be quick."

I fumble with a few items in my suitcase and decide to take the whole darned thing into the bathroom with me. I trip at the door and bang the suitcase on the toilet. I look out at Catherine as I close the door but she's not looking; she's busy unpacking. I undress.

I'm not used to showers and I have a terrible time finding the right blend of hot and cold. When I think I have it, the spikes of water shock me. But I know Catherine expects me to have a shower, not a sit-down bath.

In four minutes, I've washed myself from head to toe, five or six times in the mid-section. All the warnings and all the cautions roar into my head again: *Be gentle, don't expect too much, don't rush, don't be rough, don't put all your weight on her, don't, don't, don't . . .*

I'm out of the shower. The bathroom's still alive with her perfume. I take deep breaths of it while I brush my teeth. The bump and the cut don't look so bad anymore.

I put on my pyjama jacket, button it wrong, unbutton it, button it right. I put on my pyjama bottoms and take what seems to be years to execute a nifty bow in the drawstring.

Wait.

Do I hear voices? The Nebraskans again?

No. It's Catherine talking. Did The Shark come back?

I open the door just a crack. She's on the phone:

" —went so well, thanks to you. . . . I mean it. . . . What? . . . Well, of course I still sound the same! What did you expect? . . . No, actually, nothing's happened yet. . . . I know he is, and right now he's having a shower. . . . I will. . . . Of course! . . . No, I won't. . . . Okay, I'd better go. Say hello to Dad for me and thanks, again, Mom, to both of you. . . . Yes, I'll be *fine*! I'll call you again tomorrow. . . . Oh, you're welcome. . . . Bye, then. . . . Bye."

She hangs up the phone. She's sitting on the side of the bed, still in the peignoir and negligee.

I step out of the bathroom and say, "You called your mother?"

"Yes. She said it was very thoughtful of me."

"Do you have to report in every day?"

"No. Say, are we being a little touchy-wutchy here?"

"Sorry, I guess I'm just sort of surprised—"

"I'm pretty close to my mother, but consider that a duty call. And now it's done. Come on to bed."

She takes off the peignoir and drops it on the floor. This gesture—tossing the garment aside instead of hanging it up—strikes me as wildly sensual. She gets under the covers.

I ask, "Is that going to be your side of the bed?"

"Is that okay with you? I like to be close to a window."

"Sure. That's fine."

I go to the other side, take off my watch and set it on the desk. There's no night table or lamp on my side of the bed.

"What time are we going to get up in the morning?" I say.

"I thought we were going out for hamburgers after."

I pull back the covers on my side and get into bed. I realize I've never been in a bed with anyone, not since I was a kid and shared one with my brother, Greg. I've never even been *on* a bed with Catherine before—on a chesterfield, on a sofa, but never on a bed.

"Did you ask your mother about the guy in the madras jacket?"

"Darn it, no, I didn't. Why don't I call her back right now?"

We both burst out laughing. We're on our sides, facing each other. A door slams somewhere. I kiss her nose and eyes.

"Should we turn out the lamp?" she asks.

"Okay."

She turns away from me, leans toward the lamp and switches it off. It's so dark, I can barely see anything. She sits up, pulls the negligee over her head and tosses it onto the floor. When she gets back under the covers, I take her into my arms.

"You're shaking," she says.

"You've never been naked in my arms before."

"Aren't you going to take off your pyjamas?"

"I guess I should, shouldn't I?"

We both laugh. I try taking the jacket off while I'm lying down under the covers but it's impossible. I get out of bed, take off the pyjamas and get back in. Catherine pulls the covers up around our necks and snuggles close. I find my old pal and caress it as gently as I can.

"Why don't we skip the preliminaries?" Catherine whispers.

This comes as a shock. It contradicts everything I've read.

"Are you sure?" I say. "I mean, are you okay?" *The first embrace to be completed will depend on the bride's being fit for response after recovering from the fatigue of the wedding.*

"Of course I'm okay."

"The books say a little foreplay helps put you in the mood."

"We've had two and a half years of foreplay!"

She kisses me and pushes her warm body against mine so that even our ankles are touching. One of her legs comes up and over my hip, and she starts to pull me on top of her.

Hold it. We've forgotten something.

I kiss her nose and my old pal as I push myself up onto my knees beside her.

"What's the matter?" she says.

"You know. And I guess you'll have to sit up a minute because it's under your pillow."

"What is—oh. You got some."

"I told you I would."

She doesn't budge. "Let's not."

"I'll put it on in the bathroom, if you'd like. They're tricky devils—"

"Let's not use it."

"Cath! You said—and we agreed—"

"I know—"

"I bought a whole gross!"

"I just think it might be better—"

"Gosh, Cath, what if—"

"Don't worry about that. I'm pretty sure this isn't my fertile time."

"But it could be?"

"I could be a day out either way. But, Paul, I've been thinking. Would it be so bad? We both said we want to have a baby sooner or later."

"Later rather than sooner."

"You said how much you like babies."

"I know, but—"

"Oh, come on, it won't happen anyway."

I lie down again. It takes a few moments for me to adjust, but no longer. Catherine is so close, kissing my shoulder, coaxing me onto her. *Don't expect the first time to be a picnic.* I try to keep my weight on my elbows and knees. She spreads her legs and pulls the covers up over us again.

"I love you, Cath."

It's amazing: no guilt, no admonition from Westlake, no interruption from The Shark, no outburst from Nebraska. And lovely, wonderful Catherine isn't a bit tired or cranky and we're off on our lovely, wonderful journey down life's highway—

"Oh! Just a minute, Paul."

"Sorry, am I hurting you?"

"No, no."

"Should I come out?"

"You aren't in yet."

"I thought I was—"

"You can go in a lot further. It's just that—"

"It's all right, Cath. I understand. The books all say it might take several days to consummate—"

"No, no. I just think we're too tense. We need to relax a little."

"I can't relax *too* much or—"

74

"Just sort of shift a little that way . . ."

"Like this?"

"Yes, that's it. Now, would you mind terribly—do you think you could do—you know—a line or two from the play—"

"In the accent?"

"Yes—could you?"

"Sure. Uhh, let's see. 'I think I've got a cold coming on—we've been mucking about at the Butts all day—you can't afford to let the army catch cold, you know.'"

"That's better! Keep going—"

"'We're soldiers, we are—willing to lay down our lives for you—'"

"That's it!"

part two

Susan:
1972

1

o n e

Toronto, Ontario
Saturday, August 5, 1972

Mmm.

That feels good.

What is it? Is this part of a dream?

Something warm and moist has hold of my toe. Oh, now there's something between my toes. It's flicking in and out.

It's pressing against the sole of my foot. It's at my ankle now. It's moving up my calf.

Paul's mouth—that's what it is. And his tongue. He's kissing his way up my leg. Now the other leg. Ahh. My body's waking up, a few inches at a time.

I'm lying on my back. I've kicked off the covers—it was hot last night. I can hear the traffic over on Avenue Road.

Paul's kissing my knees. He takes little bits of flesh between his teeth without biting. He moves up, up the inner thigh while he scratches the soles of my feet.

He caresses my calves. I open my legs a little wider. He's on the bed now, kissing, caressing, farther and farther up.

I arch my body to meet his mouth.

"Oh, yes!" I cry. "Don't stop!"

He doesn't.

"Oh, yes . . . ohh!" A warm shock wave rolls through me.

"Happy wedding day," he says.

"Ohh! Promise me you'll always wake me up like that."

"I promise."

"Can we get your tongue insured?"

He gives a throaty laugh and dips his head. His lush beard joins mine.

"Come here, you," I say.

78

I run my hands through his long hair as he kisses his way up my abdomen. He teases my navel with the tip of his tongue. I'm wide awake now.

I sit up and turn him onto his back. I go down on him. He groans with pleasure. I straddle him. I'm sopping and he slides in easily. I move up and down.

I get off him and put my face against the mattress, my ass in the air. He comes at me from behind.

"Oh, yes," I whisper.

To think he used to worry about coming too soon. I taught him the best way to get staying power: do it often.

I'm on my back again with my legs around him. We work into this great rhythm. We're sweating like horses.

"Oh oh oh, Jesus!" I cry out.

We both explode.

Still fondling me, bringing me down slowly, he says, "It's after ten. I thought I'd better wake you."

"Where's Eldridge?"

"Asleep somewhere. I've already fed him."

"Is that coffee I smell?"

"Uh huh."

"Christ, you're something else."

I nibble at his shoulder.

"Sue," he says, "I'd better get dressed. Robbie's plane comes in in an hour."

"Just stay inside me a little longer—"

The telephone rings.

"*Shit*," I say.

Paul kisses my neck and gently pulls away from me. I watch him get up and go out of the room. It's scary how much I love him. He's so gentle and he gives off heat like a stove.

"Hello?" I hear him say. "Oh, hi. . . . Sure you can. Just a minute, please."

I know who it is before he tells me.

"Sue," he says, leaning into the bedroom. "It's your mother."

Mother. The human octopus. "Still wants to get this wedding into a church, I'll bet."

I get up and give Paul's cock a squeeze on my way past him.

"Hello, Mom."

"Susan, do you think I should wear a hat?" She sounds wired. Probably been up all night worrying.

"You don't *need* a hat, Mom. If it makes you feel good to wear a hat, wear a hat."

"I won't feel good if no-one else wears one."

"There won't be many there. And the wedding's at sundown. No-one will care if you have a hat on or not."

"Your voice sounds sleepy. Are you just getting up?"

"Yes, Mom."

"This is your wedding day. You must have hundreds of things to do."

"It isn't that kind of wedding."

"I wish I knew what kind of wedding it is."

I take a deep breath.

"How was your night, Mom?"

"Your father snored. And in the next room it sounded like they were chopping up the furniture. I couldn't sleep. Never can in these big old hotels."

"Get out and do some shopping. Tell Dad he can have a beer right out on the street. There're these beer gardens on Yonge Street—"

"Sure you don't want me to come over there and make some perogies?"

"Just relax, Mom. Like you were on holiday."

"When could I ever relax on a holiday?"

"Hey, I gotta go. Talk to you later, okay?"

"All right, but I'm telling you right now, I think I'm going to wear a hat."

"That's fine. And Mom? Listen, I'm really glad you decided to come to the wedding. Honest."

She doesn't answer.

"Did you hear me, Mom?"

She's already hung up.

I could throw the phone at the wall! She can make me so bloody mad. I look in the ashtray for a decent-sized roach.

In comes Eldridge, our lucky black cat, and he's purring. He stretches out on the rug. I kneel down to scratch him around the ears. The purring gets louder, sounds like the rusty cables of an old elevator.

"Coffee?"

Paul comes into the room with a steaming cup. He's dressed now, in jeans and a Ryerson T-shirt.

"Thank you. I need this." I stay on the floor as he gives me the cup. "How about some Tia Maria, too?"

"Already in it."

I take a sip. "Ahhh, that's so good."

"I have to go. His plane's on time. I'll just make it." He leans over and kisses me. I smell traces of me in his beard. "Don't worry about your mother, Sue. Everything's going to be fine."

"Hurry back." I pat his fly.

"We'll have to behave while Rob's here, you know."

"What, no *ménage à trois*?"

"*Suzy*. He's my kid."

2

t w o

I get back into bed with my coffee. Those goddam parents of mine still wish I was having a big wedding like my sister, Nadia. I'm twenty, for Christ's sake, and I know what I want, and it isn't a bloody circus.

Nadia got married when I was in high school back in Saskatoon. Before I ever dreamed about moving out here to Toronto.

It was a big Ukrainian Catholic wedding. Nadia wore white but I knew she and Kenny had been doing it for months. They had one of those presentations. The guests come up to the head table and kiss the bride and groom and throw money into a big glass bowl. The men feel up the bridesmaids while they're french-kissing them. Everybody clinks their glasses every time they want the happy couple to kiss.

What a shit night. The dancing went on forever. Polkas. Butterflies. All those lard-ass guys with their jackets off and their shirts soaked with sweat. Falling down, throwing the women around, stepping on everybody's feet. I thought I'd puke.

Bowls and bowls of potatoes and cabbage rolls and perogies and sour cream and beets and carrots. Piles of beef and ham and kubasa and tons of cakes and pies. Everything gobbled up by two hundred people who were already too fat to be healthy. All washed down with Five Star and Coke.

But the thing I hated most was greasy Kenny Stefaniuk—the goddam groom—trying to shove his tongue down my throat behind a coat rack. Wouldn't let go of me till I kneed him in the balls.

Poor Kenny. Nobody deserves to get killed in a car accident. But he was a first-class asshole to try and drive all night when he knew he had a wife and kid back home. Probably for the best in the long run, but you can't tell Nadia that.

Can't tell her there was anything wrong with her wedding, either. But I made up my mind that my wedding would be different. And

82

the guy I married would be educated, not some bohunk stubble-jumper whose idea of luxury was front steps on our brand new ATCO trailer.

I thought about weddings a lot when I was at high school. Someday some handsome prince would come along. We'd have the kind of wedding *we* wanted and then he'd whisk me away from Saskatoon Saskatchewan.

I went to all the school dances, but I never met any princes. I was on Student Council and my biggest coup was getting Radisson's department store to donate a seven-foot stuffed dog to be our mascot. The football guys liked me for that, but I never let any of them take me home. Too busy counting money or cleaning up. Most times, my dad came and got me.

When grad came along, I asked Chuck Fulton to take me. He was a guy I met on the Radisson teen council. Came from City Park High, sort of gangly, but he used deodorant and he could talk.

His parents had a cottage at Pike Lake. The summer after grad, we'd sneak off there a lot, it's so close to the city. I had this idea I couldn't be a virgin if I was going to university in the fall. Chuck made sure I wasn't.

I still get kind of mellow when I think of Chuck.

3

t h r e e

Freshman year at the U of S was a disaster. First, Chuck checked out of my life. His parents moved to Vancouver and he went with them. He promised he'd write but all I got were two postcards. I tried to find another guy just like him. Joined a few clubs, played a lot of cards, went to Husky basketball games. No new Chucks.

I took Arts and the classes were so boring, I had to pop pills to stay awake. My parents were pissed off at me all the time, for lipping off at them, never studying, never bringing guys home, having the wrong friends, not doing enough around the house. We had some huge fights.

No wonder I got mixed up with hippies. At least, they acted like hippies. They all lived together commune-style in this big old house on the South Saskatchewan River. It was on the south-east bank, which was a lot higher than the one on the other side. The high bank had lots of bushes and trees and paths. Great places to hide and make out after a couple of doobies. If anybody on the downtown side, the low side, had ever looked at the high side through binoculars that winter, they might've seen some funny sights. Like two stoned bodies up in a tree humping away in a sleeping bag. A naked guy shooting down the side of the cliff on a bicycle, and crashing into a snow bank. A gang of hippies linking arms to make a human peace sign.

I was interested in this one guy, Sean. He seemed cool, not possessive or jealous at all. He was so unpossessive and so unjealous that he encouraged me to screw his pals while he went after my girlfriends. Pretty soon, but not soon enough, I figured out there wasn't much difference between being unpossessive and just not giving a damn about somebody.

The shit eventually hit the fan. My parents found out. Found out I was smoking up all the time, found out I was screwing myself silly, found out I was on The Pill. They grounded me.

My father said he'd lock me up, maybe forever. In his eyes, the worst thing I'd done was get on The Pill. Like it was some kind of

84

insult to him, to the family, to Ukrainians everywhere.

Anyway, I got back to the grind. I wrote my exams and did okay, but pretty soon I knew I couldn't face another year of bullshit. I worked as a hostess at Radisson's restaurant and started to plot how I could avoid going back to university.

The restaurant manager, Mr. Vipond, liked me. He told me what a good worker I was. I think he just wanted to get me into the sack. But when he told me I should take a hotel and restaurant course in Toronto, a light went on. I got him to phone my father. And Dad liked the idea.

Maybe Dad just wanted me out of his sight. Or maybe he thought his hippie kid was finally straightening out. The main thing was, he put up the cash to get me to T.O.

I got into the course, thanks to a letter from Vipond. And I found this main-floor apartment in a three-storey house on Dupont, just off Avenue Road.

That first few weeks, I was lonely as hell. To pass the time, I went to hear some Yankee draft dodger rant about how colleges were squeezing the life out of us. He convinced me I had to know more about The Revolution. I took his handout and went and bought the first three books on the list: *Soul on Ice*, by Eldridge Cleaver; *Do It!* by Jerry Rubin; and *The Female Eunuch*, by Germaine Greer. I read them instead of my hotel textbooks. I didn't feel oppressed like they said I should, but I did stop wearing a bra. It made me feel politically aware and sort of sexy at the same time.

I went to a coffee house with a couple of classmates, hoping to get some great discussions going. Heard this skinny wild-looking guy pouring out stuff about folks "who were burned alive in their innocent flannel suits on Madison Avenue amid blasts of leaden verse & the tanked-up clatter of the iron regiments of fashion & the nitroglycerine shrieks of the fairies of advertising & the mustard gas of sinister intelligent editors". It took me an hour to figure out he was quoting huge chunks of Ginsberg. He said his name was Les. He lectured me on the evils of the hotel business. He told me I had to connect with my subconscious. Only then would I learn how to fight the exploitation of young people by parents, colleges and corporations. I could get to the truth through LSD. He said LSD permeated the membrane that separated the subconscious from the conscious.

Les was a nice enough guy, very caring about the Third World.

And pretty soon he was bugging me about moving into my place. It was November and his pad in Chinatown had no heat. He had these dark patches under his eyes and he was so damned thin. I felt sorry for him.

I'll never forget the sight of him arriving at my place. Had his cat, Eldridge, under one arm and everything else in a net sack: his houkah pipe, his Kleenex for the LSD hits, his Che Guevera poster, and his clothes, mainly jeans and sandals and those Joe Cocker collarless shirts. The only underwear I saw was a pair of black silk bikini shorts he said he kept for special occasions. He brought a few books with him: Ferlinghetti, Ginsberg, Corso and the other San Francisco poets, along with the odd political tract and Pynchon's *V*. When I commented on how little he owned, he said, like it was a slogan: "Possessions are the curse of the western world."

We had fun together, but, when it came to paying the bills, it was all my treat. I got pretty tired of that. He told me to ask my dad for more money but I wouldn't. He kept hounding me to quit college. I insisted I couldn't. Not as long as my father was sending me money to go. (My parents knew nothing about Les. He answered the phone by mistake once and it was my mother. I told her he was just a guy I'd hired to fix the toilet.)

Les cooked some great meals, especially omelettes loaded with green peppers. But, after a while, I figured out he wasn't good for me. He had me smoking dope or dropping acid every day. He was filling my head with slogans but I didn't feel I was learning anything. We had no money, only what my dad sent, but Les wouldn't try to get a job.

"Working for somebody is a form of slavery," he said.

One night, after slow sex and a mellow joint, I told him I'd like to have a wedding someday, outside, maybe in a pasture. He blew up.

"Work! Weddings! Where the Christ do you get such bourgeois ideas?"

He obviously wasn't much of a prince.

I had to talk to somebody. Les was getting on my nerves. Should I talk to one of the girls in my class? Shit, no, they were more screwed up than I was. There was only one person I could talk to: an older person who might know things, my Human Relations professor, Paul Hodges.

4

Only thing was, I hated having to ask a man for help. I was trying to be a good feminist. (Les said *he* was a feminist, which I guess meant he approved of women paying the bills.) But Hodges seemed like a counsellor-type. He could listen to a female student's problems without looking like he was dying to climb into her pants.

He usually wore a plaid shirt, open to the third button, and faded blue jeans. Had this great beard, partly grey, mostly brown. I liked his classes, his soothing voice and the way he walked around the room.

I got a four o'clock appointment with him, one day in early December. We sat in his office, him puffing on a pipe. The office was so cramped and so loaded with books and loose papers, I thought he might set everything on fire. He leaned toward me and invited me to talk. He had nice eyes.

I told him about leaving home and meeting Les and thinking this course was right for me but not being sure anymore. I went on and on about drugs and The Revolution and liking Les but wishing he'd give me some breathing room. I guess I talked for half an hour before I realized he hadn't said a thing.

"Hey, I'm sorry to be dumping all this stuff on you," I said.

"It's okay," he said. "Please go on."

"Can you tell me what I should do?"

"About . . . ?"

"About Les. And my parents. And this course. And the crummy way I feel when I'm not on drugs."

"Look, I'm happy to listen, but I don't think I can tell you what choices to make—"

"I figured, since you teach Human Relations, and you're probably happily married with kids of your own . . ."

"Actually, I do have a son. But he lives with his mother in Winnipeg. We're divorced."

"Oh. I'm sorry."

"It's all right. Please go on."

I checked my Timex. I was enjoying talking to him but suddenly it seemed like we were looking too deep into each other's eyes. What was I trying to do? "I think I've already taken up too much of your time," I said quickly. "I'd better be going."

He looked alarmed. Then he leaned back and smiled. A careful, almost parental smile, but his eyes were warm. "I'd really like to hear more. How about continuing over a beer?"

We went to a smoky little place near Bloor and Yonge where writers and artists hang out. He asked me questions about drugs. I couldn't believe how little he knew about what you sniff and what you smoke and what you swallow. I told him I'd never messed with needles, even though Les did. He got me talking about sex, too. All I could think was, Where's he been? Everybody at school thought he was Mr. Cool, but he sounded like he'd been living in a monastery. Which was okay, actually. I'd practically forgotten my troubles when he said:

"I've got my car downtown today. Can I give you a lift home?"

I remembered Les. I did not want to see him.

"I'm hungry," I said. "Could we get something to eat first?"

We went for a spaghetti dinner. We both had a lot of wine and I finally got him talking. He told me he and his wife were virgins when they got married. (I didn't believe him.) He told me they went out for three years without doing it. (Impossible.) He told me they intended to practise birth control but got carried away and conceived their son on their wedding night. (I believed that.) So the point was, the world had changed, hadn't it? So how could he tell me what to do?

I didn't care about that. I wanted to know what went wrong with his marriage. He sort of talked around the subject, let me fit the pieces together. I gather he and his wife worked at her dad's hotel. They competed. He could see she was better suited to the business than he was. He got out, went back to university for a Master's. That's when things went sour. They split up. She took over the hotel in Winnipeg, he landed this job at Ryerson. Then he told me how much he missed his boy. That was the sad part.

We walked to his parking spot. His car was a beat-up Austin Healey with a ratty convertible top.

"Where to?" he said.

I felt flushed from the wine. "Paul," I blurted out. "I can't face Les tonight. Could I maybe stay at your place? On the sofa or whatever. Would that be all right?"

Paul stared at me. "My place? Gosh. I—well, sure, why not. Sure."

He lived in Port Credit, the kind of bourgeois suburb Les would gladly set a torch to. Not in a high-rise, though, but in the basement of a house. When we got there, Paul said we'd have to be quiet. He wasn't sure what the family above him would think if he brought a woman home.

I said, "You mean you have to sneak me in?"

"Sorry, but yes."

I felt like a teen-ager. Shit, I *was* a teen-ager.

The bluish light in one window told us the people were in bed watching TV. He led the way up a snowbanked sidewalk. He let us in the back door. The stairs to the basement went right down from the back vestibule. The kitchen door was closed. I stifled a laugh as we bumped into walls on the way down and knocked a bottle off the stairs.

His suite was as messy as his office. Newspapers and books and magazines everywhere. A pot of cold chicken noodle soup on his hot-plate. Dirty dishes in the sink. Yet it had a kind of charm—hell, this was where Professor Hodges *lived*. Kitchen and living room sort of all one, with doors to a bathroom and a bedroom. There was a nice tobacco smell everywhere.

He poured shots of Drambuie and we sat on his green sofa to sip them. He said I could sleep on the sofa if I'd like. It made into a bed.

He sat on the edge of the sofa as if he was ready to jump up any second. There was this awkward silence. I thought he might get up, turn out the lights and leave me there. I didn't want him to. I put my hand on his wrist and said:

"Would you like to fuck?"

He looked at me as if it was the most amazing thing he'd ever heard. I expected him to grab me right there and tear off my clothes. He didn't. I thought he might at least kiss me. He didn't.

"Well?" I said.

"Do you—um—have to use the bathroom or anything?"

I could see I had to do something quick. I put my liqueur down. I took his and put it down.

"Come on," I said, taking his hand.

His bed was a standard double with a Colonial headboard. It was unmade.

"Sorry," he said. "I didn't expect—"

"No problem."

"Should I turn off the lights?"

"Don't you want to see?"

"Yes, yes, I do."

"Maybe turn on the lamp and turn off the overhead."

He did. I unbuttoned his shirt.

He said, "I don't make a habit of doing this with students, you know."

"I know."

"You know? Is it that obvious?"

I put my hand on his crotch. "I don't think you've been with a woman for a long while."

He flinched. "It's true."

In a minute, I had his clothes off and I was taking off my own. I lay down and pulled the sheet up over my hip. He knelt beside me and bent to kiss my left boob. And he kept on kissing it.

"Hey, the other one's getting jealous," I said.

"You have lovely breasts."

"They like you, too." Both nipples were standing tall.

He kissed the right one. His hands touched me with the lightest of touches. He had nice hands, but cold.

"They're freezing," I said. "I've got a place you can warm them." I threw off the sheet.

He started to probe me and I fondled him. A few seconds later, he came. In my hand.

"I'm so sorry!" he said. He produced a handful of Kleenex. "I'm too excited—"

"It's okay! Would you stop apologizing? We've got all night."

"Have we?"

"Sure. Now, just relax, okay?" And I took him into my arms and held him.

Before too long, he was hard again. I asked him what he liked and I told him what I liked and we had a nice leisurely time doing those things to each other.

When morning dawned, I lay there wide awake. For a change, my head didn't ache. I looked at him while he slept. So peaceful and innocent. I wanted to stay with him.

Then it hit me. What was I going to do about Les?

"Hey," I said, shaking my professor. "Wake up. I have to get to school."

He woke up and stared at me. He seemed surprised that I was still there. He blinked a few times, rubbed his eyes and reached for me.

"Wait," I said, sitting up. "My breath's like a sewer. Do you have any milk? Or better still, some orange juice?"

"Stay right there," he said.

He got up and went out to his fridge. He came back carrying a carton of Beep. While I knocked back half of it, he nibbled my knee.

"School?" I said, as he nuzzled me back, and he was on me and in me before you could say, "Thanks for the Beep."

"Oh, that feels so good!"

I flexed my cunt muscles. "Can you feel that?"

"Yes! And I can't believe it!"

"Believe it. And believe I have a class with you in one hour."

"Is it good for you? I mean, are you—"

"Coming? Christ, yes, but listen, I have this problem."

"Oh? Should I—"

"No, don't stop. It's not that kind of problem. I mean the problem I started to tell you about last night."

"You mean the *guy*. You can't go back to him."

"He's in my apartment."

"I know. Okay, after class we'll go to your place and—will he be there?"

"He's always there."

"We'll explain to him that you don't want him staying with you anymore."

"We?"

"I'll go with you—ohh! Oh, yes!"

"There's no need for you!—oh, wow!—for you to get involved. I can look after myself."

"That was so great."

"For me, too."

"I *will* see you again?"

"In class."

"Oh, shit, that's right!"

5

Paul made it to class, but I didn't. We decided I should skip class and meet him later. I tried to snooze in an empty seminar room, but it was hopeless. I had to deal with Les. By myself. I wrote Paul a note. "Will phone later for another appointment. Susan Walchuk." I slipped it under his door. If anyone else happened to read it, it'd give nothing away. Just another student postponing a meeting.

I hated to walk the whole way from Ryerson. I was beat, and the cold December wind cut right through my parka. But I did walk because I needed time to figure out what I was going to say. I stopped in at a Yonge Street pizza joint. Ate a whole ham-and-pineapple large and drank three cups of coffee. I cut through Yorkville, looked in a few boutique windows. Enough of that. I hunched my shoulders and headed up Avenue Road against the wind.

I wanted to be totally up front with Les. That's it, Les. There's another guy.

Oh, shit. Who said Hodges wasn't just another horny prof getting his rocks off?

I let myself in. Flute music was coming from my hi-fi. The air was rank with the stuff we called Mexican Hairless. What I saw first were Les's bare feet on the rug, toes pointed up. He was lying on the floor in his cut-offs. Eldridge sat on the chesterfield, glaring at me. I felt like a goddam wayward wife, coming home to her junkie husband.

"Hello," he said. At least he was awake.

"Hello," I said. "Sorry I didn't call."

"That's okay."

He said nothing else. I felt guilty, for Christ's sake. And strange, like I didn't belong in my own pad. I could hear the woman upstairs walking around. The flute sounded eerie. Les didn't budge. The cat folded his paws under his chest and settled down for a nap. I wanted to have a bath, change my clothes and crash. But I couldn't.

"I spent the night with a guy," I said.

"Oh." He just stayed there, stretched out. His bare chest looked frail and pathetic.

"Les, I don't like the way we're living. I mean, for one thing, I can't stand flute music."

"I never said you couldn't see other guys."

"No, that's right."

"I don't own you."

"Right on."

"Okay then."

"Okay? *Okay*? Les, it isn't okay."

"Want some lunch?"

"I had lunch."

"Sue, if you feel guilty, that's your hang-up."

"Would you get up so we can talk face-to-face?"

He looked at his watch. "I have twenty more minutes of lying prone."

"*Get up!*"

I knew I sounded like a shrew. But he did get up, slowly. He stood at attention in front of me, like a goddam soldier. He even saluted. That made me mad.

"I don't want you here anymore," I said. "I don't want you sponging off me and I've had it with drugs."

"You meet some new guy and in one night he changes your whole life? Who is he, Jesus Christ?"

"Les, the guy has nothing to do with it. You and I are through. You're no good for me."

"But, Suzy, you're good for *me*. And soon, when we all get our shit together and the working classes—"

"No! Don't feed me any more crap! Just go."

"Aw, Suzy—"

"Go."

He moved. He dragged himself to the bedroom. Groaning as if he was in great pain, he bent to pick his stuff up off the closet floor. He filled his sack. He put on a denim jacket that was worn through at the elbows. I gave him one of my blankets. He didn't look at me. At the door, he turned and flung his arm at me. His knuckles and his onyx ring caught the side of my face. I reeled backward.

"*Bitch!*"

He hurried out. It was the quickest I'd ever seen him move.

93

I flopped onto the chesterfield. My face was bleeding. I was so tired, I started to cry.

There was a polite knock on the door. Maybe the woman from upstairs?

"Who is it?" I called out.

"Paul."

Jesus, no. "Just a minute."

I struggled to my feet, got a kitchen towel, wet it and held it to my face. I didn't dare look in a mirror.

"The U.S. Cavalry to the rescue," I said as I opened the door. "Two minutes too late."

"Sue, are you all ri—oh no! That's a nasty cut. Did you call the cops?"

He stood there looking helpless. I had the urge to comfort him, even though I was the one with the wound.

"What I need is a doctor," I said.

"Which way did he go? Did I pass him?"

"Let's get to Emergency, okay? There's a hospital near here."

As we went out the door, I noticed this black lump on the armchair. Its green eyes glowered at us.

"Christ!" I said. "He's left his goddam cat!"

The cut needed five stitches. I had a shiner for a while, so I didn't go out much. Luckily, all this happened just before Christmas break, so I didn't have to go to class.

Christmas Eve, Paul came over with a pizza and a present—a gold pendant in the shape of my Zodiac sign, Taurus the bull. I loved it. I'd always thought I hated baubles, but maybe it was because I didn't have any.

I gave Paul a shoulder bag. The brief case he carried just didn't suit him.

We opened the few gifts we had from home, drank wine and sang a few carols.

He stayed the night.

A couple of days later, we left Eldridge enough food and drove to Quebec. When we weren't fucking, we hiked and ate and drank and skied.

Back in Toronto on New Year's Eve, we made a resolution to screw at least once a day whether we wanted to or not.

94

Next day, we drove to Niagara-on-the-Lake. We walked hand-in-hand along the shore, both of us turned on by the quaint old houses and how quiet everything was. I felt so goddam cozy and loved. It seemed like I was holding hands for the first time. We went back to the car and necked.

On the way home, we decided to try living together.

6

"Possessions are the curse of the western world."

Les's words rang in my ears the afternoon Paul and Roger drove up in a rented truck that was loaded to the gills. We'd agreed to live in my place because it was downtown and on the ground floor. Paul brought everything, what he'd been using and what he'd had stored. Roger Lorenz was one of his buddies from Ryerson and the right type to have along for a move—short and stocky with stevedore shoulders. When he saw my place, the look on his face said, "You're never going to get all that shit in here." But he didn't say that. He just helped haul it all in. And in it came:

This great Jesus grandfather clock left to Paul by his parents;

A teak desk with a drawer that was jammed shut;

A matching chair with a slit in its upholstered seat;

A goose-neck lamp;

A three-drawer filing cabinet filled with Psych and Soc notes, hotel menus, hotel invoices, golf score cards and about three-quarters of a gross of safes;

His green hide-a-bed;

An arborite kitchen table and two high-back swivel chairs;

An upright vacuum cleaner with a dent in the front of it;

A crooked pole lamp;

A dismantled bed and its newish looking mattress and box spring;

Three boxes of books (two titles that caught my eye were *Successful Marriage* and *Smokey Stover: The Foolish Foo Fighter*);

Three suits (from Paul's hotel days), four sport jackets and five pairs of double-knit trousers;

A stack of hangers;

All kinds of dress shirts, sport shirts, ties, clean white jockey shorts and socks rolled up in pairs;

A pair of draped trousers from the 1950s and three V-neck sweaters with holes in the elbows;

A parka with a fur-trimmed hood, an overcoat, a London Fog trench coat and two golf jackets;

A pair of black oxfords, three pairs of Hush Puppies, a pair of zippered boots, sneakers, golf shoes, overshoes and a grungy pair of toe rubbers;

A fedora, a tweed cap, a baseball cap and a beret;

A set of golf clubs with bag and cart and a towel that had a "Niakwa Golf and Country Club" crest on it;

A red tool box that had in it a hammer, a small saw, pliers, a set of screwdrivers, sand paper, a retractable tape measure and a Kennedy silver dollar;

A Swiss yodeller's hat;

A battery-operated hula dancer (souvenir of Hawaii);

A gallon-tin of maple syrup from Quebec;

An original oil painting of a geisha girl by somebody named Len Pinkus;

Some high school yearbooks;

Paul's university degrees, framed, and two portraits of his son;

A camera, binoculars and a large flashlight;

A portable typewriter with the W key missing;

A carton full of magazines, including several *Playboys* that I destroyed right away (no more jacking off over centre-folds now that I was in the picture);

A stack of LPs, including the complete works of The Seekers;

Boxes of cereal, bags of vegetables, tea, booze, some cheap wine and a dusty bottle of Chateau Neuf de Pape;

Some multi-spring exercise equipment;

Sheets, blankets and two fat pillows (I never use a pillow, except under my ass if I have to be higher in the missionary position);

Towels, cutlery wrapped in face cloths, kettle, teapot, cups, a beer stein, glasses, a set of Barbary Hotel coasters, a frying pan;

A chess game with chesspersons carved out of wood;

The shoulder bag I gave Paul for Christmas;

Two unmatched suitcases;

A cardboard accordion file full of paid bills, legal papers, cheque books and ten shares of Royal Bank stock;

And a fat Christmas candle that was a Catholic monk on one side and a foot-long cock on the other.

There was barely enough room left to stand up in.

Roger leaned around the boxes of books and said, "I don't know if the floor can support all this."

I mumbled, "Possessions are the curse of the western world."

Paul sat on the teak desk. "All right, all right," he said. He was a little edgy. "We can sell off some of it."

"But when?" I moaned. "I can't breathe."

"Let's come at this logically," said Roger. "You don't need two beds and two chesterfields. I'll give you a hundred bucks for the two you don't want."

"Sold!" I said. "If you'll take 'em away now while we have the truck."

We sold my chesterfield and Paul's bed. Paul groaned when they had to load them back on the truck. But they did take the goddam things away, out to Roger's cottage on Lake Simcoe.

After seeing them off, I went back into my place and thought the air had got a whole lot mustier. Eldridge sat on top of the book boxes, meowing like crazy. I stared at the heap of Paul's clothes on my bed. What had I done? It looked like I'd just traded one mistake for another.

7

The next few weeks were rocky. We both knew we had to get rid of more stuff, but we argued about what to keep. We tossed out some of my posters and Paul's oxford shoes and his fedora. And I made him dump all his suits.

Then I got the call that my sister's husband was dead. Kenny had been bowling in a tournament in Kindersley. Got drunk. Started home and drove off the highway. Rolled the car and snapped his neck.

When I went home for the funeral, I intended to give my parents the whole scoop on Paul. But the visit was too much of a downer.

I spent a lot of time amusing Nadia's kid, Boris, while everybody moped and cried. Nadia was a basket case. It just wasn't the right time to tell them about Paul.

When my week came to an end, Mom wanted me to stay longer. Dad said he'd change the flight and pay whatever penalty. I said I had to get back or blow the whole term.

Dad took me to the airport early. I knew he wanted to get me on my own for a talk. I waited and waited as we drove up 8th and through downtown and out Idylwyld Drive. Silence. Till we got into the airport parking lot.

"Susan," he said. "We need you here."

I wanted to leave so badly, I could taste it. "No, you don't," I said. "It's a sad time right now, but Nadia will get her life back together."

"We need your laugh. We need your help."

"Dad, this is a critical part of the year. I have to get ready for exams."

"I checked with Kelsey Institute here. They're starting a hotel course. You could transfer in the fall."

I looked at my watch. This couldn't wait. "Dad, there's another reason I can't leave Toronto. A man."

He looked startled. Maybe because I'd said "man", not "guy". "Well," he said, "I knew you'd have a boyfriend. But I'm sure he'll

99

understand. Maybe he could transfer to Kelsey, too."

"He's a professor."

"He has a *job*?"

"His name is Paul Hodges. He's one of my professors."

"Good God."

"It's okay, we're both dealing with this. It's cool."

"He's an older man."

"Older than me, yes. But not that old."

"By that you mean he isn't as old as me."

"He's a lot younger than you."

"Susan. He isn't married, is he?"

"No. He isn't married."

"Thank the Lord."

"He's divorced."

Dad squeezed his eyes shut and groaned. "You know how we feel about divorce. How our church feels about divorce. You've slept with this man?"

"Father . . ."

"This is going to kill your mother. Does Nadia know about this divorced professor?"

"No."

He put his hand on my wrist, a little too firmly for my liking. "Susan, maybe you'd better move back here right away. Before it gets any more serious than it is. He'll understand why you have to be back here with your family. And you might find out it's just a crush you have."

"Dad. I have to go." I took my arm away from his hand and opened the door. I got out of the car. My backpack was all I had for baggage and I hoisted it onto one shoulder.

"Just two more days. We'll go in and change your ticket. Is two more days too much to ask?"

"You don't have to come in with me, Dad."

He got out and spoke to me over the roof of the car. "Leave now and you may never see your family again."

"One more thing I should tell you, Dad." Other people were going by but I didn't care. "Paul and I are living together."

I turned and headed for the terminal. This was February and I had to walk through new snow into an icy wind. I pulled my scarf up around my ears. I thought I heard him call something like "You're living in sin!" But he didn't follow me.

8

I thought it was pretty cool to be disowned by my parents and living in the great T.O. with my prof. I mean, I was finally my own woman.

That feeling lasted about five days.

After a night at the pub with a few classmates, I came home and found Paul doing what he did every night. Marking papers. He was hunched over his desk in his ratty old grey cardigan. His glasses were half-way down his nose. He smelled musty, like his books. The way the lamplight hit him, I could see every grey hair in his beard and every line in his face. It suddenly hit me: Shit, I was living with a senior citizen.

Most nights, I stayed home with him. We'd sold the TV so there'd be no distractions. I'd study or read and he'd work away at his desk, marking or preparing lessons. Sometimes Eldridge amused us by jumping on the desk, rubbing against Paul's face and walking across Paul's papers. But even that got boring. The TICK TOCK TICK TOCK of the grandfather clock drove me bananas. I started going out two nights a week, to a movie or the pub.

We had a few arguments. Paul said I should phone my parents and try to open up communications again. I said piss on that. I said he should stop eating so much junk food. He didn't see why. But I lost it the night he told me Roger Lorenz was going to a conference in Ithaca, New York.

"But you made all the contacts," I said.

"I really don't mind if Roger goes."

"Why the hell don't you protest to the dean?"

"It's not that important to me."

"What *is* important to you?"

"Sue, there's no sense getting riled up."

"There you go again. You know, I really hate that. Whenever we get talking about something, you tell me not to get riled up. Jesus

Christ, I asked you a simple question. What is important to you?"

"I don't see what this has to do with—"

"Listen to you! Goddam spineless bastard! No wonder Catherine kicked you out!"

"Catherine did not kick me out."

"Oh! I suppose you're going to tell me *you* kicked *her* out."

"No. Some people can deal with these things in a civilized way. We had our differences, lots of them, but we recognized them and we didn't have to yell."

"Oh, balls. You know, I'm really getting fed up with this, you know? I'm too young to be stuck in this goddam *library* keeping quiet and watching you work. And I sure as hell don't have to sit here and listen to some bullshit about how wonderful Catherine was."

"You brought her up."

"I'll bring up more than her in a minute."

"Sue, I've got a lot of work—"

"Piss on your work! Let's go out to a goddam bar. Right now. I want to see some people and hear some music."

"You know I can't."

"Then I'm going alone."

"Wait. Maybe if I hurry this up, we could go out for a nightcap—"

"Hurry? You? Forget it. I'm going out right now."

"Sue . . ."

I grabbed my Cowichan sweater and slammed out the door. Thought I'd hitchhike over to the 401. Get picked up by a trucker and fuck his tattoos off.

I got a lift with a young couple who took me to a gas station near one of the on-ramps. A semi did stop for me. The driver was big and young and headed for Quebec City. But he didn't come on to me. Like most men, he was a trivia buff. He asked me, "Who won the Conn Smythe Trophy in the Stanley Cup playoffs of 1967?" And "Who played opposite Cary Grant in the movie, *Indiscreet*?" And "What was the score in the last game Don Larsen won for the New York Yankees?"

I knew Don Larsen pitched a perfect game in the World Series, but not much else. I got pretty tired. Seemed like Errol (that was his name—Errol) was going to go on asking questions and driving forever. I didn't want to fall asleep in his cab. I got him to drop me off at a gas station near Oshawa.

I phoned Shelly, a friend from school. She didn't answer right away. I let the damned thing ring because I felt desperate. There I was, stuck in a gas station on the freeway late at night. Surrounded by bright packages, with the attendant watching me like I was another screwed-up teen-ager on the run. Sure as hell, I was going to steal a couple of Coffee Crisps or a can of Havoline. And the telephone operator kept saying, "There's no answer; do you want me to try again later?"

I told her to let it ring and finally Shelly answered. Her voice sounded semi-drowsy, semi-pissed-off, and I could hardly hear her over Three Dog Night.

"For Christ's sake, Sue. I told you, when the phone rings seventeen times, I'm either out or *busy*."

"But you're home and how busy could you be at this time of night?"

"I'm in a bubble bath smoking dope with Rod."

"Okay. I'm sorry. Look, I need you to come and pick me up. I walked out on Paul."

"You what?"

"Jeez, I'm too tired to explain. Would you come and get me?"

"Where are you?"

"At the first Oshawa exit on the 401."

"You gotta be kidding."

I convinced her that she had to come for me. It wasn't as if I'd interrupted anything special. Shelly was always in the shower or on the kitchen table or out on the balcony floor with somebody. (She lived in this downtown high-rise and her dad paid all the bills.) I had a cup of lousy coffee and ate a box of chips while I waited. Chatted with the attendant. He said he'd seen The Beatles live in Montreal. Sat in the seventh row and couldn't hear the music for all the screaming. Then he started asking me trivia crap like which White Album track I thought Eric Clapton played lead guitar on.

Shelly arrived looking bright-eyed as usual. She has jet-black hair cut in bangs that are too long. She's forever pushing them out of her eyes. She has a big soft lower lip that's permanently coated with scarlet lipstick. She was wearing a fake fur and leotards.

We drove back to town.

I said, "Shelly, I'm not sure about Paul anymore."

Shelly snickered. "You're nuts."

"I don't know if a young woman like me should get into such a settled-down life."

"Is he a good lay?"

"No problem there."

"You'd prefer a young guy with no hair on his chest."

"Maybe."

"You want to trade?"

"For Rod? I thought he was God's gift."

"You ever tried to talk to Rod? 'You Jane, me Tarzan.' Guy goes about as deep as nail polish."

"Who wants deep? I need a nice superficial relationship for a change."

"Bullshit."

"Can't I stay with you for a couple of days and think this thing through?"

"Sure you can."

When we got to her place, Rod was still there, all six-foot-three of him. He was all of eighteen, still in high school. We listened to some Janis Joplin and shared a joint. They asked me if I wanted to do a three-way thing in bed, but I said definitely not. So I had to lie there in my sleeping bag listening to them. I got this tremendous longing for Paul's arms around me.

I couldn't stand it for very long. Shit, it was getting on for three in the morning, but I took Shelly's car and went home.

I crawled into bed about 3:30. Paul came alive instantly. Jesus, he felt like a roaring fire. I don't know where we got the energy, but we slammed into each other's arms. No questions, no apologies. We just swung into the sweetest fuck of our lives.

As we lay there tangled together afterward, Paul said, "We need to make some changes. Some plans."

"Like what?"

"I don't know. Maybe we should get married or something."

"Get serious!"

"We could have a wild and crazy wedding."

"You *are* serious!"

9

nine

The idea turned us on. That was all we talked about for days.

"I'd like our wedding to be simple and natural," I said.

"It should be outside somewhere," he said.

"In a park. In a cow pasture."

"The reception, too?"

"No, I think we'd have the people back here."

"When?"

"Early August?"

"You don't think it'd be too hot in here?"

"People expect it to be hot at weddings. If it's hot, they won't stay too long."

"How many should we invite?"

"I don't know. Let's make a list."

I went to the desk and got a pad and pencil. Paul sat on the hide-a-bed and I sat on the floor, my back against his shins.

"We'll start with you and me," I said. I wrote our names side-by-side at the top of the page.

"Then the best man and the maid of honour," said Paul.

"We don't want a best man or a maid of honour."

"We don't?"

"None of our guests is any more special than anyone else. At weddings these days, all the guests are considered 'best people'."

"Are we going to be that theatrical?"

"It isn't theatrical. It's just getting away from stupid middle-class traditions."

"All right. So let's start our list. You go first."

"No, you."

"Okay. How about Roger and his wife?"

"Could we face her after the way he's been screwing around with Deirdre?"

"But he's my closest friend at Ryerson."

105

"Let's leave him off the list for now, okay?"

"Um. Okay."

"What about your department head?"

"Don? He doesn't even know we're seeing each other. And he does not approve of faculty marrying students. No, not Don. What about your parents?"

"My parents? Get serious!"

"They'll be happy to hear we're getting married. They'd probably come."

"I don't want them to come. I'm dying to send them an announcement *after* the wedding."

"But surely we have to invite your sister."

"No way."

"Well, there's Deirdre. You have to invite Deirdre."

"I haven't seen her since she announced she was going to have an abortion."

"Deirdre? I didn't know she was—is it Roger's?"

"She thinks so."

"Well, I can understand not inviting her if Roger's wife was coming, but we've already —"

"I don't even like Deirdre. Deirdre is a jerk."

"Shelly then?"

"That kook? She hasn't spoken to me since the night I took her car home. Says she didn't give me permission. She was stoned, for Christ's sake."

"Hey. We need a minister."

"That's right. We don't have a minister."

"You know what? We don't have any friends, either."

It was true. Under our names, the page was blank. I kept thinking of Les, the only real friend I'd had in Toronto before Paul. Well, I sure as hell couldn't invite Les.

"Let's face it," I said. "We keep to ourselves too much."

"Is it our age difference?"

"What should that matter? Let's start inviting people over."

"Who should we start with?"

"I don't know. Let's sleep on it."

We went right to bed and held each other very tight.

10

_t e n_

"Could I speak with Paul Hodges, please?" It was a male voice I didn't recognize.

"He won't be home for about an hour," I said. "Could he call you?"

"Yes. Would you please ask him to call Hugh Godfrey?" He gave me a number.

When he saw my note, Paul said, "Hugh Godfrey? Oh, for God's sake! It's The Shark!"

He leaped to the phone. He was so excited, he dialled the wrong number three times. When he reached his friend, he found out that The Shark's company had transferred him to Toronto. The Shark and his family were already living here. Paul kept jabbering and laughing and feeding me information. I'd never heard him get so loud. I made sure he invited The Shark and his wife over for an evening.

They came two nights later. By then, Paul had told me more than I ever wanted to know about them. The Shark could blow perfect smoke rings, swim the width of the Red River and build anything. He married Frances, the woman he met at Paul's wedding. He built himself a house in south Winnipeg. Stayed with the first company that he went to work for after Grade Twelve, an insurance company. He was some kind of whiz with numbers and moved up the corporate ladder while Frances stayed home having babies. Paul lost track of The Shark when he split with Catherine. I wasn't sure how I was going to react to a bloody insurance man who kept his wife barefoot and pregnant.

When they arrived, Paul hugged both of them like they were long lost relatives. Frances was pale and tall, with her hair cropped short. She had a great smile. The Shark had sloped shoulders, long arms, hair way shorter than most guys wore it. Instead of a chin, he had this blob with a dimple in it. And yet he was good-looking in a toothy

107

sort of way. They were both dressed in trendy sports clothes—sweater, shirt, slacks. Paul and I stayed with our usual jeans and T-shirts.

"The *times* this guy and I have had together!" Paul said. He kept his arm around The Shark way too long.

"The *drunks* we've had!" The Shark said. "Remember the tally-ho where all of us were so smashed, we left Allan in a snowbank?"

"I was the guy who went back for him. Remember the time you and Steve drove Frances's dad's car into Lake Winnipeg?"

"Remember the girl they raffled off at my stag and I won?"

"He didn't do anything but take her for coffee," Frances said. "At least, that's what he tells me."

I said, "I'll bet they didn't raffle off a guy at your shower, Frances."

They laughed—kind of nervously, I thought.

Paul changed the subject. "How's your dad, Shark?"

"Max is still selling. Still has a couple of good soap lines. He and Mom still go skating every Sunday in the winter. Last time I talked to him, he was hustling money for somebody's political campaign."

"Remember what a nut he was on scavenger hunts?" Paul said. "Sent me to North Dakota one night just to pick up a can of Hamm's beer."

"You were the one!" Frances said. "We could never figure out if it was you or Steve."

"How is Steve?" Paul asked.

"Keeps flitting from job to job," said the Shark. "Last I heard, he was selling real estate. You know his marriage to Joy didn't last—has a new woman friend we haven't met. Poor girl."

The three of them went on and on, raving about old times. I felt sort of out of it. Threw in the odd laugh like I was their audience. I got the drinks. Frances looked at my chest a lot. I don't think she approved of going braless. Or the words printed across my T-shirt: "Professor's Playground". But she kept smiling.

When Paul went to the kitchen to fix up some snacks and The Shark followed him, Frances said, "Got him well-trained, haven't you?"

"Oh, no. We take turns."

"You wouldn't catch The Shark dead in the kitchen. He says that's my domain and his is his basement workshop."

"We don't have a basement."

"I like your place. Cozy."

"Cluttered, you mean. Sort of Hippy Haven?"

"To be honest, I'm a little envious. Of your freedom, I guess. We have to keep up a certain image for The Shark's position. And we have four kids. The move was hard on them, but we've got a nice place here and we're settled now. Sometimes, though . . . well, do you know what I mean?"

I thought I did. And I was beginning to like old Frances. "Yes, I think so."

There was a burst of laughter from the kitchen.

"The Shark was so glad to get in touch with Paul again," Frances said.

"I guess it's tough on friends when a couple splits up. You know Paul's ex-wife pretty well, don't you?"

"Yes. We used to see quite a bit of her before we were transferred. Now we exchange letters."

"She's doing well in the hotel business?"

"Catherine has really made her mark in the catering end. If you have a function to plan in Winnipeg, Catherine is *the* person to call. The Shark used to go to her for all his company's conferences. He adores her."

Paul reappeared carrying a tray of veggies and dip. The Shark brought us fresh drinks.

"I can't get over this guy's beard," The Shark said. "Long and bushy just like one of those Smith Brothers cough drop guys. Which one had the great beard, Trade or Mark?"

He and Paul broke into hysterical laughter.

"The company won't let The Shark grow a beard," Frances said. "He's dying to."

"Listen, folks," Paul said. "Sue and I have some news and you two are going to be the first to hear it."

"Sue's expecting," The Shark said.

"Not that I know of," I said.

"I know!" Frances said, clapping her hands like a little girl. "You're going to get married."

"Absolutely right," I said. "And we'd love it if you two would come to the wedding."

"We'd be delighted," Frances said. She squeezed my hands and kissed my cheek.

"That's terrific," The Shark said. He shook Paul's hand and lightly kissed me while Frances kissed Paul. "Can I tell some of the people back home? I'm going to Winnipeg next week. Does this mean you're engaged?"

"You could say that," I said. "But there won't be any rings. Paul and I consider them symbols of bondage."

There was an awkward silence. Paul frowned and The Shark rolled his eyes.

"Shark, this calls for a toast," Frances said. She was fiddling with the rings on her left hand.

"To Paul and . . . and Susan!" The Shark said, raising his glass.

Later, when Paul and I were in the kitchen making coffee, Paul said, "What's this about bondage? Aren't we going to exchange rings?"

"No," I said. "Think of the money we'll save. Come on, smile! We've got our first official wedding guests."

11

Next morning, the doorbell woke us. It was Deirdre.

Deirdre's great-looking, with legs that won't quit, but that day she didn't look so lovely. She wore a dirty poncho and some kind of burlap minidress. Her streaked hair was a mess and her face was pasty-white.

"He was a butcher," she sobbed. "God, I feel so shitty."

"Come in," I said.

Paul made coffee. We had her feeling better when the doorbell rang again. This time, it was Roger.

"Is Deirdre here?" he asked.

"I don't think she wants to see you right now," Paul told him.

"I've been looking all over for her. I have to see her."

Paul looked around the door at Deirdre. She nodded. Roger came in looking as awful as she did, with puffy face and red eyes.

"I haven't slept," he said. "Last night, I had a family meeting and told them I was leaving. I told them all about you, Deirdre, and how you're pregnant with my child. I told them I was leaving so that we could have this baby together."

Deirdre wailed.

Roger was nonplussed. "What's wrong?"

"Roger," I said, "didn't you know Deirdre was having an abortion?"

Roger flopped down onto the hide-a-bed looking wasted. Paul and I tried to soothe the two of them with words and coffee and shots of scotch. To take their minds off their problems, I told them about our wedding plans.

Deirdre took Roger's hand in hers and said, "I hope you're going to invite us."

The guest list was growing. Things were falling into place.

It was Deirdre who put us onto a minister. She said he was a friend of hers.

Father Phil came over for tea, reeking of incense. He looked about

111

thirty, but his hair was thin and there were flecks of grey in his beard. He had a thin nose with nostrils that flared every time he spoke. He was dressed in a caftan, jeans, sandals and a red headband with a black cross drawn on it. The hair on the sides of his head was long, nearly to his shoulders.

"You know, I can say whatever you want me to say," Father Phil told us. He spoke out of the side of his mouth like a gangster. "I mean, we don't have to use any of the ritual words and phrases if you don't want to. Like, it's up to you, you know?"

"You mean we don't need any scripture?" Paul looked surprised.

"No sirree."

"That's good," I said. "We'd like it to be natural and simple."

"Fine and dandy. Everybody who's there can say something if they want to. Or not. Whatever you like. All you need is a licence, okay? And blood tests and some witnesses. And, you know, some money to pay me." He popped a whole butter tart into his mouth.

"Shouldn't we at least have an outline of what we're doing?" Paul asked. "It'll be a little hairy, trying to wing it through the whole service."

"Maybe so, but look, don't call it a service, okay? I mean, this can be a *happening*. Folks can break into song if they want. They can tell us something funny about you or about themselves. You know, like, they can do magic tricks or copulate on the lawn. Say, where are we holding this gig?"

"We thought maybe in a nice field somewhere," I said.

"I've got the perfect spot. I teach a Philosophy of Religion class over at the Glendon Campus of York University. I mean, that's a grabby spot in summer. How about it?"

I said, "Sounds okay to me."

Paul said, "Could we see it before we decide?"

"Sure. I know you'll love it. Anyhoo, as long as your guests enjoy themselves and vouch for the fact that you two have made an agreement, I mean, you know, that's all you need."

As we talked, he leaned over and picked up Eldridge off a cushion. Normally, if a stranger tried to pick up Eldridge, he'd be asking for a nasty scratch. But Father Phil had some kind of hex on the cat. Eldridge settled down in his lap and let him pet him and even fool around with his tail.

"You're going to want to make a promise or two," Father Phil said as he scratched Eldridge around the ears. "You know, 'I promise to take out the garbage.' 'I promise to stop what I'm doing every so often and think of the Lord.' 'I promise never to fake an orgasm.' Whatever. Maybe you've got some favourite poems or something. Do you like Kahlil Gibran or Rod McKuen?"

Paul and I both shrugged.

"Pure unadulterated crap, both of them. Give me Donne!

'License my roving hands, and let them go,
Before, behind, between, above, below . . .
To enter in these bonds, is to be free;
Then where my hand is set, my seal shall be.'

Who could say it better?"

After he'd drunk three cups of tea and loudly pissed in our toilet, he tore a corner off the front page of *The Globe and Mail* and wrote the time and date of the wedding on it. At the door, he said:

"Let me know what you think of Glendon. Say, a pity Deirdre had to have an abortion. It was my kid, you know."

12

"Hello?"

"Hello."

"Who's this?"

"*Who's this?*"

"That's what I said."

"You don't know who this is?"

"No, so maybe I should hang up."

"Go ahead. Hang up on your mother."

"Mom!"

"It wasn't my idea to phone. It was your father's."

"Oh? Well, Mom, this is a surprise."

"Your fiancé said to call back tonight."

"My *fiancé?*"

"Yes."

"You mean Paul."

"The man you're marrying, yes. I think he said his name was Paul Hodgeson."

"Hodges, Mother. You mean Paul phoned you?"

"Yes. Didn't he tell you?"

"Mother—"

"If you don't believe me, ask him."

"He's out getting groceries." The bastard. "So I gather he told you we're getting married next month."

"He said he thought we should know, which is more consideration than we get from our daughter."

"Mom, if you just called to start in on me again—"

"I don't want to argue, Susan. I phoned to tell you that your father and I have given this a lot of thought and we've decided to come to your wedding."

I couldn't talk. I looked out the front window. No sign of my darling rat-fink husband-to-be.

114

"Susan, your sister and your little nephew want to come to your wedding, too. We're going to be one big happy family again."

"Is Dad there?"

"No. He's downstairs fixing Boris's car seat. Do you want me to get him?"

"Are you sure he wants to come to my wedding?"

"He wants to see this wedding with his own eyes. Then he'll believe his daughter is married and he'll be able to sleep at night."

"He . . . I . . ." I was stuttering. How could Paul do this to me?

"Paul sounds like a nice man."

Just as she said that, I saw the "nice man" go by the window.

"Mom, I'll call you back, okay?"

The door opened as I hung up the phone. I lunged at him, my fists flying. One grocery bag fell. He tried to protect himself with the other one. Apples tumbled to the floor. Slices of whole wheat bread flew. Cans hit my legs and feet. Milk spilt. A ketchup bottle fell and broke. I pounded his arms and shoulders. He stood there and took it, and that made me more furious.

"How could you call them?" I yelled. "How could you?"

"Who? Who did I call? Wait a minute, who?"

"Who! Who! You sound like a goddam owl! You know goddam well who. I never said you should call them. I said I didn't want them at this goddam wedding!"

I kept punching.

"Susan, wait. I knew you wouldn't phone. I thought maybe if your mother phoned you—I mean, you can't let something like this go on. It gets harder and harder—"

"You invited them to the fucking wedding!"

"I didn't! I just wanted to re-establish contact—"

"Liar! You invited them. She phoned to say they're all coming, including my goddam sister and her snot-nosed brat."

"Susan. Hold on. I'm sorry I didn't tell you. But I just couldn't go through with the wedding without ever at least talking to your folks."

"Maybe we shouldn't go through with it. God, I can't even trust you."

"I'm sorry. I didn't invite them, though. They've invited themselves."

"Are you listening to me? I said maybe we should cancel the whole thing."

"No, we shouldn't. I'm crazy about you."

"And I'm just crazy, right? Can't even handle my own parents. Oh, *shit*."

I stopped hitting him. He put down the tattered grocery bag and took me in his arms. I cried a little. So did he. And then we made love.

13

My mother, father, sister and nephew arrived yesterday. Paul and I met the train. They came that way because my dad works for the railway, has for twenty-odd years. Mom and Dad had a bedroom but Mom said she didn't sleep a wink. She sat by the window all night and made faces at the wild animals. Dad slept like a railway tie. Nadia and Boris had a roomette and she said it was hell having to pack up the bed whenever she had to pee.

What struck me about my parents when I saw them on the Union Station platform was how short they were. Maybe it's because I've been living with a six-footer. I thought they'd shrunk. I walked right past them in the platform crowd. Mom had to grab my arm. Here was this tubby woman, shorter than me, wearing a white summer hat with a cloth coat. She was carrying a Radisson's shopping bag that bulged with knitting and Boris's toys. Her pudgy face had only one wrinkle, a deep one between her eyebrows.

"It's nice to see you again," she said as we hugged, "even if you don't recognize me."

Over her shoulder, I saw my father. He was loaded down with four ancient suitcases. Carrying heavy stuff used to be a piece of cake for him, but since he'd been moved to a desk job his muscles were getting flabby. He was sweating. This man I remembered as big and scary was all hunched up, his glasses knocked crooked by the crowd. He wore brown pants and a bright floral sport shirt that made him look like he'd just come from Hawaii.

"Mom, Dad, this is Paul," I said.

"Here, let me help you with those," Paul said.

Dad dropped the larger suitcases—they only had a few inches to fall. Paul took the smaller ones and set them down and he and Dad shook hands.

"Do I get to kiss my daughter's fiancé?" Mom said. She stood up on her tiptoes and Paul bent down to her cheek. "No, no, on the lips!

117

Mmmm. We're so glad Susan's marrying someone—ah—mature."

Dad and I gave each other a self-conscious hug.

"What's the weather like here?" he asked. "It's been raining a lot at home."

"Will you look at that?" Mom nodded toward a hippy couple, all scruffy jeans, tattered hair and bangles.

Next to them, I guess Paul and I looked like yacht club members in our clean shirts and pants. Well, not quite.

Nadia came walking up behind Dad. She was carrying Boris, who was squirming like mad. Nadia used to be so careful with her looks. Her print dress and brown hair were a mess. She looked like she might break into tears any second. She handed Boris to Dad and flung her arms around me. I could feel her shaking.

"Nadia, this is Paul," I said. "Paul, this is Nadia. And that's Boris."

"Let's get this stuff to the hotel," Dad said. "Then we'll all go out for dinner. Someplace nice, and I'm buying."

They were staying at the Royal York. While Dad and Paul got everybody registered and settled in two rooms, Mom quizzed me. She'd done this on the phone every day since that day she broke the ice. She wanted to know how she could help me. Could she make this for me. Could she cook that for me. She'd sew a dress or make decorations or whip up a three-tiered cake. I kept telling her that I wasn't having a wedding like Nadia's. She freaked right out when I told her I wasn't getting married in a church. She made it sound like I was breaking the law. Was I going to have flowers? Only those growing on the campus. Did that mean there wouldn't be a flower girl? Right. What about a ring-bearer? No ring-bearer and no rings. No rings? I told her not to worry. Just come and enjoy.

One time, Dad came to the phone and asked if I wanted him to give me away. I told him as nicely as I could that he didn't own me. I wasn't his to give. He asked me what in blazes the father of the bride was supposed to do? I said he just had to come and be himself. The good news was it wasn't going to cost him a cent.

Now that they were here, Mom asked some of the same questions. I guess she hoped some of the answers would be different. She said she was hurt that I hadn't asked her to make my wedding dress. I said I wasn't going to wear a wedding dress. She said she was hurt about that, too.

The six of us went to a nice-enough restaurant not far from the hotel. Boris kept sliding off his booster chair and landing in a messy heap under the table. He pulled off our shoes and jabbed our legs with celery stalks. Could've been a real pain in the ass, but we needed the distraction, we were having such a tough time facing one another. The only safe topic was the weather, and even that reminded my family how long we'd lived together ("Paul and I had snow coming in the bedroom window"). Dad couldn't hide his dislike for Paul's age and Paul's divorce and Paul's job—teaching wasn't a man's work in my father's eyes. Mom got on me about not having an aisle to walk down and not having Dad give me away. Nadia, when she wasn't bawling or going under the table after Boris, took Mom and Dad's side on everything.

Paul tried to speak in our defence. I know he tried. He just couldn't get a word in. When my mother and I went to the car, she said, "He's nice, but he doesn't talk much, does he?"

By the time Paul and I were heading home, I was uptight. I gave him hell for not talking. I cursed the wedding, I cursed my stupid family, I cursed Paul for being so old, so second-hand and in such a sucky profession. He said it'd do us both some good to mellow out on some dope. When we got home, I slammed the door and kicked Eldridge. But Paul calmed me down, as he usually did. I put on his favourite Seekers LP and we toked together. I told him we were goddam well going to get through this fucking wedding and live happier ever after if it killed us.

14

I'm dressed in a prim blouse and my dress jeans, waiting for Paul to come home from the airport with his son. I'm pacing back and forth, more nervous about the kid than the wedding.

I hear a car door slam. I check myself in the bedroom mirror. What exactly am I supposed to look like? A mother? A nice girl? *Hi there, I'm your dad's roommate.* Jesus, I don't have a clue what a thirteen-year-old boy looks like, never mind what he wants in a stepmother.

The front door opens. I smile, trying to look friendly, not sexy. I slouch so that my breasts don't stick out too much. And there he is.

"Hi there," I say, holding out my hand. "I'm Susan."

He's tall—well, taller than me. Almost as tall as his dad. He's good-looking, with blond hair that's beginning to darken. A bit gawky, but no zits, no whiskers. He has Paul's eyes.

"Hello," he says. "I'm Rob."

He looks at me. Am I younger than he expected? Too young? Too shapely? We shake hands.

Paul brings in a suitcase and an athletic bag. "Rob's plane was right on time," he says.

"How was the flight?" I ask.

"Bumpy," Rob says. "We hit a lot of air pockets. People's coffee was jumping out of their cups."

"Wow. Did yours?"

"I don't drink coffee."

He's dressed in a blue blazer, grey slacks, a narrow red and blue tie, white button-down shirt and black oxfords. The typical bourgeois kid, Les would call him. This is probably what Paul looked like as a teen-ager. Before he turned teacher and found out jeans and a beard were the quickest way to tell students he wasn't The Enemy.

"He played his game most of the way here," Paul says.

"Game?"

120

"A hockey game you play with dice. Rob invented it. He compiles scoring statistics, even writes up the games."

"Who do you play it with?"

"My friend, Tim, some of the time. But mostly I roll the dice for both teams."

"He has a whole league of eight teams with a schedule and everything," Paul says. "He made up the teams and all the players. His rules simulate a real game—there are power plays and fights and injuries. One of his favourite players got killed."

"Cool!"

Rob stands there looking a little embarrassed.

"Maybe you could show the game to Sue later," Paul says. "Let's get you settled first. This makes into a bed and that's where we'll sleep tonight. You get the bedroom, so you can crash anytime you want to."

He takes Rob into our bedroom and lays the suitcase on the bed.

"Your dad and I'll have to use this room for changing our clothes," I say. "So we'll take turns, okay?"

"Okay," Rob says.

"One big happy family," I say. I promised myself I wouldn't talk any shit and, just like that, it slips out. Why am I nervous? "Can we get you some lunch?"

"No, thank you."

His mother likely told him not to accept anything from us. Not even food. Probably has his suitcase full of sandwiches and home-made pies.

I say, "You want to change into something more comfortable?"

"Mom told me . . ." He blushes and starts over. "I was going to wear this to the wedding."

Should I tell him a better outfit for this wedding would be a T-shirt and cut-offs?

"We've got a few hours to kill," Paul says. "Maybe you could change into something casual and you and I could go for a walk. Or . . . ?" He looks at me for a suggestion.

"Maybe take the ferry over to Toronto Island?" I say.

"Sure," Paul says.

"Okay," Rob says.

He goes into the bedroom and Paul closes the door.

Paul whispers to me, "What do you think?"

"I like him. He's almost as good-looking as his dad."

"That athletic bag is full of his game. Statistics on every player, write-ups, action shots he drew and coloured. Calls it the Tundra Taiga Hockey League. He's dreamed all this up since I saw him last."

"When was that?"

"Last August. He spent a month with me while Catherine went to England. His passion last year was chess."

"We don't need to feel we have to entertain him. When he gets bored, he can play hockey with himself."

The phone rings. I answer it, figuring it's Mother.

"Hello." It's a man. "Um—is this—uh—is Paul Hodges there, please?"

"He sure is." I hand the phone to Paul.

"Hello? . . . Greg! Where are you? . . . Yes, that was Susan. . . . Yes. . . . You're here? In Toronto?"

It's Paul's brother. We invited him, thinking he wouldn't come. Paul says Greg figured it was Paul's marital problems that killed their mother.

"Sure," Paul says, "come on over. Robbie's here."

A noise comes from the bedroom. Sort of a clickety-click, like a baby's rattle. Clickety-click and then nothing and then clickety-click again. Is this the sound of two Tundra Taiga teams taking to the ice?

Paul gives directions to our place. I gather Greg's here without his family. I go to the kitchen to put the kettle on.

There's a knock on the door. The only person who never rings the bell is Shelly. She's become a regular visitor since we invited her to the wedding. I go to the door and open it.

"Ahhh—the blushing bride," Shelly says. "Good morning, good morning." She hands me a pile of four or five cake-size boxes. "The goodies I promised you. This one's cheesecake and watch that, it's strudel, and the pies."

"Thank you, thank you, and Shel, it's afternoon."

She's looking gorgeous but hot in her knitted maroon minidress and matching leotards. She goes over and hugs Paul just as he's hanging up the phone.

"Hey, man," she says, "today's the day you make all that fucking legal."

"Shhhh!" Paul says, pointing a thumb at the bedroom door. "My son is here."

"Well, sorrrr-ee!"

I take the boxes to the kitchen and make room for them in the fridge. I pour a shot of Tia Maria into a glass of milk, stir it and take it to Shelly.

"Yum, thanks, Sue," she says. "First one today. Aren't you having one?"

"I'm not sure. I keep asking myself, Do I want to be drunk for my wedding? And I keep answering, Yes! But with this kid—"

Another clickety-click.

The doorbell rings. Paul goes and it's Deirdre and Roger, with more food.

"What is it with you guys?" I say. "I told my mother nobody had to bring anything. You trying to make a liar out of me?"

I take the two cold plates of veggies and fruit and Deirdre follows me into the kitchen.

"Roger's wife is still bugging us," she says. "She's threatening to kill herself if Roger doesn't go back to her. Roger spends his whole life on the phone with her. I tell him, What's the big deal? Let her do it and give us some peace."

"You really don't want her to."

"Can't she just let us get on with our lives? Happy wedding day, by the way."

We go back into the living room and find the bedroom door open. Shelly, Roger and Paul are in there with Rob. He's changed to a red and white muscle shirt and white pants and sneakers. He's demonstrating what makes the clickety-click sound: a pair of dice in a plastic bubble mounted on a spring. The spring has a suction cup on the bottom end. He has the thing stuck on an ashtray and all he has to do is flick the bubble and it shakes the dice for him.

"I was just finishing the game I started on the plane," he says.

Paul says, "The Olyutorsk Oxen beat the Fort Chimo Flying Frenchmen 3 to 1."

Shelly says, "The boy needs a drink after all that excitement."

Paul shows Roger Rob's complicated rules and directions. Shelly and Deirdre take turns flicking the dice-bubble. Rob seems embarrassed and I get him to come out to the kitchen.

"They're all kids at heart," I say. "Shelly's going to want to have a game. I hope you won't mind. Want a beer?"

"No, thank you. Coke'll be fine, please."

"Cocaine?" It's supposed to be a joke but Rob blushes.

"Coca Cola," he says.

"We don't have any cocaine. We do have Coca Cola." I get some out of the fridge. "Ever tried drugs?"

"No way."

"Good. Your dad and I smoke up the odd time, but he got me off the hard stuff. A great guy, your dad."

"I know."

"Rob, this wedding . . . you've probably been to a church wedding, haven't you?"

"Yes."

"Big Anglican wedding?"

"My Uncle Wally's was."

"Well, we aren't getting married in a church. Did your dad tell you that?"

"Sort of."

"We're getting married outdoors, on a college campus. Not Ryerson, another one. We'll have a tent handy in case it rains. We'd like everybody to say something at the wedding. Do you think you could say something?"

"Like what? Gosh, Mom didn't mention—"

"Nothing long or fancy. It's not a speech. Maybe something you remember about your dad—anything. You'll hear what the others have to say. You know the man your dad calls The Shark?"

"Uncle Hugh?"

"Yes—well, he and Frances—Auntie Frances?—they'll both be there tonight and they'll both be saying something."

"Do we have to say it to God?"

"No, no, it isn't a prayer."

Paul comes into the kitchen. "Hi. Just getting drinks for Roger and Deirdre."

"I was telling Rob how informal the wedding is going to be."

"Great. Say, Rob, Shelly wants to play your game with Roger. Is that okay?"

"I'll have to show them how."

In wanders Eldridge. Where the hell's he been hiding?

"Hey, you've got a cat!" Rob says. "I love cats."

We're all sitting around our place drinking and laughing. Shelly and Roger have had their game; one of Rob's imaginary players, Jack Kweenking, scored four times to lead Krasnoborsk Killers to a 9-2 romp over Beeston Beagles. My mother has phoned twice. She called to tell me Boris did a Big Job on the toilet for the first time. She called back to ask what solo was being sung. "No solo," I told her. "Just Shelly's guitar music." Deirdre's feeling a bit ill. I think she's mad it's me getting married and not her. Shelly's embarrassed the hell out of Rob by asking him if he's still a virgin. I'm drinking Caesars.

Greg Hodges arrives. He's wearing old-fashioned plastic-frame glasses, a knitted tie with an orange shirt and tweed sport jacket, baggy pants and scuffed shoes. He's missing one of his bottom teeth. First thing he tells us is the leather patches on his elbows do cover actual holes. I get the impression he tells this joke on himself all the time.

As soon as Shelly finds out he teaches Math, she gives him a costing problem. It's been bugging her boss at the Park Plaza, where she's working for the summer. They go to the kitchen table to work on it. About a minute later, I catch Shel dipping into the food.

"Time everybody split," I announce. "The party's supposed to be *after* the wedding."

15

f i f t e e n

It's evening and here we are ready to do our thing on the Glendon campus. Nadia, Boris and The Shark got here early and followed the nature trail to this fantastic ravine over by the tennis courts. They're just coming back now and The Shark has Boris on his shoulders. There's a bit of a wind, enough to pick up gum wrappers and student hand-outs and blow them across the quadrangle grass. My mother's hat blew off and Greg's gone after it. Shelly's doing a good job of amusing my mother and father with a spiel about hotels. Robbie, Paul, Frances and I are sitting on a blanket chatting and watching for Father Phil. Roger and Deirdre haven't got here yet.

Here comes Father Phil now. He's just stepped out of a cab at the Bayview Avenue gate and he's heading toward us in flowing white robes like a yacht under full sail.

Paul's wearing new jeans and a white, balloon-sleeved shirt with undone laces at the V-neck. And this wide black belt with a buckle as big as a shield. Also patent slip-ons.

There's an old custom where the bride wears a shift—sort of a thin cotton slip. That's what I'm wearing. For now, I've got my old raincoat on over it. And, as usual, I'm barefoot.

"Greetings and hallucinations," says Father Phil. He swoops into our midst carrying a battered black book. "Is everybody here?"

I tell him we're just waiting for Deirdre and her friend.

"She's, you know, a dear girl," he says, "but, like, she has trouble with priorities. Shall I go ahead?"

"If you have to."

"Why not? It's starting to get dark. ALL RIGHT, FOLKS! GATHER ROUND. I mean, like, MAKE A CIRCLE, OKAY?"

The circle forms. I'm beside Father Phil and Paul's beside me. Rob comes over to his dad's side and next to Rob is Greg, then Frances and The Shark, Shelly, Nadia and Boris, Dad, Mom and back to Father Phil. Shelly has her guitar hanging by a strap from her shoulder.

"Hi, everybody," says Father Phil, adjusting his headband. "We've all come here this evening to share something very beautiful. I mean, we're here in the presence of God to be with Susan and Paul on this very happy occasion."

While he talks, I slip off the coat and let it fall to the ground. Everyone stares at me. I wish I hadn't been so dramatic. But people always look at the bride, don't they? So what if I'm wearing a cheesecloth slip instead of a fussy gown? Mom and Nadia gasp and Dad, as usual, looks mad.

"Maybe I should explain something right off the top," Father Phil says. "Instead of blowing a lot of bread on a gown and a train and everything, Susan's brought back an old custom. They used to call it 'the smock wedding'. They believed that if the bride's barefoot and dressed in a smock or shift, the groom can't be liable for her debts. I mean, in those days, the guy automatically acquired an interest in the woman's personal assets. Well, Susan here is, like, telling us by the way she's dressed that she brings no dowry, no debts, no property to this marriage. Only love."

"What about him?" my dad snaps.

"Good point—uh—what's your first name?"

"Mike."

"Good point, Mike. Paul maybe should be standing here in his shorts, but the fact is, he is bringing a certain number of, you know, accumulated assets into the marriage."

"It's an insult to God," my dad says.

"Oh, no, on the contrary, God wouldn't mind if we were all out here in our birthday suits. It's our hang-up that makes us hide behind clothes, not His."

"Excuse me," says my mother. "My husband and I are sorry, but we're not used to our daughter's strange modern ways."

"Don't apologize—uh—?"

"Natasha."

"Don't apologize, Natasha. We want everybody to be their natural selves here today. Anyone who wants to say something, you know, just speak right up."

"Hey, I don't blame anybody for being a bit surprised," Shelly says. "If I hadn't been to a few different weddings lately, I'd be sort of wondering what's going on, too. But things change, right? And I can't blame Suzy and Paul for not wanting to spend big bucks on hoop skirts and veils and tuxedos and baubles, bangles and beads, can you? So let's enjoy, okay?"

Paul's hand touches mine, feels how cold it is, squeezes it. Shelly starts picking out notes from Led Zeppelin's *Stairway to Heaven*. Where the hell is Deirdre?

"O-o-o-kay," Father Phil says. "Well, we'd sure like God to give His blessing to Paul and Susan and to all of us sharing this happy time with them."

He turns to me and smiles. It's my cue.

"Most of you have met," I say, "but Paul and I'd like to tell you a little more about everybody here. My father and mother, Mike and Natasha Walchuk, have come all the way from Saskatoon and I'm glad they came. They gave me a good upbringing and I hope they'll take some credit for the fact that I can think for myself and I'm not afraid to try different things. My sister, Nadia Stefaniuk over here, was always good to me when we were kids. She's a great mother to my little nephew, Boris. We're so glad Boris feels right at home—no, Boris, you can have your turn on the guitar in a few minutes. Providing the music is my talented school pal, Shelly Goldfarb, who's also a great cook. You'll taste her strudel later. Another friend, Deirdre Hannah, is supposed to be here, and she could arrive at any second. If a helicopter flies over, don't be surprised if Deirdre jumps out."

"And lands in the ravine," says Father Phil. "Okay, great. Paul?"

As Paul introduces Rob, a young man in a York University sweatshirt and shorts comes walking across the grass and stops to watch a few feet behind The Shark. It's twilight but still light enough for me to see he's nobody I know. He taps his sneaker to the beat of Shelly's guitar as she moves into Three Dog Night's *Joy to the World*.

Paul tells a little about Rob's hockey game and Greg's love of fixing cars. He credits Frances with being the brains behind his insurance executive buddy, Hugh "The Shark" Godfrey. "Then there's my colleague, Roger Lorenz, who's supposed to be here. He's probably in that helicopter with Deirdre."

"And I'm Father Phil," says Father Phil, as everybody looks up to see if there's a helicopter in the sky. "You know, you're the people who know Paul and Susan best and I know you love them and I know they love all of you. You've all helped them become who they are. So you're all involved in this marriage, whether you like it or not. I mean, you ain't physically part of it—last time I looked, there was only room for two in their bed. But we do want you to share any thoughts or feelings you have, right now, with the rest of the gathering—which I see has increased by one."

He's referring to the guy in the sweatshirt.

"Father Phil," I say, "he isn't . . ."

But Father Phil isn't listening to me. "Come into the circle, brother," he says. "You must be one of the people we're expecting."

"Well—er—no," this guy says, looking sheepish but still stepping forward.

Father Phil isn't listening to him, either. "That's it, step right up between Shelly and—Hugh, isn't it? Yes. All right, who'd like to go first? You can say whatever you like, you know. Recite a poem, read a passage from a book, sing . . ."

Shelly stops playing. You can hear the wind in the trees and the traffic over on Bayview where it runs into Lawrence. Boris makes an explosion noise and giggles.

"Um . . . may I say something?" It's Rob. We talked him into staying in his casual clothes.

"Sure, fire away, m'boy."

"I didn't really prepare anything."

"Best that way, m'boy. Say whatever's in your heart."

"I—well—I guess all I wanted to say was I'm glad I'm here. I think this wedding is really neat. I don't see my father much now that he's here and I'm in Winnipeg, but I hope we'll still be able to get together. . . . I do miss him. I hope he and—and Susan are going to be really happy."

The kid's got me blubbering. I wipe my eyes with the back of my hand.

"Do you realize that Paul and I go back to grade school?" It's The Shark speaking. "He was a year ahead of me but we used to try to get thrown out of our classes so we could meet in the hall. He's the kind of close friend you can discuss the world situation with. I'd call him to get help with writing a report or just for a good laugh. Give us one minute together and we're back in Rosie's Snack Bar in Winnipeg eating hot chicken sandwiches after a double feature at the Vogue theatre. I'm glad we were moved to T.O. because we've been able to renew our friendship and meet Susan. Sue, you've got yourself one very solid fellow. Much happiness to both of you."

"The first time I saw Paul," says Shelly, "I thought, there's a guy I wouldn't mind sitting through a whole Argo game with. He just looked like a guy who could talk about something meaningful. Instead of the usual ess-aitch-eye-tee most guys hand you. Suzy and I both drooled over him in class, but she got to him before I did. And they've been great for each other. Paul's made Suzy more mature and Sue's kept Paul young, right? If they want to have a baby and they do have a baby, what a baby that will be!"

Shelly claps her hands and I have a feeling she might compose a song with those words.

"I . . . ." Nadia takes a step forward and her voice cracks. "I wish both of you a happy and healthy marriage." She steps back, her head bowed.

"Yeah," says Greg, and he mumbles something.

"Could you repeat that?" says Father Phil.

"I just said, 'I wish my brother and his new wife all the best.'"

"Can I say something?" It's the guy in the sweatshirt.

"By all means," Father Phil says.

I can't believe this. My mother gives me one of her wide-eyed looks and shakes her head.

The guy starts to talk: "I just wanted to say that I'm Roman Dansey, and I'm taking the Writers' Workshop here, and we've got this short story assignment for Monday. A bunch of people from my class went downtown tonight, but I figured that's no way to get started on a story, not unless you're going to wander around downtown and maybe get a handle on the pulse of the city. So I thought I'd stay here—I mean, that's why you come to these things, isn't it? The setting's perfect for getting down to work. Oh, I know there are some people who just come for a good time, like this doctor's wife from Cleveland, but I'm here to work. So I sit in my dorm—this room I have all to myself—and I stare out the window at all these fantastic trees and I keep thinking, What a perfect setting for sitting down and writing! I'm from Calgary and you might think that's a good place for sitting down and writing, and it probably would be all right if I didn't have a wife and two little kids to worry about. My wife's a wonderful person. She believes in God and she believes in me and she thinks we can have peace in our time if we work at it. Well, you could've knocked me over with a hammer when she said I should go to this writers' workshop. I paint houses and work at the post office at Christmas and do odd jobs for our local service station and I make ends meet but she knows how much I'd like to be a writer. She said I could take some of our savings and come here and get to be the new Arthur Hailey. We've had a week and you know what? I'm scared. I'm afraid I'm going to let Pattie down because I can't think of a thing to write. And it isn't as if I'm goofing off. I mean, I see some of the others partying—like the woman from Cleveland sneaking into the room of the guy from Wolfville—but I stick to my knitting, if you know what I mean. Still, nothing comes. I stare at the paper and I go for a walk and I come back and stare some more, and I fall asleep in class because I haven't been able to sleep the night before. I start to think that maybe this writing business ain't for me, but how can I go home and face Pattie and tell her that? So here I am tonight, eh, out for a walk, hoping some kind of inspiration will hit me like a bolt out of the nut, and lo and behold, here, right in front of my nose, is this group of people in what I figure is some kind of religious rite. I say to myself—this is the honest-to-goodness truth—I say to myself, There's your short story happening right before your eyes! I say to myself, Maybe it's a peace rally of some kind, but then I come closer and I'm kicking myself for not bringing a pad and pencil because I should be writing things down as I hear them. I should be describing this! Professor Eggleston says even when you're on the bus or in the pub you should have a pad and pencil handy so you can write down some of the natural witticisms and stuff that people say to one another. Back home, all I ever overhear on buses and in pubs is 'Whatdeya think the Stampeders'll do this year?' and 'The old lady wants me to pick up a quart of milk on the way home' and 'I think we're in for a dry spell, don't you?' I don't know if it's my hearing or the places I go to, but I just never seem to pick up any gems. So here I am, wandering across the campus at sundown and panicking about another night of writing, and here's a short story happening right here. So, if you don't mind, could I maybe ask you a few questions so's I can get some of the details right? Like, it really knocks me out that you're actually having a *wedding* here—I mean, it is a wedding, isn't it? I guess I wasn't born last Tuesday, I got that figured out, haven't I? I've heard of this type of wedding but I've never been to one, and, you know, Pattie goes to lots of weddings—some she isn't even invited to!—so she's just going to love the story if I can get it just right. So, let me ask you a question or two, okay? Like, I figured out that you're the bride's mother and father, am I right?"

131

Mom and Dad stare at him. They can't believe he's stopped talking.

"You're right," I say.

"And you're the bride."

"Right again."

"Let's see—I'm not sure—are you the groom?"

"Yes, I am," Paul says.

"Then who're the groom's parents?"

"They're dead."

"Oh, I'm sorry. And who is the best man?"

Father Phil says, "There is no best man, no maid or matron of honour. There are only best people, and that's everybody here."

"Fantastic! Okay, now—"

"You are welcome to stay and celebrate with us," Father Phil says, finally taking charge. "We have others to hear from, now. Who'd like to speak next?"

Frances puts up her hand as if she's in school. "I have a poem. It's a long poem by Edmund Spenser called *The Epithalamion*, but I want to give you just a little part of it. It's kind of a wedding night blessing." I expect her to pull out a book or a sheet of paper, but damned if she doesn't recite it!

"'Now welcome night, thou night so long expected,
That long day's labour doest at last defray . . .
Spread thy broad wing o'er my love and me,
That no man us see,
And in thy sable mantle us enwrap,
From fear of peril and foul horror free.
Let no false treason seek us to entrap,
Nor any dread disquiet once annoy
The safety of our joy.'"

"Isn't that nice!" my mother says. She probably thinks the poem sounded a lot more like a church service than what she's heard so far.

"Anyone else?" Father Phil says. "Mike?"

My father shakes his head but Mom gives him a nudge. He looks over at me and says, "Susan, you are my daughter and I wish you happiness. And you, too, Paul."

Maybe he feels better about this now that everyone's said nice things and the sun's down and the darkness gives me some modesty.

Father Phil says, "Okay, thank you, everybody. I'd now like to, you know, throw in a few verses from the *First Book of Corinthians*."

He opens his book and reads: "*Love is patient; love is kind and envies no one.*" Shelly starts playing *Love is Kind, Love is Wine*. "*Love is never boastful, nor conceited, nor rude; never selfish, not quick to take offence. Love keeps no score of wrongs . . .*" He finishes the reading and says, "It'd be a perfect world if everyone remembered those words and lived by them."

He puts his book on the grass and steps between Paul and me. He takes our two hands.

"Okay, you two," he says. "I know you've felt the thrills of your love for each other, but you've considered the consequences of marriage, too, so let's hear it. Do you take each other to be husband and wife?"

"Susan," Paul says, "I love you and I take you to be my wife."

I take a deep breath and say, "Paul, I love you and I take you to be my husband."

We look at each other. Though it's dark, I try to tell him with my eyes that I've just made a promise I intend to keep.

Father Phil says, "Will the two of you give yourselves fully to the other and be consoling and forgiving to the best of your ability?"

We're in the middle of answering when I notice a couple of people running across the campus toward us. Roger and Deirdre!

"Paul and Susan have exchanged promises," Father Phil says. "Oh, hello, Deirdre. Welcome. And um—?"

"Roger," says Paul.

"Right, Roger. Hey, the two of you are kind of late, but do step into the circle . . . that's it, open the circle for—that's it. O-o-o-kay, as I was saying, we've heard the promises. Now, if the rest of you will repeat after me: We're glad we've witnessed your promises to each other . . ."

Everybody except Paul and me says, "We're glad we've witnessed your promises to each other." And, led by Father Phil, they tell us they accept us into the community as husband and wife. And they promise to help us and be responsible to us. Following this, Father Phil tells me it's my turn to speak again.

"I'm just so grateful that all of you could be here today. And I'm just so glad that my mom and dad are here to see for themselves how much I love this man." I feel tears on my face and I fling myself at Paul. I kiss him as hard as I can. He feels sturdy and warm and terrific.

Everybody applauds.

"This isn't only a wedding," Paul says. "For me, it's a rebirth." He holds me close at his side. "Now, we want to continue this celebration, so, please, everybody come over to our place for a party."

Shelly pushes past Deirdre so she can hug me. Her guitar jabs me in the breast. "Ouch!" I cry.

"Oh, sorry," Shelly says. "Suze, the wedding was beautiful and you are beautiful."

Over her shoulder, I say to Deirdre, "You turkey. What the hell happened?"

"Oh, Sue, I'm really sorry. It was Les. He came over to our place and demanded to know where the wedding was. We had a horrible time getting rid of him. We finally did but we were sure he was following us. We had to go up and down streets and cut through back alleys to make sure we'd lost him."

I feel my knees go weak. Shelly moves on to Paul and I want to take Deirdre aside, but the writer gets between us.

"Congratulations!" he says, and he grabs me and kisses me.

In quick succession come Greg, Rob, The Shark and Frances to hug me and wish me well. The writer kisses Deirdre and starts interviewing her. Roger's snapping photos like crazy, trying to make up for what he missed. I push Les to the back of my mind and brace myself for The Big Four.

"Mom," I say, "was it so bad?"

"Susan," she says, holding me. "It's over. You're a married woman." What's over? I wonder. The wedding or my life of sin?

Nadia makes it a three-way hug. She's crying.

"Your father is proud," Mom says.

"Is he, Mom?"

She breaks from me and gestures to Dad. He's holding Boris, who's asleep on his shoulder. He gives Boris to Nadia and holds me at arm's length.

"I like your man, Susan," he says. "I think he loves you. The one thing any father wants for his daughter is that she'll be happy and I know you are."

"Oh, Dad, thank you." I hug him.

"Just one favour I have to ask," he says into my ear.

"What's that?"

"That someday, when you're ready, you'll come to Saskatoon and get married by a real priest in a church of God."

16

It's nearly four in the morning.

The reception is over. It was a replay of the party we'd had earlier. Paul and I are both drunker than we should be on our wedding night. We stumble into the hide-a-bed and pull up the covers.

"We're married," Paul whispers groggily. He giggles, then turns on his side.

I lie back and think about it. Married. To my prof. Who is old enough to have a son not that much younger than me. But he is, nonetheless, a man who seems to love and accept me as I am.

A sudden creak startles me. I sit up. The bedroom door is opening.

"Dad?"

I wait for Paul to answer. After a few seconds, I realize he's dead to the world.

"Your dad's asleep," I say. "Anything I can do?"

"Uh, no . . ."

I hear him walking back to the bed. I reach for my T-shirt and jeans and slip them on. I go into the bedroom and watch him climb into bed. The room is dark but there's moonlight coming through the curtains.

I say, "We'll remember this wedding for a long time."

He's sitting up in bed but he doesn't speak.

"Can I get you anything?"

"No, thank you."

"You okay?"

"Uh . . . yes."

"Really?"

"Well . . . I'm sort of confused."

I sit down on the bed, feeling maternal. I reach for one of his feet sticking up under the covers. I squeeze it.

I say, "It's not every day that your old man gets married."

"It's not that so much . . ."

135

"What else?"

"It's . . . um . . . "

"Come on, tell me."

"I . . . I think it's being in a different place."

"I'll stay in here with you."

"You don't have to."

"It's all right. You try to get to sleep."

Rob moves down in the bed and puts his head on the pillow. I stay at the foot of the bed, waiting for a change in his breathing that'll tell me he's asleep.

Every once in a while, I sneak a look at him.

His eyes are wide open.

part three

Catherine:
1981

1

Nottingham, England
Saturday, August 8, 1981

Something—perhaps the mental alarm clock that I've relied upon for years—wakes me at precisely seven o'clock. I lie on my back, scanning the beige walls, the brown drapes, the cream-coloured coves of yet another hotel room. Beyond the drapes and the bay window are the houses and shops of suburban Arnold, and beyond those, the rolling Nottinghamshire hills. I listen for any sounds from the room that adjoins mine. My son, Rob, is asleep in there—if he came home after his night out with the men.

I watched BBC television last night until it went off the air, about midnight. After my bath, I lay in bed reading and fell asleep. (It wasn't the book that sent me to sleep; Iris Murdoch's *The Sea, The Sea* is so good, I portion it out to myself in twenty-page segments.) I didn't hear Rob come in.

Since I can't sleep, I rise and go to peek into his room through our connecting door. He is lying there, apparently fast asleep, turned away from me. For a few moments, I stare at his broad shoulders, the blondish curls at his neck. How many times, I wonder, has Fiona seized those curls in ecstasy?

At two o'clock this afternoon, in an eight hundred-year-old church, my son is marrying an English girl named Fiona Bryson. They met in Garmisch Partenkirchen, West Germany, and they have travelled all over Europe together—even Greece, where I have never been. They made their way back to her hometown, moved in with her parents, found employment and surprised everyone by announcing wedding plans. It seems a little crazy for Rob to spend the night at my hotel, but I asked him to and, with a half-grin that planted me squarely in my own generation, he agreed.

I close the door softly and cross the room to plug in the kettle. This room is equipped with all one needs for making tea or coffee for two: cups, saucers, spoons, tea pot, electric kettle, tea bags, packets of coffee, powdered milk, sugar, all grouped on a tray. I put on my wine-coloured robe over my pink nightgown and tie the sash. Till the kettle boils, I brush my short, greying hair, watching myself do this in the dresser mirror.

I make coffee, consider for a moment whether this will be the day I stop using sugar, and stir both milk powder and sugar into the coffee. I carry the cup over to the chair by the window. This instant stuff is far removed from the strong, delicious coffee I had last month in France and Germany, but it will do.

From my handbag I take a letter, one that caught up with me here. I have read it several times and now that I've had a night's sleep, I want to read it again. I open the drapes to let in the daylight. Again today, the sky is overcast. I unfold the letter.

July 29

> *Dearest Catherine:*
> *Sitting here by the pool, I've been looking out over the blue water of Indian Arm, watching a sailboat come from the direction of Deep Cove. It went behind an island—the one they call Boulder Island—and I swear it didn't reappear. It might have stopped at Belcarra Park, but I have a view of the only dock. Where did that boat go? I tell myself it couldn't just disappear, but it troubles me.*
> *What troubles me more, of course, is the way you vanished from my life those long, long weeks ago. You seemed to be loving Vancouver. I know you loved our morning swims, and I will always have a picture in my mind of you lugging rocks and digging dirt as the two of us, side by side, built the steps down to the water.*
> *You seemed so marvellously relaxed on those walks we took along the seawall, your incomparable face turned toward English Bay, the wind ruffling your hair. Now, when I take Mort on long jaunts from Denman to Prospect Point and back, I think how infinitely more enjoyable it was to have you along with us. I have to lie to myself that it's the place I love, that I'm privileged to be able to walk freely among the sun-worshippers and watch the gulls swooping over the water. I lie to myself that walking good old obedient Mort is the real pleasure of a summer day. But, without*

*you, the walking (even on Robson Street!) is monotonous, and Vancouver—
which was vibrant and multi-coloured when you were here—is drab
and grey and lifeless.*

I've taken the boat out only once since you left.

*When I got to Second Narrows Bridge, I thought, Why am I doing
this? It was a perfect day for sailing, yet it was all wrong without you.*

*That two weeks you spent here was a watershed in my life. You know
that. I hoped it would be for you, too. I hoped you would be back here
soon (I know you still have clients here).*

*I dream about rushing off to meet you somewhere exotic. Even Toronto's
hideous Terminal Two could be magical if it was where we planned to
meet. I hoped your last letter was going to be the one that named a place.
Instead, it let me know that you wanted to get away by yourself, "to lose
yourself in Europe", as you put it. That saddened me, yet I do respect your
right to be on your own. I know your travels will not be all pleasure;
you'll be taking note of old customs and new procedures in every hotel you
stay in.*

*I didn't go to bed last night so that I could watch the Royal Wedding
live on TV. It started around 1:30 in the morning here. You had said you
were definitely going to be in London, so I kept my eyes glued to the
screen, ignoring Charles and Diana and searching the crowds for you. (I
videotaped the whole thing and maybe when you have a chance to see it
you'll be able to pick yourself out of the crowd.)*

*I was impressed with the Archbishop's little speech on the meaning of
marriage. It was a nice touch when he said, "All couples on their wedding
day are 'royal couples' and stand for the truth that we help to shape the
world and are not just its victims . . ."*

*By the time you read this, you'll be with a "royal couple" of your own.
Please give my very best wishes to Rob and Fiona, and tell them I'd like to
fly them somewhere as a wedding present. I'm sure they have honeymoon
plans, but they might consider a quick flight to Vancouver or Montreal
(if Montreal continues to be your home base) after all the excitement has
worn off.*

*Here's a better idea. Why don't you come here, with your son and
daughter-in-law, for another wedding. Yours and mine.*

*The furniture business has become a bore. I've had a good offer for the
stores as a package deal, and I'll sell them all so that nothing can distract
me from you.*

Please marry me.

I love you madly and I look forward to hearing from you, any time, any way.
Mort sends his greetings.

With all my love,
James

My eyes are moist, but not because of his sentiments. What I feel is more pity than anything, or perhaps anguish. I fold up the letter and return it to my handbag. In the few moments it takes to finish my coffee, I recall the effort I put into amusing those two, Mort and his master. I had swimming races with Mort (a playful water spaniel), end to end in James's pool. I took him for walks on afternoons when James was at work; Mort pranced with a regal gait, telegraphing to the housebound dogs that he was king of the neighbourhood and causing them to snarl and bark at him from any available window. I threw a tennis ball for him to fetch and loved his little bark as he dropped it at my feet and urged me to throw it again. Some mornings, I was wakened by Mort licking my face.

James also had to be amused. Most of the time, he pampered me, making the meals, doing the housework, shopping for groceries. He insisted I tell him about my work, even though he didn't listen but simply watched me while I talked. Some mornings, he woke me with a nuzzle and a whimper, and this meant he wanted "breakfast in bed", his pet name for suckling at my breasts. There were times when I woke with a start, unsure which was at me, man or beast.

The truth is, I grew to love Mort more than James.

I take my coffee cup to the bathroom and wash it out. The dark brown remains dilute and disappear in the surge of tap water. My feelings for James were like that—a residue at the bottom of my heart, lying there for some months before being diluted by my European trip and finally disappearing in London. Poor James. He deserves better imagery.

Returning to the room, I drift over to the window and look out. In the playground-park across the street, a man throws a stick and his dog retrieves it. Paul often spoke of buying a dog for Rob, but I'd never go along with the idea. Now that I know how playful yet well-behaved dogs can be, I wish we had bought one. Paul would howl at the sight of me enduring one of Mort's kisses.

I always liked Paul's laugh. The sound of his all-out laughter could lift my spirits. Whenever I try to recall the good moments in my marriage, I think of the two of us laughing. Those were the high points, when something struck both of us as wildly funny at exactly the same time. I wonder if we'll be able to laugh that way when we see each other later today.

That is one problem with James; he doesn't laugh very much or say anything very funny. He is much too earnest. I noticed that the first time we met, at the home of mutual friends, Charleen and Frank Scanlon (Charleen was one of my bridesmaids). I was in Vancouver on business, doing what I do best, suggesting a new promotional package for a hotel that had a good location and sagging profits. Charleen would not let me leave town without meeting Frank's widower uncle. James did appeal to me, but I think it was because he was one of those brave risk-takers who had started with one tiny store and built his business into one of the more substantial shopping-mall chains. I liked talking business with him, but he had this disconcerting way of taking my hands in his, right in the middle of a discussion of Theory Y management or computerized inventory.

It suddenly seems important that I answer James's letter right away. I look inside my handbag for a pen and come upon the postcard that Rob sent me a few weeks ago:

Hello, Mom. We love Greece! The small-town merchants
give you brandy or ouzo when you enter their shops. The
taverns give you free food when you buy a small bottle
of retsina. One place gave us fish, bread, cheese,
olives, oranges. Sculptures amazing. Language gap huge.
To be understood, we have to use hands and feet and draw things.
Can say Greek words for "thank you" and "good", which are all they
want to hear. You wouldn't like the male domination, but they do
accept the liberated antics of foreign women. Love, Fiona and Rob.

All this is jammed onto a single card in Rob's small but legible handwriting, the message spilling into the address area, the last sentence running around the perimeter of the card. All that information but not a word about where they were sleeping.

I take a writing pad from my brief case and, at my window seat, pad on knee, I write:

Aug. 8/81

Dear James:
Your letter arrived three days ago at Fiona's, and her mother gave it to me yesterday. I went over there for afternoon tea (an outrageous spread of tarts, cakes, buttered breads, biscuits, pastries, meats, cheeses, tomato slices, cucumber slices, deviled eggs, lettuce, carrots, chocolate wafers, grapes, pears, apples and on and on). I met Mr. and Mrs. Bryson and the bridesmaids and Fiona's dear old grandparents (Mrs. Bryson's parents, the Middletons, who contradict each other continually). Though I've been in England for two weeks now, it took me a while to adjust my ear to their accents. I am amazed at how much accents can vary within such a small radius and from social class to social class. Most of the Brysons sound as if they are direct descendants of the Romans; they pronounce the "u" sound in words like "some" and "rum" the way you say the last word in the Latin sentence, cogito ergo sum. *They say, "Are you all right?" instead of our "How are you?" and I want to answer, "But I haven't been ill."*
The more differences I see, the better I like them. McLuhan was wrong; the world is not a global village.
I expected to meet Paul at the Brysons', but he wasn't there. Rob had taken him out for a driving lesson, of all things, and they met Rob's best man for dinner (you remember Arthur Wiley) before joining the rest of the men at the pub. I wish Paul and I could have met yesterday to rid ourselves of the initial awkwardness.
No-one has mentioned if Paul's wife is here, and I haven't asked. She wasn't at the Brysons'.
Your letter. It lies folded beside me like a morning rose. You are a dear man, James, and your letter is lovely and loving.
Thank you for saying you respect my right to be on my own. This time in Europe has made me see how important it is for me to be independent. It thrills me to know that whatever I've accomplished I've accomplished on my own. If my father is in Heaven, he will be so proud to look down and see his daughter travelling all over, advising men on how to manage their properties, and now taking this vacation in the Europe he knew only as a soldier in World War I.
Though there are times when I am lonely, I cherish being able to go places where no-one knows me. Driving a Mercedes down the autobahn

at 160 k.p.h. can be exhilarating. And, yes, the list of ideas I have gathered in the smaller hotels is filling up my journal.

Thank you for taping the Royal Wedding. I camped out on the street for a day and a night and met some other whacky monarchists doing the same. I am sure I could pick myself out on the tape because I was wearing a red toque and standing near the Vaudeville Theatre on The Strand. I had a perfect view of the procession but it went by much too quickly. Even so, I was caught up in the euphoria. Some of my new friends and I fought our way to The Mall and managed to be fairly close to the Palace when the whole family came out on the balcony. My head is still bursting from the sights and sounds and smells of that day.

James, your proposal is flattering and direct. You know how much I like directness. I think selling the stores would be a mistake; a man like you needs his daily fix of business negotiation, just as I need the planning and training seminars I do for people.

The time we had together was made especially good by the fact that we both had been working hard and we needed some diversion.

Here I am complimenting you on directness and shying away from a straightforward statement of my own. All right, then. The answer to your proposal is, I'm afraid, No.

Please be assured that no other approach could make me answer differently. I simply do not intend ever to marry again.

I shall tell Rob and Fiona that you are thinking of them on their wedding day. You certainly do not have to give them a...

I stop to re-read what I have written. Maybe I am too blunt. Or have I been blunt enough? James will search the sentences for a phrase, a word, a syllable that he can translate into hope. Making no reference to Mort seems harsh, but how, after all, does one gracefully turn down a marriage proposal?

I re-read the paragraph about the Royal Wedding and smile at the second sentence: "*. . . met some other whacky monarchists . . .*" How we couch our communications in half-truths! We believe that the whole truth would hurt, and of course it would. I could never write, "*Cultivated a rambunctious actor young enough to be your son and shared a sleeping bag with him.*" If only we didn't have to explain our actions.

I look at my watch—time to wake Rob. As I lean into his room, he turns over, flings one arm out and grunts. He is having a dream. I wonder if all his dreams include Fiona these days, or does Lise pop back into them now and then? In many ways, this son of mine is fully mature, but, as I watch him now, he seems still a child. I have no idea why he wants to get married so young.

2

t w o

Rob and I take the stairs down two flights to the restaurant, a long, maroon-carpeted room with three rows of tables-for-four. A young waitress in white blouse and black skirt leads us to a table at the far end of the room. Five or six of the tables are occupied by women whose badges indicate that they are delegates to some sort of convention.

"Would you like the full English breakfast or the Continental?" the waitress asks.

Rob looks at her and they smile at each other. His slightly dishevelled blond hair and his sleepy face contrast with his crisp new yellow sport shirt and his tan jeans. There is nothing flirtatious about his expression or hers; I have noticed an admirable lack of guile in the younger generation's social encounters.

"The full English breakfast, please," I say. "Bacon and eggs, sunny side up."

"The same for me," says Rob.

After the waitress has taken the rest of our order and left us, I scan the room and take note of the cherry-red placemats and serviettes that match the shades on the chandelier lamps. The decor might suggest a bordello if the women at the tables were less animated and not so obviously dressed for committee work. One near us is explaining her theory of who is behind the attempted assassinations of Reagan and The Pope.

I say to Rob, "Hung over, are you?"

"I'm dying for coffee."

"You said you were going to take it easy on the drinking."

"They treated me as if I was some cowboy from the Wild West who was expected to drink them all under the table. You know the size of the beer mugs?"

"The pints?"

"Yes. It isn't easy to drink even one after a big dinner. They got me

146

up to six. And then we went to Patrick's and his mother served us scotch, 'neat', as they say—without ice, without mix, without water. Straight."

The waitress brings us a pot of hot coffee and a smaller pot of hot milk. (I will make a note of this practice in my journal alongside the one describing the brightly-coloured trash bucket that the Germans set in the middle of the breakfast table as if it were a centre-piece.)

Rob takes a deep breath of the coffee fumes and says, "Ahhhhh." He pours my coffee and his own and bends to sip his. "Mmmm."

"Are you ready to have a conversation now?"

"What have we been having?"

"A lot of moaning about your stag party. I'm surprised at the Brysons wanting to segregate the sexes the night before the wedding."

"It wasn't my real stag party. You know we had that two weeks ago. Tell me, Mother, how was tea?"

"The food was delicious and the people were lovely. Fiona's father was there for a while—before he dashed off to be with you fellows—and he told a few funny stories. I like him very much. Fiona's mother couldn't sit still, but she's one of those active little women you love instantly."

"She reminds me of a squirrel."

"What a thing to say about your mother-in-law-to-be!"

"I've always liked squirrels. How was Fiona?"

"Terrific. She seems so much more sure of herself than she did when the two of you came to Montreal. Do you think she's one of those people who shine brightest on their own turf?"

"I'm the wrong one to ask. To me, she's super all the time."

The waitress brings our breakfasts. The bacon is thick, undercooked and curled up at the corners. The two eggs ("farm eggs" the menu calls them) are the colour of the evening sun in summer. Between our two plates the waitress sets a metal holder bearing eight slices of hard unbuttered toast, and beside that she places a little china pot of marmalade and a dish of wrapped cubes of butter.

"Will there be anything else?" she asks.

"More coffee, later, please," Rob says.

"I'll come back then."

I begin to eat. The eggs taste good.

"Mom, tell me about London."

"Oh, I did the usual things and some crazy ones. Tea in the Palm

Court at the Ritz. The changing of the guard. Took a taxi through the parts of Battersea where they rioted—store fronts boarded up or covered by iron grill-work. Did you know that, since the trouble, a fashionable night club that used to be called 'Bennett's' has been re-named 'Riots'? Isn't that typically English, somehow, to—"

"I mean the wedding. How was the Charlie and Di Show?"

"Glorious! The pageantry, the glitter, the patriotic fervour, the well-behaved crowds, the Household Brigade with their swords and their matched brown horses. It was marvellous to wallow in the happiness that everyone was feeling, everyone, from policemen to punkers."

"Did you say you spent the night in the street?"

"Yes . . ."

"Alone?"

"There were hundreds of people—"

"I mean, was there anyone with you?"

"I befriended several. Really, you should've come down. It was quite a spectacle." I am conscious of deflecting the question.

"You know I can't get excited about royalty. All that money they spend—"

"But surely an event like a royal wedding is worth every penny if it rallies the people. The English haven't felt so excited and proud for years."

"Is it true that they had doctors check out Di to make sure she was still a virgin?"

"I don't know—I hadn't heard."

"Do you approve of that?"

"I suppose it's pretty vital to a royal family—"

"Mother, do you think Di sent *her* doctor to check out Chuck? I thought you were dead against double standards."

"I am, but you've shifted the topic. I'm not defending the methods used for royal match-making. I'm applauding the way the Royal Family has stimulated the British ego and the British economy at a time when some stimulation was badly needed."

"Well, all right. So what else have you been doing?"

"I drove up to Scarborough to see the latest play directed by Alan Ayckbourn. It's a new Peter Tinniswood comedy called *You Should See Us Now*. You'd love it. It's wonderfully funny, and it makes an intriguing point; that some of us are born adults and some of us

never grow up. It's true of a lot of people we know—which reminds
me . . . Rob. You've kept me in suspense long enough. How is your
father?"

"I was beginning to think you were trying to avoid talking about
him."

"I haven't seen him for six years. I'm curious."

"You should've seen him drink last night. He'd had a bad time
with the driving lesson."

"Wasn't it you who took him out?"

"Yes, in Fiona's car. It's a standard transmission and I'm used to
gearing down and pulling on the handbrake at every intersection the
way Fiona and her dad do. Well, Dad could not get the hang of it,
but, worst of all, he had no idea where the left side of the car was."

"Not everybody adjusts quickly to driving on the other side of the
road. Give him a day or so and he'll master it."

"I don't know—he was completely rattled. Twice I had to yank
the steering wheel out of his hands or we would've hit a parked car."

"Oh, dear."

"Mind you, I took him on a pretty tough course—two-lane
country roads, dual carriage-ways, three-lane highways with the
middle lane just for passing, congested streets with cars parked with
two wheels up on the curb, round-abouts—I thought he should
experience every kind of situation. He nearly went nuts. I've never
seen him like that. We stopped for coffee and he was white as chalk
and shaking all over. When he came out of the cafe, do you know
what he did? After those two solid hours of English driving, he
reverted right back to North America—he said, 'I won't let this beat
me, I'm going to show you I can do it,' and he jumped into the
passenger seat."

I can't help myself—I laugh.

"Last night at the pub," says Rob, "he swore he'd never try driving
in England again."

"Why did he want to drive in the first place? There are lots of
other methods of transportation, most of them very reliable."

"He said he wanted to take a trip into the countryside, at his own
pace, maybe to Wales or Scotland. Now, he figures he can't. Last
night, he kept knocking back beer and shaking his head and moaning."

"How did he look otherwise?"

"Okay. A bit fatter around the middle. He's back to a beard, but the short, trim kind."

"Did he say why he didn't bring his wife?"

"Who said he didn't?"

"No-one has said a word about her. She didn't come to tea."

"Dad and Susan are staying right here in this hotel. I guess everybody avoids saying anything for your sake—I know I have. Mother, Susan didn't go to tea because she hasn't been feeling well. . . . She's pregnant."

3

Why am I so angry? Why am I *furious*? Because the Brysons didn't tell me that Paul's young wife is here with him? Because Paul and Susan are staying right here in this hotel? Because Rob, my own son, thought he was being kind by not mentioning it? Because Susan is going to have a baby? Because she and Paul are going to flaunt this pregnancy at the wedding and take the attention away from the bride and groom? From what I hear, she loves to cause a scene, and she's probably six months gone, with a belly out to here, and she'll no doubt appear in one of those T-shirts that have "BABY" emblazoned across the front and an arrow pointing down to the bulge. Is that why I'm mad? Or am I simply jealous?

I've never met Susan. Rob once showed me a photograph of her, taken on a New York street when he, she and Paul drove down there to see some plays. She was striking a pose in front of a limousine and its uniformed driver and she was not at all what I'd expected. I had always visualized someone pretty—turned up nose, wide blue eyes— maybe a little off-beat, but definitely pretty. In the photo, Susan was quite short and plain; she was squinting into the sun and maybe that distorted her face, but her clothes were ragged, her feet bare, and her hair seemed to be the colour and texture of hay.

Am I angry because she can have a baby while I, thanks to a tubal ligation and middle age, cannot?

All this speculation prevents me from speaking as we go back to our rooms. Rob, sensing my mood, walks a pace behind me. I'm uncomfortable every step of the way, knowing that, at any moment, Susan and Paul could come around a corner or step out of any door.

At my room, I say, "Rob, would you come in here for a minute, please?" I want to tell him how we're going to handle this Paul-Susan situation, but I'm not sure what I'm going to say.

"Mom, I have to have a shower. Arthur will be here very soon."

"Oh, come on in, just for a second."

I unlock the door and enter. The first thing I see is a bouquet of red roses arranged in a glass vase on the desk. Their scent is everywhere. I assume they are for Rob and Fiona, sent to the wrong room. While Rob closes the door, I walk over to the flowers and see a little envelope leaning against the vase and the name written on it: "Ms Barber". I open the envelope and take out the card. Written on it are the words, "With love," but "love" is crossed out and "affection" written under it, but "affection" is also crossed out and "fervour" substituted. Then the name of the sender: "Barry."

"I'll bet I know who sent those," Rob says. "James, the incurable romantic."

I consider pocketing the card and nodding that yes, they are from James. From an early age, we believe that, in a pinch, a little lie will save us no end of explaining and anxiety. I am not pleased to be put in this situation by a man I have only recently met, especially when I made no explicit reference to him in our earlier chat about the Royal Wedding. The timing is particularly bad because it scuttles any chance of a serious discussion with Rob about his father.

I tell him, "They're from someone else."

At first, Rob looks aghast. The young like their elders to be settled in their relationships; a few years after Paul there was David, and when that didn't work out Rob was very critical of the variety of casual associations I cultivated. He showed great disappointment when I emerged from my Vancouver interlude without a ring. He claimed to like James even though they had nothing in common.

His face gradually breaks into a smile, the smile of someone who has learned a fascinating secret. I turn away from it.

"Mother, you *rascal*!" he says. "You've been cheating on poor old James."

"Rob, the flowers are from someone I met in London—it's nothing, really. And it's over with James."

"Who is this guy in London?"

"He's an actor; his name is Barry Lambert. He was quite pleasant to me and made it easier to endure the masses of people."

"An actor! Mom, you should've invited him up here for our wedding. You could've upstaged Dad."

"Rob. It's time for your shower."

4

"Mom, check this!"

"Howdy, Mrs. Hodges."

I look over at the door connecting our rooms and there stands Arthur Wiley, Rob's best man. Freckled, sandy-haired and pudgy-cheeked, he looks like a child playing dress-up in his rented grey tails, his striped trousers and his top hat. Rob stands behind him wearing only a towel. His hair is wet from the shower.

"Arthur," I say, "you look splendid."

"Thank you, Mrs. Hodges, thank you." I've told him to call me Catherine but he never does.

Arthur and Rob went to McGill University together and graduated with B.A.'s, but Arthur has gone on to Toronto to take Law. He flew over especially for the wedding.

"I hear the gang of you drank the pub dry," I say. "Would you like some coffee?"

"Yes, please," Arthur says, coming into my room. "One can become awfully fond of Theakston's Old Peculier and wonder why the next day. Think fast!"

He turns and twirls his top hat at Rob. The hat does not make a good frisbee and it dives to the floor beyond Rob's reach.

"Not a nice thing to do with a top hat," Rob says. He retrieves it and tries it on. "A good fit. I think this is the one I had on in the shop."

He says "shop", not "store". Yesterday, he said, "I'm not bothered" instead of "I don't mind". Staying with the Brysons is having its effect.

"Well, I won't trade," says Arthur. "That one is definitely mine."

He lunges for it. Rob twists out of reach and dives back into his room, leaving the towel in his wake.

Arthur is on the phone and Rob is shaving, with his bathroom door wide open. I have come into his room to deliver Arthur's coffee.

153

In bikini underpants, Rob looks athletic and virile but oddly vulnerable. A feeling that some might call the maternal instinct comes over me. Strange that I should feel it now. He could meander all over Europe, sleeping in alcoves and culverts and anonymous women's arms, incommunicado for weeks at a time, and I wouldn't feel a single pang. Often I doubted if I had ever been a mother and I was proud of that, proud to be unshackled. I was certain that my lack of possessiveness helped Rob achieve maturity. But now, I want to hold my son back, protect him from the world. But it is already too late.

Arthur hangs up and begins to dial again.

"Who are you phoning *now*?" Rob says with mock-anger.

"Patrick. I want to see if he still remembers which church it is."

"Have a little faith!" Rob pantomimes shooting him with his Foamy shaving cream can.

"I'd pay attention to your shaving if I were you," I say. "Your father came to our wedding with a big cut on his chin."

Rob says, "That's the first time I've ever heard you say anything about your wedding."

"He arrived at the church with a bump on his forehead, too. He and his brother and his dad played golf that morning and a ball hit your father. He wondered if the cut and the bump were some sort of divine punishment."

"For what?"

"Good question. For being a fool? I don't know."

"I don't see how he could've been a fool. He fell in love with you, didn't he?"

"*Touché*. But he also fell out of love with me."

"I'm not so sure about that."

"Well, it's all academic now."

He has finished shaving and he dabs his face with after-shave lotion. Arthur is explaining something to Patrick, making it sound as if ushering is some serious military manoeuvre.

"Mom," Rob says, "you will promise not to get into some crazy argument with Dad, won't you?"

"I'll be on my best behaviour. Events like this are carried off quite naturally these days. Princess Diana's divorced parents attended her wedding and it was handled with no fuss or bother at all. I'm quite looking forward to talking with Paul."

"And Susan?"

"And Susan. By the way, how far along is she?"

"I don't know—five or six months, I think Dad said. Remember, I haven't seen her lately, either."

"I hope she'll let your father and me have a few words alone."

"Sure she will. You'll see, she's open and friendly with everybody. But, Mom, when you're talking to Dad, don't mention his driving lesson, all right? He'll know damned well it was me who told you about it."

Rob and Arthur have gone. When I kissed Rob goodbye, I held onto him a little too long. I could tell by the way he tensed up that he thought I was being too emotional in front of Arthur. In a matter of two hours or so, I will see him at the church, taking part in a ritual that people still consider meaningful. When I told my friends I wished my son were not taking this step at so young an age, they said I should be thankful that he's getting married and not simply moving in with Fiona. They said I'm lucky that his bride isn't pregnant (as far as we know). Nevertheless, as lovely as Fiona is, I do not feel thankful or lucky at all. I have only one child and he is leaving me.

He left me several months ago, but that was different. After he graduated from McGill, he worked as a labourer in a construction project just long enough to accumulate funds for a trip to Europe. He said he needed time to decide on a career. I hoped he would spend time in France polishing up his French, then come home and either take post-graduate work or help me in my business for a while, maybe program my computer for me. Instead, he met Lise, his Montreal girlfriend, in Frankfurt (I think they had secretly planned to meet), but they split up in Munich, and, on the rebound, he fell for Fiona, who was hitchhiking to Rome. They spent most of their time travelling. (Tomorrow, they are off again, this time to Barcelona.)

They have rented a little semi-detached house in Woodthorpe (like Arnold, a suburb of Nottingham), and Fiona has a good job in a bank, but there is still a question of what Rob will do—he is not even clear on what Immigration will let him do. He keeps talking about moving back to Canada but, if they do, will they live anywhere near me? Somehow, I doubt it. That's why I clung to him for an extra few seconds.

I am alone. Lying around in my underwear is a luxury I never permit myself at home. Sloth, I have always believed, is the number one cause of fat; a lazy body becomes overweight and out-of-shape. Fanatic that I am about physical fitness—regularly going for long walks, doing aerobic exercises, playing tennis—I have indulged in this kind of relaxation often on this trip.

I lie on the bed, thinking of Rob, letting scenes from our life together flash through my mind: the time I forgot that I had left him on the changing table and I darted to his room just in time to catch him—literally catch him—as he rolled off; coaxing him to stay with the teacher on his first day of kindergarten; urging him to "Hit 'em! Knock 'em down!" when he played defence in peewee hockey; comforting him after I'd had a shouting match with Paul; explaining to him—after Paul had moved out—the biological facts about wet dreams; badgering him to tell me something *bad* about Paul's new wife when he came home from their wedding; watching him win a first-place ribbon in the high-school high jump; sharing his elation when The Shark had Rob's hockey game professionally designed, then sharing his disappointment when the marketers told us the rules were too intricate; patting myself on the back as he received his degree— I had graduated, too! with a diploma in single parenthood; our many, many animated conversations about Rene Levesque and separatism and bilingualism, and then his silence when I knew he must be sleeping with Lise; his crazy, costly visit home with Fiona to announce they were going to be married in the summer and have the wedding in England . . .

Ahh—weddings.

They are such artificial celebrations, yet they have an ineffable charm. Weddings bring unlikely people together, often from distant points. People renew old acquaintances, others meet for the first time, and usually the two extended families look as if they come from different planets. I have been to interminable Roman Catholic weddings and succinct United Church weddings and second-marriage weddings that took place in hotels and teen-age weddings that took place a short drive from the maternity ward (even in this age of easy access to contraceptives). For a while, it seemed as if every wedding I went to had a service written by the couple. I've heard *Bridge over Troubled Waters* played by organ, guitar and trumpet, as well as on tape in the original Simon and Garfunkel version.

As a manager and then as a consultant, I've catered or planned hundreds of weddings, and, while some of the same things always happen, each seems to have an energy all its own. It doesn't matter what the economic, social or ethnic circumstances are; it doesn't matter if the bride is seven months pregnant and wearing a skin-tight jersey dress or the groom is high on mescaline and wearing a T-shirt with a tuxedo drawn on the front, nothing upsets the inner energy. Grooms stumble over their vows, brides weep, soloists sing flat, best men drop rings, ministers lose their places, and everyone judges the performance of everyone else against some mystical—if not divine—standard that is not to be found in the Amy Vanderbilt or Emily Post etiquette books; it's floating in the air like radio waves.

I've had one wedding and I do not intend ever to have another. It is a once-in-a-lifetime experience, like birth, death and defloration. I might marry again someday, but I will not have another wedding. I had a storybook notion of weddings, seeing mine as the end of my youth, a wonderful whiz-bang climactic ending, and the beginning of my life as a mature adult. My wedding was perfect; we were a handsome couple, married by a handsome minister, and everything went well (though we could've done without the sexist joke that ended Doctor Bolton's toast—the implication that everything will be rosy if the groom is the breadwinner and the bride likes to be fondled). It was a 1950s wedding full of innocence and wonder and surprise in the couple's relationship. What is innocent or wonderful or surprising in a 1981 relationship? Young couples would have us believe that "It's best to know what you're getting into," to use that vulgar phrase. "You wouldn't buy a car without taking it for a test drive." I doubt the relevance of that analogy; I've seen too many jaded looks on the faces of contemporary brides and grooms, and divorce statistics are getting worse, not better.

Curiously, even with today's sophistication, intelligent people still make public promises that are impossible to keep.

In my 1950s wedding ceremony, I vowed to obey and serve Paul, and I did obey and serve him for a while, perhaps six months— probably longer in fact but not in spirit. I made his meals, darned his socks, washed his clothes. But, when Rob was born, I gave the son much of the attention that the father coveted. There were things I stopped telling Paul about—gifts of money from my father; weekly coffee klatches with a group Paul disliked; rebuffing his so-called friend, Steve, who insisted whenever we were alone that he and I were destined to have an affair. Still, I was content with the roles of wife and mother until my father put pressure on me to help him with the hotels and Paul developed a yearning to leave the business and become an academic. Through the next few years, as my heart frosted over and I contemplated separation, I never once recalled my wedding vows. Even though Mr. Westlake had done as much as anyone could to drum into us that this was a serious, sacred lifetime commitment, I never consciously thought, Good God, I have stopped living up to my vows.

Now that adultery, separation and divorce have become so commonplace, how can anyone in a congregation keep a solemn face when the bride and the groom promise to cherish each other, forsaking all others, until death? What prevents the congregation from laughing out loud?

5

I am bathed, dressed and growing anxious when Cyril Grey, husband of Fiona's Aunt Molly, phones me from the front desk. The Greys have been delegated to take me to the church.

In the hotel lobby, Cyril greets me with a red face, an embarrassed smile and a stiff handshake, as if there is something illicit about our meeting. Before we head outside, I talk him into leading the way and letting me take my rented car so that I will not have to rely on others later.

As Cyril pushes open the main door and holds it for me, I see someone familiar crossing the street, approaching the hotel. For a moment, I feel disoriented. It cannot be—but it is—The Shark! He sees me, smiles at the startled look on my face, glances at Cyril.

He says, "Hello, Catherine," as if we see each other all the time.

"Hugh! What are you doing here?"

We embrace on the pavement, oblivious of passers-by. He smells strongly of English leather cologne. Still holding each other's arms, we break apart to have a good look. He's wearing wire-framed bifocals, and his handsome face is more jowly—his chin has nearly disappeared between the jowls. His hair is as thick as ever, but greying. There is a tic in the crow's feet of his left eye.

"I couldn't miss this wedding," he says. "Rob's one of my favourite kids—you know that."

"Is Frances here?"

He hesitates. "No, Fran didn't come. Actually, I'm combining this with business. I drove up from London this morning and I'll have to hustle right back after the service."

"Hugh, you can't. You have to stay and be my escort—oh, forgive me. Hugh, this is Cyril Grey, the bride's uncle. Cyril, Hugh Godfrey, an old friend of mine."

"How do you do, Cyril," The Shark says, shaking Cyril's hand.

"Are you all right, then, Hugh?" Cyril pulls off his cap and his

159

face reddens again.

As I watch them, I recall seeing The Shark's photograph in *The Financial Post*. I remember thinking that he didn't look at all like a shark—but why was that picture in the paper—oh, that's right. Hugh Godfrey was recently made a vice-president of the insurance company where he's worked all his life.

"I believe congratulations are in order," I say.

"Why?"

"The vice-presidency?"

"Oh, that. It's been nearly a year now. Not many of us uneducated bums make it these days."

"Hugh, please stay for the reception. I have a lot of catching up to do on your family. You and I can sit together."

He grimaces. "Gosh, Cath, I'd love that . . . but . . . hey, I'm already ten minutes late to pick up Paul."

"Oh, that's why you're—right. Well, I won't hold you up."

"I'll see you at the church."

He enters the hotel and I follow Cyril to a car parked down the street.

"Seems like a nice enough bloke," Cyril says.

"Mmm," is all I say. Damn Paul, insulating himself with his flower-child wife and his old friend. Why didn't Frances come? I'm sure they can afford it.

"Are you all right, Catherine?" says Molly from the passenger window.

"I'm fine, thanks."

"You do look loovly," she says, giving my light blue dress and white cotton jacket a quick inspection. She is fifty-ish, with large teeth like Fiona's mother's. She's wearing a brimmed beige hat.

"Thank you," I say, feeling blatantly hatless. "You look very nice, too. I was telling your husband I'd like to take my own car, if that's all right. I'll follow you."

"Oo ah, you suit yourself, loov. I shall keep an eye on you, shan't I? So's our Cyril doesn't get too far ahead of you."

I fetch my rented yellow Cortina from the hotel parking lot and follow their blue Princess through the streets of downtown Arnold, which is bustling with Saturday afternoon shoppers. Cyril drives too slowly, giving me signals well in advance, while Molly makes a series of confusing gestures which I ultimately ignore. There's a light drizzle, barely enough to require the windshield wipers.

It's fortunate that I have someone to lead the way, because anger clouds my vision. I can tell myself that this situation is no-one's fault, that the circumstances of this event were bound to throw us together, that I have been in uncomfortable situations before, that I am my own woman, ready for anything. But I still feel furious.

We come to a street with red-brick row housing on the left and, on the right, a grassy hill with the ancient church squatting on its crest. I concentrate on the sleek torpedo-style back end of the Greys' car, feeling less confident about driving in this country the closer I get to the wedding.

"Int it a loovly old church," Molly says, after Cyril and I have parked our cars up the street.

"It is," I say.

"Aye, it is an' all," says Cyril.

We walk up the cement sidewalk toward the lush green grounds. Along the perimeter of the churchyard is a knee-high brick wall that is crumbling with age. Scattered about the yard are some ancient gravestones, their inscriptions obscured by weather and time. The church looks venerable but by no means imposing; even with its tall, square bell-tower, it has neither the community-dominating quality of the churches you see in French Canadian towns nor the outer signs (flags, kiosks, scaffolding) of a tourist attraction. This is one of the phenomena of England—the great age of buildings still in regular use.

Groups of people stand outside the main entrance, despite the drizzle—Molly says, "They do like to have their little chin-wag before they go in." I see the value of hats, to protect your coiffure from the incessant dampening. My hair is too short to be spoiled, though, and the rain is more mist than downpour.

Cyril chats with a man who resembles Molly—the same plump cheeks and large front teeth. The man looks at me and smiles. Many of the women seem to be looking at my hair—or rather the absence of a hat on my head. Molly introduces me to the man, her brother, and two younger women, but I don't catch their names.

" —Barber just had a nice trip on the Continent, didn't you, loov?" Molly is saying. "And, oo—she saw the Royal Wedding—could've reached out and tooched the carriage, couldn't you, me dook?"

"Oo, *could* you?" says one of the young women.

"What was Lady Di like, was she loovly?" asks the other.

"Yes, yes, she was as nice as her pictures," I say, "better, in fact. I was close—well, not that close—"

As I speak and watch the street, I recall Mrs. Bryson's question of the evening before: Will you be sitting with Rob's father in church? I said, Yes, of course I will.

"I think Charles was marvellous, too, don't you?" the first woman says.

"I wish the Queen would step down and let him be King," the second one says. "There's talk of that, you know."

A car comes up as close to the church as it can and stops. A man jumps out of the back seat and opens the front passenger door. He leans in, takes the hand of a woman whose bare leg slowly emerges, reaching its foot and flat-heeled shoe to the road. The man's movements tell me before I see his face that this is Paul. The woman, clad surprisingly in a prim, white-collared, middy-style blue maternity top and blue skirt, must be Susan. Her blond hair is styled in a pageboy with bangs cut straight across her forehead at the eyebrows. She is wearing a white hat set back; from this distance, she looks about fourteen years old.

Paul has her arm in his. He is attentive in the extreme. As they approach a patch of mud at the edge of the road, I expect him to whip off his suit jacket and spread it out in front of her. She is walking with gingerly steps, as if at any moment a chasm will open up and down will fall Susan, baby and all. Their progress is ridiculously slow.

"She's not been well," Molly says. "They say she's a loovly girl, though, really they do."

Paul's hair and beard are neatly trimmed, and his blue three-piece suit fits him perfectly. He looks more natty and healthy than I expected.

Impatient to have this encounter over with, I step out from the group to greet them. "Hello, Paul," I say, my hand extended. "Hello, Susan."

"Hi there!" she says.

"Catherine," he says. Since Susan is leaning on his right arm, he takes my hand in his left and squeezes. "It's good to see you. Sue, this is Catherine."

"Rob *does* look like you," says Susan. She shakes my hand. "Now I see why that kid's so handsome."

162

"Thank you." Disarming as her comments are, I cannot ignore her condition. "How are you feeling?"

"It's been a bitch of a pregnancy," she says, with the sunniest of expressions on her pretty, make-up-free face. "We tried and tried for so long, and I started to worry that something was wrong with me, because I knew how fast Paul knocked you up. But one of those little buggers finally caught, and then I had a miscarriage. And another miscarriage. The doctor told me I should stay in bed this time, and I've been good about that, but did I want to miss Rob's wedding? No way, José."

6

"Hello, I'm Molly Grey, the bride's aunt."

Molly steps up to Susan and gently touches her arm. *Thank you, Molly, your timing is perfect.* Paul releases Susan so that she can accept Molly's handshake.

"I ran into The Shark at the hotel," I say to Paul.

"Yes, he told us."

"I'm amazed that he came all this way. Too bad Fran couldn't make it."

"Uh—yes."

"Does Rob know?"

"That The Shark's here? No. The Shark wanted it to be a surprise. Did you know I work for him now?"

"No!" The professor, my former husband, Susan's hippy husband, in an insurance company?

"He needed someone to take over his food operation. I thought I was getting a little stale in the classroom, so I took it on, along with Personnel."

"You must be pleased," I say neutrally.

"*Pleased?*" Susan says, turning away from Molly. "You should see the *bread* he's pulling in now. Hey, hadn't we better get inside? Here comes the you-know-what."

The white Rolls Royce bearing the bride is coming up the street and from the opposite direction comes The Shark. Noticing the Rolls, The Shark breaks into a little trot that takes him into our midst. Some of the people are going into the church.

"You'll sit with us," I say, taking The Shark's arm.

"No—no—"

"Of course you will," Paul says.

"We should wait till the others are in," I say.

"Paul and I'll start in now," Susan says. "We're slower than cold molasses going up the Down escalator."

"See you inside," Paul says, taking Susan's arm.

Out of the Rolls step Fiona's mother and father and, with Mr. Bryson's assistance, Fiona, in a formal white gown, which her mother fusses over, adjusting the waist, tugging the hem, while her father tries to keep the train away from the car door and the mud on the road. Fiona seems to be labouring a little; she is not smiling and, despite her make-up, her face seems drained of colour. I try to ignore this as The Shark and I inch our way toward the heavy oak doors behind the crowd.

"Tell me about your family," I say to him.

"Oh, Lord. Let's see. Rick's got an NHL scout after him. Barb could be the next Nadia Comaneci. Sam won a trivia contest on CBC and he's down in Nashville right now soaking up the country music atmosphere. Kim—poor Kimmy can't do much else but put on weight, and Kate—well, she's seven years old and she's already giving us trouble the others never did."

"I can't believe Kate is seven. It seems like yesterday I changed her diapers the time Fran came to stay with me—I think it was just before I moved to Montreal. How is Frances? A pity that she couldn't come with you."

"Fran hasn't been a hundred percent lately. She's worried that she might have to have another operation."

"Oh no. I must write to her."

"I wish you would, Cath."

We are inside the ancient church. It feels dank.

"This is the first time you and Susan have met, isn't it?"

"Yes."

"What do you think of her?"

"I don't know—more wholesome than I imagined, perhaps. She doesn't look—what is she, thirty?"

"Twenty-nine, I think."

Patrick, one of the grey-clad ushers, politely tells us to wait a moment while Willie, the other usher, escorts the last of the non-family guests to a pew. The maid-of-honour, dressed in pale mauve, comes into the vestibule looking red-faced and ungainly. I think her name is Deborah. With her are the two bridesmaids—or flower girls—two youngsters about twelve years old. One is Fiona's sister, Nora; I don't know the other. Mrs. Bryson comes in, sees me and waves, her eyes wide, her nose twitching like a squirrel's. Paul and Susan have almost reached the front pew. As I walk down the aisle beside Patrick, my hand in the crook of his arm, I say to him, "This is a wonderful old church, isn't it?" and I notice there are not many people on the groom's side. I feel the congregation turning to look, to have a good look at the hatless Canadian divorcee.

In the front pew, with The Shark between me and Paul, I kneel and silently say a prayer: Lord, please look after Rob and Fiona and see them through the bad times. There *will* be bad times. Please give them the strength to cope—that's the important thing. I sit back in the pew and look up at the carved wood, the stained glass, the vaulted ceiling. I wonder if the cross-beam above the altar is the original one.

A young blond man appears at the front of the church holding a video camera to his eye. A length of black cord connects the camera to a power-pack strapped to his waist. He points the camera up the aisle. I regard this electronic recording of everything as tacky, but Rob and Fiona insisted on it.

A door opens to our right and out comes the minister, with Rob and Arthur. The cameraman swings around to catch their entrance. Rob looks wonderful. Arthur's lopsided grin tells me that he has already had one drink too many.

The organ begins to play *Here Comes the Bride*. All of us turn. Deborah comes slowly up the aisle, not with the hesitation step of our day but with a regular walk. Even so, she seems to be having trouble staying on her feet—she is noticeably wobbling. Fiona and her parents follow, one on either side of her, and behind them are the two girls carrying the train. Patrick and Willie have stepped into a pew at the back. I glance at Rob and see that he has noticed The Shark and he telegraphs this to me with a wink.

Fiona has reached our pew. She isn't as beautiful as Lise, but she has wide blue eyes and a perfect *retroussé* nose. She has a look of complete trustworthiness about her, but at this moment she seems less than confident, even worried. Has she been sick? Or is this a severe case of the jitters? Surely she isn't having misgivings.

As Fiona reaches Rob's side, Rob looks at her with a smile that fades into a frown of concern. The minister, a short, balding man with a ruddy complexion and black-framed granny glasses, whispers a greeting to Fiona and directs the Brysons to a spot behind her and Rob. The organ is silent. Someone coughs and a baby giggles. The minister clears his throat.

"Dearly beloved," he begins, in an accent that suggests his university background ("be-lavvid", not the Midland "be-loovid"), "we are gathered here in the sight of God and in the face of this congregation, to join this man and this woman in Holy Matrimony."

These are the same words that Reverend Westlake used in my wedding, twenty-three years ago. I note in the wedding booklet that there is now a choice of vows for the woman: she can still "obey him, and serve him, love, honour and keep him", or she can "love him, comfort him, honour and keep him". Rob and Fiona have chosen the second.

Fiona speaks her promise in a barely audible voice.

In a louder voice, Susan says to Paul, "Can you hear her?"

When they exchange rings, I recall the fight that Paul and I had over whether ours should be a double-ring ceremony. I said I thought it might be nice; he said he had never worn a ring and he preferred tradition. I agreed that the double-ring idea was likely just a fad promoted by jewellers and a gold band wouldn't look good on his finger. (Over the years, I have seen how easily men slip off their rings when they want to appear single.)

We sing a psalm and the minister blesses Rob and Fiona. The bridal party, followed closely by the video cameraman, moves into the vestry to sign the register. We stand and sing two hymns (I can hear Paul's tenor voice, right on key, and The Shark's suppressed monotone), and we sit, waiting for the newlyweds to appear.

"I was worried that Fiona wasn't going to make it through the service," I whisper to The Shark. "She looks so pasty white—I feel sorry for her."

"Stage fright, maybe."

"I hope that's all."

"Does this bring back any memories?"

"It certainly does. I have this vivid recollection of changing the groom's diapers."

"I mean—"

"I *know* what you mean."

He says something to Paul and Susan but I don't hear what it is. He says something else to me but it's lost in the commotion of Rob and Fiona and the others coming out, led by the cameraman, who walks backward down the aisle, keeping his lens focused on the newlyweds. They are going to have a permanent record of Fiona's peaked face.

The organ music grows louder and the church bells ring. We rise to our feet and The Shark reaches out to shake Rob's hand. As soon as the bridal group starts down the aisle, Mrs. Bryson comes to me, tears spoiling her make-up.

"Fiona's been poorly all day, poor thing," she says. "Couldn't keep her breakfast down." She blows her nose in a tattered Kleenex.

I am about to say "I thought she—" but I change it to "She bore up well. She looks lovely."

Mr. Bryson and the Middletons come up behind Mrs. Bryson, masking concern for Fiona with winks and smiles. The five of us move down the aisle behind the attendants, who are doing their best with the train. I notice Sidney, a young man who knew Rob at school and turned up unexpectedly yesterday on his way to Israel, and I feel a little sad that more of Rob's friends couldn't be here.

On the way out, we pass a room in which several young men yank the ropes that ring the bells. The sound is old-world and wonderful. I will be able to tell people that my son and daughter-in-law were married in an eight hundred-year-old church where they rang the original bells for them. (It would spoil the story if they weren't the original bells, so I won't ask if they are.)

Outside, the drizzle holds off while Deborah's brother, Clive, assembles people for still photographs. Rob and Fiona excuse themselves for a moment to speak with The Shark.

"Rob looks terrific," Paul says to me. Susan is talking to Mrs. Bryson. "He's turned out well, Cath. You deserve all the credit."

"Thank you, but I think a lot of it is his own doing."

"Look at him. *Married.* I suddenly feel old."

"Amazing that The Shark came. Did you have a hand in that?"

"No." He doesn't elaborate.

"Rob, sorry, you've got to come for photos," Arthur says, stepping between the groom and The Shark. "We have to hustle. The next wedding's due in a few minutes." He looks over at Paul and me. "Parents' shots next, so don't go away."

"Okay, okay," Rob says. He shakes The Shark's hand. "Got to go. You're sure you can't stay for the reception?"

"I have to drive back to London this afternoon. God bless you both. Come and visit us in Toronto."

"We shall," Fiona says, managing a sweet smile. She kisses The

Shark on his left jowl.

Arthur whisks his charges over to a line-up comprised of the Bryson clan. The video cameraman follows Arthur so closely that he must be recording little more than the back of Arthur's head.

"Do you have time for a drink?" I ask The Shark, who is lighting up a cigarette. "A coffee for the road? I want to hear more about your children."

"I exaggerated about Barb," he says. "She *could've* been the next Nadia Comaneci if she hadn't quit everything and moved in with a painter—the kind that paints houses. Rick *is* going to make it in hockey, but Sam's obsession with trivia made him flunk Grade Ten. Frannie and I used to worry until we discovered good scotch."

"Paul, does he really have to leave so soon?"

Paul looks at The Shark; some communication I don't understand passes between them.

"He does," Paul says.

"That's ridiculous," I say. "He has time for a drink. Let's the four of us—"

"The pubs are closed," Paul says.

"What's the big hairy problem here?" Susan wants to know.

"I thought . . . the four of us could go up to my room for a drink," I say, amazed at myself, "but Hugh says he can't—"

"Oh, for Christ's sake, Shark," Susan says, "bring Deirdre with you. We're all grown-ups here."

The two men look ill at case. I am stunned.

"I *knew* I should've planned this differently," The Shark says. "All right, all right, I'll see all of you in Catherine's room. I've got to go."

He dashes off. It's an unusual sight: a middle-aged Canadian insurance company vice-president running around and between groups of wedding guests as he crosses a damp English lawn in a light blue suit and black oxfords, trailing smoke like a tramp steamer. For a moment, the guests and the onlookers take their eyes off the bride and groom to watch The Shark jog down the wet road.

I recover from the shock enough to say, "She must be really something to make him run like that."

"She's an old friend of Susan's," Paul says. "A real hard-luck case until The Shark took her on as sort of a protégé. Last month, she was our top salesperson." He snickers as if making light of a difficult situation will ease us through it. That was always his first impulse.

I do not smile. "I suppose Frances has no idea," I say.

"Everybody *but* Fran knows," Susan says. "I think she just doesn't want to know. Hey, Catherine, you don't have to entertain us, you know. I mean, all of a sudden you've got yourself a party."

"It's all right."

"It's time to do the parents," Arthur calls over to us. "Sorry, but we've got to rush."

The bride for the next wedding is arriving. I didn't notice the wave of new guests moving onto the grounds. Coming up beside Rob and Fiona's white Rolls Royce is a horse-drawn carriage. An overweight young bride and her father step down from the carriage and start up the sidewalk.

Once our photographs are taken (including one with Susan on the end of the row), all the Hodges-Bryson guests move out onto the street—the verger has made it clear that confetti can only be thrown when we are off the church grounds. As I throw my confetti with a zest intensified by my bitter disappointment with The Shark, I hear Susan say to Paul:

"Do you realize you'll be nearly seventy when *our* kid ties the knot?"

7

Deirdre is tall, perhaps an inch or two taller than I, and she is gorgeous. Her straight blond hair (dyed) is parted on the right side so that the locks on the left fall across her eye, except when she tucks them behind her ear, as she does now. Her brown eyes, framed in expertly applied mascara, look directly at me. Her lips are full, painted in a scarlet shade that matches her blouse and skirt. Her eyebrows have been darkened and shaped. Just above her upper lip is a tiny mole—a perfectly situated beauty mark. She stands straight, but she is much too thin. Her hips are contoured, but her arms and legs lack curves; she may well be anorexic. Yet my attention can't stay long on her limbs; her face is too striking, and she knows how to hold her head to achieve the maximum effect with her hair.

We're in my hotel room. Deirdre lowers her red handbag to the floor by its shoulder-strap as she sits on the end of the bed. Susan has sat on a straight-back chair; The Shark and Paul sit on either side of Deirdre, moths drawn to the bright light. I pour gin for everyone except The Shark, who wants coffee. Everyone looks uncomfortable; this gathering reminds me of those pathetic groupings that materialize in hotel rooms at conventions after the bars and the hospitality suites have closed for the night.

"Mind if I smoke?" Deirdre says, tossing her head with all the grandeur of a champion racehorse.

"No, no, of course not," I say.

From her handbag she takes a package of Benson & Hedges cigarettes. Her scarlet fingernails are long and perfectly manicured. "Anyone else?"

"I will," says The Shark.

He takes a cigarette from her package. The rest of us watch her hold up an ornate lighter, start it, light his cigarette and then her own.

"Well," says The Shark. "Here we are."

171

"Yes," says Paul.

"Talkative bunch," says Susan.

I busy myself with the kettle for The Shark's coffee. "How is Allan?" I ask.

"God, didn't you know?" says Paul.

"He died," says The Shark. "It was pretty awful, I guess. He drowned in somebody's pool in Regina."

"Oh, no!"

"I hadn't seen him or heard from him in years," says The Shark. "A mutual friend in our Regina office sent me the obituary."

"Who is Allan?" Deirdre asks.

"You had to ask!" Susan says. "When these two guys get going on Allan—"

"Paul and I went to school with him," says The Shark.

Silence. We all listen to the kettle. I fetch an ashtray for Deirdre and The Shark. Paul sips his gin. Susan puts her untasted drink on a table.

"Isn't it funny, the way nobody can think of anything to say?" Deirdre says, shaking her hair loose from her ear. She lifts her chin and strokes the front of her long neck. "On the way up here, Jaws couldn't talk about anything else but seeing you people."

Jaws? Of course—The Shark updated.

"Listen to this gal, will you?" says The Shark. "She slays me."

"Gal?" says Deirdre.

"Cath," says The Shark, "before you go to a lot of trouble with the coffee—I've got some Johnny Walker in the car. Mind if I go and get it?"

"I'm sorry all I have is gin—that's all I drink in the summer."

"You know, people, I feel the shits," says Susan. "If I'm going to this reception, I'd better go to our room and lie down."

"Lie down here," I say.

"No, it's okay. The Shark'll give me an arm—"

"Don't be silly, Sue," Paul says, jumping to his feet. "I'll take you to the room."

"Don't you want to stay and reminisce?" Susan asks. To me, she says, "This guy can reminisce your ass off."

"I'll be back," Paul says.

"Look," I say, rather hopelessly, "no one has to—"

"I'll be right back," says The Shark.

"See you later, Catherine," says Susan, grimacing as she stands.

The three of them go and I am left alone with Deirdre. We sip our gin.

"Mind if I brush my hair?" she says.

"Not at all." This day is rapidly becoming the worst of my whole life.

Deirdre goes to the dresser mirror carrying a brush from her handbag. She bends forward from the hips and brushes her hanging hair straight down. After twenty or thirty vigorous strokes, she swiftly resumes an upright stance, tossing her hair back into place. She leans in close to the mirror, checking her lips and eyes.

"My contacts are hurting me," she says. "We didn't sleep much last night and I left them in."

I am not sure how to respond. I utter a little grunt that is meant to sound sympathetic but not too sympathetic.

"These transatlantic hops are killers on contact-wearers," she says. "I meant to take them out when we . . ." She smiles at me in the mirror. "Know what Jaws does when he comes?"

I wish with all my heart that she would tell me something else, perhaps something about insurance—double indemnity, anything—

"I have no idea," I say.

"He laughs. Oh, not a big, booming belly-laugh. This little giggle. At first, I thought he was being derisive. Like I didn't measure up or something. But he tells me it's kind of a nervous reflex. It does put me off the rails a little, though, do you know what I mean?"

"Deirdre, I don't think I want to discuss this."

She turns to face me, pushing the hair off her forehead.

"Is there something about me that bothers you, Catherine?"

"Well . . . I wondered . . ."

"What?"

"Do you work for Hugh?"

"Not directly. John Forrest is my immediate supervisor. Hey, I didn't get where I am on my back, if that's what you're thinking. I'm a damn good salesperson and I work hard. Jaws and I don't even see each other in Toronto. And we're not in love or anything. I like *making* love, and so does he, but we meet only when it's convenient—out of town."

"No matter how broad-minded I try to be, it still bothers me when I find out that a good friend of mine is cheating on his wife, who is also a good friend of mine."

"He says our relationship is good for his marriage."

"What utter garbage!"

"Listen, there's something I should tell you before they come back. Jaws says he thinks Paul still loves you."

"The Hugh Godfrey I used to know would never speak such drivel."

"He wouldn't put me on."

"What earthly good does it do to tell me this?"

There's a knock at the door. For a moment, I'm immobile, and it's Deirdre who goes to answer it. The Shark comes in with his scotch and a shot glass.

"May I pour you one, Cath?" he asks.

"No, thank you."

"Deirdre, I know you don't want any." He tosses back a shot and wipes his mouth with the back of his hand as if he is John Wayne. "Ahh."

"Looks like I'll be driving back to London," Deirdre says.

I am irritated by the signs of intimacy in her words and her glances, the suggestion that she knows him better than his old friends do. There's another knock on the door, and this time I go. "Hi," says Paul, as he comes in.

"How is Susan?" I ask.

"Okay now. She threw up."

"Paul!" says Deirdre. "Poor thing. Should I go to her?"

"No, no, she'll be okay. She said she'd like to be left alone so she can get a little rest."

"Fiona's been sick, too," I say. "Did you notice how white she was?"

"She did look kind of strained," says Paul.

"If she's anything like Susan, she'll be okay," says The Shark. "Susan's a hell of a trooper. She'll be dancing up a storm at the reception. Want a shot of this, Paul?"

The two of them share the same shot glass. I'm too angry to offer one of the hotel glasses. Their drinking of straight whisky and Deirdre's pretty posing—her constant playing with her hair—drive me to the breaking point.

"Paul, why did you bring Susan?" I snap. I immediately sense that they misunderstand me. They all think I'm jealous. "You're endangering her life and the baby's. You should never have let her leave Toronto in her condition."

"Wait, Cath," Paul says. "Surely you of all people don't mean I should've forced her to stay home. She likes Rob. She very much wanted to come to his wedding. All right, so she hates to admit there's anything she can't do."

"You *insisted* that she come," I cry. "You wanted to flaunt her pregnancy."

"Oh boy," says Deirdre.

"Cath, Cath," says The Shark, playing the role of mediator. "You're being a little unfair. Please, we all came here as old friends—"

"He'd do that sort of thing," I persist. "He'd want to bring her here to show me what a *man* he is. It wouldn't occur to him to try to talk her into staying home."

"She wanted to come here!" Paul barks. "I knew Rob'd be glad to see her and I thought, with my help, she could come."

"A sensitive, understanding man would've put the health of two people ahead of his ego—"

"Wouldn't that have been sensitive and understanding! To insist she stay home!"

"Next you're going to tell me the vomiting has nothing to do with the baby—it's something Susan ate."

"Oh!" Deirdre exclaims.

"Listen, listen, you two," says The Shark.

I turn on him, a flash of fury visible in my eyes. I am about to tell him to take his whore and his bastard friend out of my room, but I stop. He has a gentle yet firm grip on one of my hands.

"We're forgetting Rob in all this," he says. "None of us is perfect, but we did come a long way for Rob. Let's not spoil his day."

"He won't know," I mutter.

"Shark, Cath's right in a way," Paul says. "I should be with Susan right now instead of knocking back the booze. You and Deirdre have a safe trip back."

He shakes The Shark's hand and leaves.

There is a long silence. I feel like a fool. "I over-reacted," I say, eyes cast down. "I'm sorry. I promised myself I wouldn't."

"I'm just as much to blame," The Shark says. He glances over at Deirdre, who is turned to the mirror and is applying fresh lipstick. "We'd better be going—those M roads can be crazy."

I suddenly want to talk with him, ask him about his marriage, fish for some information about Paul and the way Paul feels about Susan and his job...and me...

"It was good to see you, Hugh," I say.

On her way out, Deirdre stops in front of me. "I guess I didn't help the situation much," she says, "but I'm glad I met you." She kisses my cheek. I resist my impulse to pull away.

As they head down the hall, I hear The Shark give a little giggle and it instantly brings to mind the image of the two of them fornicating: Deirdre astride the supine Shark, her lean torso bouncing, her thigh muscles straining, her blond hair flying, until his signal— that laugh—tells her to cease, and she collapses onto his chest, her smoker's lungs gasping for air.

I go into the bathroom and, suddenly weary, I lean on the sink and look into the mirror to see if I recognize this person.

There is a smudge of Deirdre's scarlet lipstick on my cheek.

8

e i g h t

A waiter hands me a glass of sherry as I enter the banquet hall. A waitress checks a hand-drawn diagram and shows me that I've been assigned to the head table. I note that Mr. Bryson will be on one side of me and Patrick on the other. I will not have to converse with either Susan or Paul at dinner.

"Time for the receiving line," Arthur tells me.

He escorts me over to where Paul is standing. Susan has been deposited in a chair some distance away.

"I'm sorry about my outburst," I say to Paul.

"Don't be silly. I think you may be right. She shouldn't be here."

"Let's try to make the best of this."

"Yes, let's."

As the guests file past us, Paul gradually perfects an introduction for me: "Have you met the groom's mother? Catherine Barber." I don't have to do much introducing; most of the guests know Mr. Bryson, who is standing beside me.

"That lad of yours is just what the doctor ordered for our Fiony," he says to me, quietly, so that the bride doesn't hear him. "Aye, he is an' all."

"Your daughter is so pretty."

He and I continue to exchange compliments at the head table, where we sit facing the sixty or so guests and enjoy a hearty roast lamb dinner.

"Fiona is the perfect bride," I say. "Demure and wholesome."

"She was a shy little thing," Bryson says, "and 'e di'n't 'alf change that. Have you seen the snap 'e took of 'er on the Riviera with nowt on 'er top?"

We converse on this level for most of the meal. Patrick speaks to me only once, and that is to ask me to pass the mint sauce. Bryson seems to want to discuss our offsprings' sex lives, but he's approaching

177

the subject from a distance and I am content to leave him out there. I eventually learn that he is going to give the Toast to the Bride; I don't recall having ever heard of a father toasting his daughter, but Bryson says it's common in England. By the time it's his turn to speak, he has drunk great quantities of wine and I wonder if he's going to be able to stand up.

He not only stands, he gives a magnificent speech, bringing tears to everyone's eyes with touching anecdotes about Fiona's childhood. It occurs to me that this man feels exactly the same mixture of joy and heartache that I do.

All of us stand to drink the toast.

Rob answers, speaking too informally. He hesitates often, doubles back, pauses for long periods, clears his throat; he stops in mid-thought so often that I ache to finish his sentences for him. At a point where he seems hopelessly lost, Arthur interrupts him to present him with a manila envelope. From it Rob pulls a framed photograph. When he looks at it, he blushes and lets out a booming laugh. Arthur passes the photo around and, when it reaches me, I see that it shows Rob naked in a locker room, holding a sock at just the right level to hide his genitals. I show the photo to Mr. Bryson; we laugh and pass it on.

Rob can't stop guffawing. He obviously didn't expect anything like the photo. He tries to be serious: "I really want . . . oh golly—to thank—a ha ha—to thank my—um—parents—uh huh—ha!—Mom and Dad—for—for oh haw huh huh—for . . . I mean—you know— coming all this way—um uh—to be with us."

He stifles another chortle with a swig of water. The laughter spreads to the guests. They seem to be laughing with him, thank goodness, not at him.

Arthur takes over, glancing at crumpled notes as he tells us how Rob met Fiona. He says they have done so much hitchhiking, their thumbs are permanently bent. Rob holds up a bent thumb (his double-jointed one) to prove it. Arthur tells a few jokes, including one about Rob's "equipment" that makes both Rob and Fiona blush. Everyone laughs and applauds loudly. Arthur reads some telegrams: my mother and her new husband, Senator Dudley Foss, have sent a long one about "health and happiness and hands across the sea"; there's one from Paul's brother, Greg ("May God give you all the riches of a good life"); one from my brother, Gord, and his wife, Jill ("We hope you get busy and hatch a nest of Monty Pythons"); and one from my brother, Wally, and Dodie, the secretary he left a wife and four kids for ("Best to be loved and never tied down, but better to be wed than dead").

"You'll save us a dance, now, won't ye, Mrs. Hodges?" Bryson says to me when the formal part of the evening is over.

"Of course."

I go over to Rob to kid him about his speech. We both laugh. The guests mill around while the waitresses clear everything away and the music man sets up for dancing.

"Wasn't that picture of Rob a gas?" Susan says from behind me. I turn to find her right there with Paul. "Hey. it's lucky I got out of your room when I did. Did Paul tell you? I upchucked on the rug."

"Yes—"

"I feel okay now, but I don't think I should dance, do you?"

"I wouldn't advise it."

"Promise me you'll dance with Paul—he tells me you two used to do a hot jive. Me, I've got two left feet when it comes to that old stuff."

Standing near the bar, alone, I watch the banquet hall employees move furniture to the sides of the room, opening up the centre for dancing. Paul has taken Susan back to the hotel, but she said he would definitely be back. She didn't say goodbye ("Catch you tomorrow, eh?") because the plan is that we will meet Rob and Fiona for brunch before they leave on their honeymoon. It seems strange that we're going to see the newlyweds tomorrow; I remember more innocent times when the day after was cloaked in secrecy. The bride and groom would have vanished. The honeymoon was some sort of cocoon in which the caterpillar couple could hide, and they'd burst out two weeks later as mature social (not to say sexual) butterflies. That little nicety has disappeared, along with the mystery and the surprise.

Molly comes over to chat with me ("What did you think of Paul's little wife, then? Seems more than six months along, if you ask me"), and soon the music man, a portly young chap in a swelling red T-shirt and baggy jeans, plays the first tune, loudly. Bryson comes looking for me. We wait for something less contemporary; before the next dance, the music man announces that Rob and Fiona will start it. At the music man's call of "Mablethorpe!" Rob and Fiona will break and select new partners, and this will continue until everyone is dancing.

"They are a pair, they are," Bryson says.

For this moment, Rob and Fiona are symbols of all newlyweds, gazing into each other's eyes, smiling (Fiona seems in much better spirits), functioning together in harmony, under the scrutiny of a roomful of witnesses. They are, publicly, a team. This, it seems to me, is more representative of the wedding of two human souls than the stiff, sombre reciting of vows.

"Mablethorpe!" says the music man.

Rob releases the bride. He spots me and walks directly over. Fiona selects her father.

"Having fun, Mom?"

"Yes, I am. I'm glad you and Fiona and the Brysons decided on music and dancing. I wish my wedding had been more like this."

"Why wasn't it?"

"My mother convinced me that dancing at a wedding was somehow unsophisticated. But not until we'd had a few heated arguments about it."

"Mom—uh—listen. Fiona's acting kind of weird."

"Oh? I think she looks much improved—"

"She's pretty good at keeping that smile on her face. Oh, I think she feels better, but she's grumbling a lot."

"It'll pass. The day is a strain when you're on show the whole time. Just make sure you keep your cool."

"Mablethorpe!"

I leave Rob and pick Cyril Grey. He has no feeling for rhythm and his heavy brogues come down on my feet three or four times before "Mablethorpe" allows me to escape into the arms of Arthur. I have danced with Arthur before and I know he can be light on his feet. Tonight, he isn't.

"Sorry, Mrs. Hodges."

"Don't be silly. Arthur, you've done a good job."

"It's real nice of you to say so."

"I mean it."

He lurches too far to his left and says he's sorry again. I am able to keep my own balance and half-support him as well.

"Mrs. Hodges?"

"Yes?"

"How did you ever stay so great-looking?"

"Arthur! What a lovely thing to say!"

"I can't figure out why the hell Mr. Hodges would ever leave someone like you."

"Mablethorpe!"

"We don't have to switch partners, do we?"

"Those are the rules."

"I could dance with you all night."

"Flattery becomes you, Arthur."

"Keep dancing with me, okay?"

"We'll dance again later."

From Arthur I go to Fiona's father.

"It's a bit of all right, i'n't it?"

"It's delightful."

"You're a jolly good dancer, Mrs. . . . ."

"Call me Catherine."

"If you'll call me Ernest."

"I will."

"Catherine's a loovly name."

"Ernest, my waist is up here."

When the music ends, and I have danced with three more men (Patrick and two unknowns), I head for the sidelines. Before I can sit, a fox trot begins and Ernest comes over to claim the dance that I have supposedly been saving. This time, he keeps his hand at mid-back and is the quintessential gentleman. The fox trot ends and he offers to buy me a drink.

"I'll have a pint of lager, please."

"A pint? Are you sure? Ladies usually prefer a half-pint, in a stemmed glass."

"Ernest, I think you're guilty of a little male chauvinism here."

"*Chau*-vinism? I'll give ye chauvinism." He sets off for the bar chuckling to himself.

But he does bring me a pint, and one for himself. We chat and sip our beer and we dance again. I notice Paul reappear. Deborah comes over to claim Ernest for a quickstep and I take the opportunity to go and see Paul.

"How is Susan?" I ask.

"She'll be fine."

"And the baby?"

"Kicking."

The music man's next selection is slow and I ask Paul to dance. He's apprehensive at first, but we gradually move into the old reliable, all-purpose "Arthur Murray's Magic Step". He seems tense and rather careful about moving in too close.

"Well," he says. "This is a milestone, isn't it?"

"What, our dancing together?"

"Rob's wedding. It's the end of a generation, the end of—"

"Our responsibility? I suppose so."

"You and I may never see each other again."

"Do we want to?"

"It might be a good idea to keep in touch."

"I'm sure we will. Once the first grandchild is born . . ."

We both turn silent on that thought. I want to talk with him, but it seems difficult. At the end of the dance, Mrs. Bryson steps in to take Paul for the next.

"Miz Hodges?"

Arthur is at my side, taking my hand. We dance and he holds me close. Under his breath, he sings along with Engelbert Humperdinck—*The Last Waltz*—into my ear. His chin is warm and moist against my cheek. I can smell his deodorant. None of this is unpleasant; in my current state of mind, being held close by a physically fit young man is not unpleasant at all. Halfway through the song, I feel something hard and insistent against my abdomen. I try to move my pelvis back and away from it, but it follows.

"Miz Hodges," Arthur murmurs into my ear, "have you ever considered having a relationship with a younger man?"

Into my head comes a flash of Barry Lambert—so appealing out on the street surrounded by patriotic Londoners, so pathetic in his cluttered flat—and I shake with suppressed laughter.

"Miz Hodges, I'm serious."

"Arthur, you're an excellent best man and a fine dancer."

"You do like me, then."

"Of course. I've always liked you."

"Then—"

"Arthur, let's just enjoy the music."

When Engelbert's song ends, I look around for Paul.

"Excuse me for a minute," I say to Arthur.

"Miz Hodges . . ."

I leave him and head toward the washrooms. I see Paul engaged in conversation with Willie and Willie's girlfriend.

"Excuse me, Paul," I say. "Could I speak with you a moment?"

"Sure. Have fun, kids." He nods to the young couple and we walk two or three steps away from them.

"Paul, would you consider going out to a pub?"

"You and me?"

"It's one way to get away from Arthur."

"*Arthur?*"

"He's had a little too much to drink, I'm afraid. Besides, there are a few things I'd like to talk over with you."

"Sounds ominous."

"Don't *you* want to talk?"

Before he can answer, Fiona's parents approach us.

Alice Bryson says, "I was telling Ernest, wasn't I, Ernest, that your Rob combines the best features of both of you."

"Aye, he does, an' all," Ernest says.

We are joined by Rob and Fiona, who both look too warm. Most of the young men have taken off their suit jackets, but Rob has not. Fiona apparently intends to stay in her gown the whole evening— brides never change into going-away outfits anymore. Rob boisterously dances me out onto the floor to a rock and roll beat.

"Would you and your friends object if your dad and I went off to the pub?" I ask him.

"Together?"

"Believe it or not."

"Well, you are consenting adults, aren't you? Promise me you won't rehash all the old arguments."

"I promise. Rob, we're thinking of leaving soon."

"Before the end of the reception?"

"Yes, in the next few minutes. There are a few things I want to discuss with your father before we both cave in. We'll be seeing you tomorrow."

"Right."

"Is Fiona feeling better?"

"I think so. But do say goodnight to her before you go, won't you?"

"Certainly."

"And Mom. Be nice to Dad."

9

_n__i__n__e_

Outside, Paul and I come upon Willie and Patrick decorating the newlyweds' getaway car. They have filled the interior with crumpled newspapers and tied the doors shut with rope that is wound round and round the chassis. They have written messages ("Doomed", "This Vehicle Does Not Stop", "Just Married: Do Disturb") on the windows and the trunk with shaving cream and they have tied streamers to handles and bumpers and hood ornament and aerial, but the cream and the streamers are turning messy in the drizzle. They have tied cans and shoes to the rear axle.

Paul and I have come upon this scene in a shadowy lane we chose as a short cut to my car. Willie and Patrick are debating whether to take off the front wheels. They tell us they have pilfered the key to Rob and Fiona's house and hidden all the lightbulbs and bedclothes. They scattered confetti through every room and hid a kipper in a warm place. They even scrambled the house number. My impulse is to tell them how nasty they are, but I refrain. Rob and Fiona will be inconvenienced, but what will it matter to two former vagabonds who have already slept together in foreign fields, alcoves and culverts?

In my rented car, I check the map for the quickest route to Woodthorpe. Rob has recommended a pub there called The World's End. We start on our way.

"Do you want to look in on Susan?" I ask Paul.

"She said she'd phone the banquet hall if she needed anything. She told me not to worry—we won't be late, will we?"

"No."

"I see you have no trouble driving in this country."

It seems strange to have him on the same side of me as he used to be in the old days when *he* did the driving.

"I had problems at first," I say. "Then I got used to it."

"I tried it and I was terrified. It was like learning to drive all over again. Did Rob tell you?"

184

"He said he'd gone out with you in Fiona's car."

"He didn't tell you I was a basket case by the end?"

"He didn't use those words, no."

"I'll bet the two of you had a good laugh about it."

"You'll be all right next time. Just rent an automatic transmission like this one. It's much easier."

A silence falls over us. It's dark now and I try to remember where to turn.

"Why do you want to drive, anyway?" I ask. "You can reach most places by bus or train."

"Susan and I want to drive through Wales—if she's up to it, I mean. We've heard so much about the Welsh countryside. And we want to go at our own pace."

"The roads are narrow. It's beautiful, but take a bus so that you can enjoy the scenery."

"We might."

More silence. We both know I'm on the verge of saying that Susan should not be going anywhere. And I don't think Paul likes the idea that I can drive these English roads and he can't. He can probably feel the old tension mounting the way I can, the anxiety that always develops between us. I wonder why on earth I am driving down an English country lane in the dark of night with the man I divorced over ten years ago.

I think of the Welsh property I may invest in: The Hovey Arms, a place I loved at first sight when I was in Britain last year. It's a solid, comfortable place half a mile from the village of Maentwrog, in the Vale of Ffestiniog. Spacious rooms with a view of rolling green hills dotted with sheep. A cozy pub. A proper English dining room. Another large room for relaxing in front of the TV and sipping your coffee and liqueur. It's the kind of place that I'd love to run after I've had my fill of freelance consulting, a place where I can mingle with the folks who come down every night from Blaenau. And it's so close to the sea (the sea, the sea!) and Caernarvon Castle to the west, and the pretty town of Betws-y-Coed to the north-east.

The World's End is busy, but at least the sounds emanating from it are human voices talking and laughing. (In Canada these days, there are few taverns or bars where you can carry on a conversation. Rock groups bombard you with their amplified sound; so-called exotic dancers, both male and female, grind through lugubrious performances; on special nights, you can be distracted by wet-T-shirt contests, mud-wrestling, and perhaps an amateur strip-tease.) The crowded parking lot is lighted by a string of red, green and yellow light bulbs. Both of us are silent as I find a place to park. It isn't until I've turned off the engine that Paul speaks.

"Cath, do we really want to go in there?"

"I think we do. We have things to talk about. Didn't Rob's wedding make you feel a little nostalgic?"

"You know it did, but—"

"Come on. I'm sure we both have things we want to ask each other."

We step out of the car and lock our respective doors. We walk across the parking lot side by side and I recall Paul's bad habit, when we were married, of walking a step ahead of me. He holds the door for me as we enter. We decide against one room—I think they call it the "snug"—which is smoky and far too crowded. All the seats in the second room—the "lounge"—are taken, but there is room to stand. We stop at the bar to order pints of bitter and two patrons step aside to allow us access. The barmaid handles the pump with studious attention, as if each pint is a work of art—almost brimming and topped with froth.

"Cheerio," I say, clinking my mug against his.

"Cheerio."

"Ahh, that's good. Canadians think it's served too warm, but I love it. If I lived here, I know I'd drink too much of it and—say, that's a problem you've never had, have you? You can eat or drink anything and never put on weight."

"Oh, come on, I'll bet you could still fit into your wedding dress."

"I loved that dress, despite all the arguments I had with Mother about it. Do you remember all the trouble she gave me?"

"She was a dominant force, all right. Didn't Reverend Westlake have to put her in her place a couple of times? There was a fine fellow. What ever became of him?"

"He's had a parish out in Victoria for years. I should look him up the next time I'm out there."

"I think he had high hopes for us as a couple."

"He'd likely be more understanding than most people."

"If you ran into him in Victoria and he asked you what went wrong between us, what would you say?"

"What do you think I'd say?"

"You'd probably blame me. You'd say I was immature, got married too young."

"Is there a right age? I think it was difficult for you, marrying the boss's daughter. My family forced you into the hotel business. We thought you had the potential to make it big in business—I know I was devastated when you said you wanted to go back to university and be a professor. You were playing it safe at too young an age."

"Now I'm out of teaching again."

"And working for The Shark. Paul, what's got into him? Where did he find this Deirdre?"

"Rob must've told you about our wedding—Sue's and mine?"

"'A hippy wedding,' I think he called it. Was that unkind?"

"Not at all. It's what we wanted. Outdoors, on a beautiful campus, everyone participating. Well, The Shark was there, as you probably know, and so was Deirdre. She'd just had an abortion and was mixed up with a colleague of mine at Ryerson. For some reason, Deirdre was attracted to The Shark—who knows why? Probably because he was this powerful businessman and her boyfriend was a sad sack of a professor."

"But she knew The Shark was married."

"So was Roger, the guy she was seeing. She just likes married men, I guess, I don't know. Anyway, Roger eventually went back to his wife to save her sanity and Deirdre started bugging Susan and me about using our contacts to get her a job. We thought that's what she wanted—a job—but I guess she was after The Shark. Well, Sue isn't shy when it comes to things like this, so she just flat-out told The Shark to find a job for Deirdre. Frankly, she did the same for me. And The Shark came through for Deirdre—this was maybe three or four years ago—just low-level clerking jobs at first. Well, she's had several other men friends over the years, but, when I went to work for The Shark, it was obvious to me that Deirdre's relationship with him had become rather special. By then, she'd moved into Sales."

"But he's an executive with a fairly conservative company, and he has a gregarious wife who's expected to share the social obligations. How does he get away with this?"

"The Shark isn't parading young lovelies through a bedroom next to his office or anything. No one ever sees him with her in Toronto. Those who know what's going on justify it on the grounds that Fran has been sick for a long while. Some even believe that Fran knows and approves. Whether she knows or not, The Shark is always discreet."

"You call coming to Rob's wedding with Deirdre *discreet*?"

"He didn't bring her to the church, did he. But, come to think of it, I don't know why he'd bring her over here at all when he knew he was going to be seeing you. He's been carrying a torch for you for years."

First Deirdre tells me The Shark thinks Paul still loves me. Now Paul tells me The Shark loves me. Has everyone gone mad? What am I supposed to do with this kind of information?

"It's true," Paul says. "He's virtually told me as much. He only married Fran because she was a good friend of yours."

"That's ridiculous!"

"He's kept in touch with you, hasn't he? Taken you out for dinner on occasion?"

"A few times, if one of us was in the other's town on business. We got together as old friends, nothing more."

"Maybe he wanted you to find out about Deirdre. Maybe it's his way of telling you things are more or less over with Fran and he's not ready to be put out to pasture."

"I think you're reading too much into it. He's just another successful man who wants to show off young women as if they're symbols of wealth, like cars and jewellery."

"There's a place to sit. Should we take it?"

"Yes, quick."

The two of us scamper to a table that a departing couple has vacated.

"I think I'll have a scotch chaser," Paul says. "Will you?"

"Why not?"

I watch him go to fetch the drinks. Some of the shy mannerisms he used to have are still there, but he seems more sure of himself, somehow. I scan the room: most of the people are middle-aged like us, well-dressed like us. One of the men has a wonderful laugh that rises above the din of conversation and sets a happy tone for the room. Saturday night is Happy Night in so many parts of the world.

When Paul returns with the drinks, he says, "Didn't The Shark go to your mother's wedding when she remarried?"

"Yes, with Frances. They were invited because Fran was always one of my mother's biggest fans."

"How *is* your mother?"

"Very well. She and The Senator went to Singapore on their honeymoon, with side trips to Nepal and Hong Kong. Neither of them had ever been to Asia, and he managed to tie it in with government business. I thought they would both contract exotic diseases, because Mother has so many allergies, and The Senator has suffered through every malady known to man. But both said it was the best trip they'd ever taken—they even hiked a short distance up Mount Everest."

"Your mother sold the hotels after your father died?"

"Yes. She wanted me to take one over, but I'd already developed my own business too far. Now she's right at home as a doyen of Ottawa society. Her wedding was a major social event, complete with honour guard."

"Steve always said your mother would end up in Ottawa."

"Have you heard from Steve lately?"

"No, but I understand he's separated from his second wife and back in Winnipeg. You won't believe who he's living with."

"Who?"

"Becky Wyatt."

This comes as no major surprise. Becky Wyatt is one of those people who hover out there on the periphery of your life, like a housefly in your window, and occasionally flit into your midst. She offered comfort when Paul thought he needed to be comforted, when he had left the Barber hotels and we were already living apart.

"I hope they're both happy," I say. "Steve never seemed happy when I knew him. He tried to put up a good front—"

"Are you happy, Cath?"

He's turned the tables on me. This is one of the questions that I was planning to ask him.

"I love my work," I say. "You know it takes me right across the country now and even into the States. I work hard and I see results. I'm able to take trips like this that combine business and pleasure. I was in London for the Royal Wedding and then I drove around Western Europe, staying in the smaller hotels in smaller cities like Maastricht and Mittenwald and Marktheidenfeld and Alchenfluh/Kirchberg. I have a notebook full of ideas I picked up—"

"I mean your personal life. How is James?"

"James . . ." I hesitate because I'm startled by Paul's mentioning him. Of course, Rob would've told Paul about James. "James has been good for me . . . but he doesn't understand how highly I value my independence. How about you, Paul? How are things going between you and Susan?"

He downs his scotch. "Good, great," he says. "It's hard for me to believe I'm going to be a father again, after all these years. Sue's talked me into taking part in the delivery. We've been going to Lamaze classes. And guess what. She's got me taking photographs of the various stages of her pregnancy and she wants shots of the baby coming out . . ."

My stomach gives an involuntary lurch. I remember when Rob was born, over twenty-two years ago; Paul was at the hospital but he stayed in a waiting room the whole time. They called it "The Father's Room". I didn't want him to see me looking unfeminine and unpretty. I had this instinct that childbearing was an animal process that would somehow degrade me in his eyes. A nurse let him know that the baby was a healthy boy, and he wasn't allowed to see me or his son until the baby was cleaned up and I had had my face wiped and my hair brushed and my lipstick applied.

"Having a baby around will keep you young," I say. I stand up. "I'll fetch the next round."

"No, no, let me—"

"Stay right there."

I suddenly feel lonely and barren. It's good to be up, moving through the jabbering, rollicking crowd. When I order the beer and the scotch, the squire gives me a look that says, "Another blinkin' feminist knockin' back pints like a bloke." Some of the male customers, their faces glowing in the bar lights, smile or wink at me. A group starts singing *I've Got a Loverly Bunch of Coconuts*. I take first the beer to the table and then the scotch. Paul is chuckling.

He says, "Remember how you and I used to take Rob everywhere when he was a baby?"

"We weren't going to let a child tie us down."

"Cheerio." He takes a long swig of his pint. "We seldom got a sitter, did we? We never went to a party without the little guy. He'd fall asleep wherever we put him down—strange bedrooms, nightclub banquettes, other people's laps. One night—I think it was a party at The Shark's—we couldn't find him, remember? He'd fallen asleep on the bed where the guests stacked their coats and some latecomer actually threw a station wagon coat over him and he didn't wake up. We were pretty worried for a while; I don't know where we thought he could've gone."

"No wonder he has no trouble sleeping in French fields and Greek alcoves."

"I'd carry him in from the car and we'd take off his clothes and put on his pyjamas and he'd never wake up."

"You did that for *me* once, remember? At Frances's parents' place near Kenora. It was our annual bash to welcome winter. There was no heat and no running water but we stayed overnight in sleeping bags—Allan and Pris and you and me and some other couple and Fran and The Shark. I got drunker than I ever have in my life."

"And I changed your clothes."

"Because I'd been sick all over them."

We both laugh.

"We all slept in the living room," I say. "You and I were surrounded by those six other people and we did it, remember?"

"'Did it'. Sounds pretty quaint in this day and age, doesn't it?"

"We weren't that brazen on our honeymoon, were we? Remember the couple that wouldn't leave us alone?"

"Jack and Greta? Or was it Gretchen?"

"Greta, I think. We met in a restaurant. They were on their honeymoon, too. We had a mountain chalet and they had a plain motel unit down on the highway. Our bed was in the front room, and one morning they came barging in—why wasn't the door locked?"

"I don't know. Maybe we didn't lock doors in those days. But in they came, about a minute after we'd made love. You were naked in the bathroom and I was naked in the bed and neither of us could reach our clothing."

"The two of them sat there talking to us as if it were a regular tea-time chat, me with my head poking out of the bathroom door and you with the covers yanked up around your neck. Why didn't we ask them to get our clothes for us?"

"I think we were petrified. We probably felt as if we'd been doing something wrong."

"Or something they hadn't done yet. They nonchalantly made themselves coffee. We finally had to ask them to leave so that we could get dressed."

"All that time we spent with them and then we never saw them again."

Paul goes to pick up two more pints. It's apparently almost closing time and there's so much I'd like to discuss.

Paul returns with the beer and says, "Cath, there's something I've always wanted to ask you."

"What's that?"

"On our wedding day, Steve said something to me in the car on the way to the church. He . . . he implied that you weren't a virgin. He said he'd heard that your old boyfriend Ray had 'put the blocks to her', to use Steve's cute turn of phrase."

"Your good old best friend, Steve."

"I told him he was full of shit."

"You were right."

"I *knew* you were a virgin."

We've had too much to drink—that's why we're discussing this.

"No, Paul, I wasn't."

"What!"

"Paul," I say, putting my hand over his, "it was so important in those days that a bride be a virgin. I knew how important it was to a young man like you . . . but, if you'd ever asked me, I would've told you the truth."

"I thought you'd have told me if—"

"You didn't want to know."

"If it wasn't Ray, then who was it?"

"Does it really matter now?"

"Well, no, of course it doesn't—but—"

"Polonius Martin. My English prof."

"*What?* Oh no. Not him. *Christ.*" Paul bangs his glass mug down on the table, spilling some of his beer and some of mine, and causing people near us to turn and look.

"Paul, it isn't important."

Why did I tell him? To get back at him for showing up here with his pregnant wife? I should never have kept it a secret from him in the first place. I had a crush on Polonius Martin in first year university. The smell of his pipe, the way he broke into Shakespearian quotations and virtually acted them out in class, the look and smell of all those books of his crowding the sagging shelves in his office. At eighteen, I was a pushover for academia and erudition and all the trappings—

tweed jackets, leather elbow-patches, messy hair, and musty books with hundreds of pieces of paper stuck in them to mark quotable passages.

"He was married," Paul says. "Where did you—"

"In his office."

"No!"

"We didn't get together very often. Not at all once you and I started seeing each other. I realized how stupid I was. I'm sure I was just one of a series of student seductions for him."

"But you invited him to our wedding."

"I talked about him at home a lot. Mom and Dad had met him at a couple of university functions and they liked him. They wanted to invite him and they would've asked a lot of questions if I'd insisted we not invite him. They knew nothing about my involvement with him. Maybe now you can see why I hated the idea of your becoming a teacher."

"Polonius Martin! I never liked the bastard—"

"It doesn't matter now. It never mattered."

People all around us are saying goodnight and leaving. As Paul and I stand, he staggers a little and I reach over to take his arm.

10

I drive carefully along the darkened country road. We reach the Nottingham outskirts and I ask Paul to find the map in the glove compartment. Since there is no grid system in this city, the streets seem like a maze, a labyrinth, as they do in most European cities. Paul navigates, the Nottingham map open on his lap, the glove compartment light on.

"Polonius!" he cries out. "God!"

"Check the map. Don't we—"

"Oh, yes. Turn left."

"Remember the times we used to drive all night? To Texas, to the west coast, to Florida. "

"You used to pack all kinds of snacks. As long as I was eating, I could stay awake—"

"Rob and I would sleep—"

"And I'd do all the driving."

"And you'd keep waking me to check the map—"

"And I didn't know about Polonius Martin! Make a right turn up here."

I shouldn't have told him about Polonius. How can I ask him about his job, about how he feels about me, now that his head's full of the past. Maybe we need another chance to talk when we're both sober; maybe I should offer to take him and Susan to Wales.

Paul says, "Polonius Martin's the last guy I ever—do you know who I used to worry about? The guy who came to our wedding in a madras jacket. I used to think he might be someone you'd had a fling with and you weren't going to admit it. Remember him? And the woman in the white dress? Did we ever find out who they were?"

"I think we did. She was a friend of—oh oh. What's this? What does that sign say?"

"Notts County."

"Check the map again. You've got us into the soccer stadium parking lot."

The outside door of the hotel is locked, but we have a key. It takes a concentrated effort for the two of us to insert the key in the hole. There is one dim lamp burning in the lobby, barely enough to light our way to the cage elevator.

Paul says, "Let's see. I think we press this button."

"Wait. We have to have both doors closed first."

"Are you sure we aren't too heavy for this thing?"

"We'll soon see, won't we?"

Shutting the inside door requires a certain manipulative skill, but we master it after several noisy attempts. We press the button and the elevator slowly ascends. Being able to see the thickness of the ceiling as we go past it makes us giggle. I feel as if we are rising to the heavens in the rickety basket of a balloon. We come to his floor first and we have another good laugh when we both fumble with the door to let him out.

"Good night, Cath."

He leans forward to kiss me lightly and something—perhaps guilt about the Polonius secret, perhaps pure devilment—causes me to reach my hand up to the back of his neck and hold him there. And open my mouth against his. And use my tongue. To his credit, he doesn't leap back in astonishment. He responds. It's a long, long time since we kissed like this. I hold him against me, letting him kiss my eyes, my ears, my throat. His urgency is youthful—it's Arthur's, it's Barry Lambert's—

"Paul—Paul—we'd better—"

"Say goodnight?"

"Yes—"

"Okay—but . . . okay . . ."

"Good night, Paul. It was great fun."

He backs out of the elevator looking bewildered and so sad that I wish I hadn't started anything. He stands there watching as I shut the first door and the second door and I press the button. The elevator jerks and clangs and starts to rise.

11

Lying in my hotel bed, I feel battered, drained, woozy from drink, yet completely awake. I turn to my place in the Murdoch novel. I read a line and I read it again. And again. I will blame the beer and the scotch for that episode in the elevator. In some respects, it was the right way to end such a preposterous day.

The telephone rings, startling me.

"Hello?"

"Hello, Mom."

"Rob! What in heaven's—"

"Mom, I'm sorry to wake you—"

"No, no, it's all right, I wasn't asleep—"

"Mom, I . . ."

"Rob, I can hardly hear you. Is that music? Where are you?"

"That's just a tape. I don't want Fiona to know I'm calling you. I feel pretty dumb, bothering you like this, but I had to talk to somebody. Fiona's locked herself in the bathroom."

"No—"

"I told you she was acting weird. Well, when she saw what they'd done to our car, that was bad enough, but when she saw the house, she freaked out. She can't believe friends could do so many terrible things. She's still in her wedding dress, crying her eyes out. She says she's never felt so horrible in her whole life. I can't do anything to make her feel any better. Mom, this has got me beat. What should I do?"

I want to scream, *Come home! Come back to Canada with me!* "Rob, this night isn't important, remember that. Don't think of this night as having any significance for the future. It's just an ordinary night and the main thing is to get through it. Stay calm. Be—"

There's a tap-tap-tap at the door. It's after two in the morning—who can this be?

"Rob, just a minute, there's someone at the door."

"Mom! Mom, for God's sake, don't answer it!"

"Hold on."

"Mom—"

I set aside the phone and the book, step out of bed and walk over to the door. "Who is it?"

"It's Paul."

Oh, no. "Paul, it's late. I'm in bed."

"Could I see you, just for a minute?"

I put on my robe and open the door. He stands there with a crooked, sheepish grin on his face and a bottle of scotch in his hand. He has taken off his tie, his jacket and his vest.

"Let's have a nightcap," he says.

"Susan—?"

"Fast asleep."

"Paul, Rob's on the phone."

"Huh?"

"Rob. Your son. He's on the phone."

Paul looks at the phone lying off the hook on the night table. He takes a step back as if he might run away. "I'd better not—"

"Oh, come in."

I go back to the phone and Paul comes in and closes the door.

"Mom! Is that Dad?"

"You guessed it."

"Is Susan there?"

"No."

"Mom, what's going on?"

"I don't know. Would you like to speak to your father?"

Paul waves wildly and shakes his head.

"Mother. I don't believe this. Why would you—why would Dad—"

"Rob, your father wants to speak with you." I cover the mouthpiece with my hand. "Paul, Fiona's locked herself in their bathroom. Rob's not feeling very good about it. I think it would help if you gave him some reassurance."

Paul grimaces but takes the receiver from me. "Hello? Hi, Rob, how are you? . . . So your mother says—look, I don't blame her, I mean, kippers, for God's sake. Is she still crying? . . . She is, eh? Poor kid. . . . Well, let me tell you what *my* dad told *me*. I'll always remember it. He said, 'Son, don't expect the first time to be a picnic.' Well, I guess it isn't exactly appropriate in your case, but a wedding night

takes on a whole lot of extra importance, regardless, doesn't it? . . .
Be calm, Rob, and be civil. If—if she wants to stay in the bathroom,
let her. You've got to get some rest—you have to drive a long way
tomorrow, don't you? . . . That's the spirit. . . . Okay. . . . Yes, you too.
. . . Good night—"

"Let me speak to him!" I cry.

"Oh—Rob? . . . Rob, your . . . he's hung up."

"I wanted to talk to him again."

"Sorry." He hangs up the phone.

"How did he sound to you?"

"I don't know. Kind of weird—disappointed, maybe. I think he
was more concerned about you and me being together."

"Maybe it'll take his mind off Fiona."

"What do you make of her?"

"I don't think she's an unstable girl. She may not be quite ready
for marriage. I'm worried that they're bored with each other, that this
reaction of hers is caused by the terribly anti-climactic nature of their
so-called Big Day. They live together and travel together and suddenly
they have this ceremony and celebration and when they get home
and they're alone again, what has changed? Nothing. Oh, sorry, I
forgot you and Susan lived together first."

"It's okay—I think I agree with you. Hey, would you like a
nightcap?" He dangles the bottle of scotch in front of my face.

"Paul, it's late."

"There's something I have to tell you."

Jaws says he thinks Paul still loves you. "Couldn't we discuss it
tomorrow?"

"In the pub, you asked me how things were between Susan and
me, and I said they were great."

A heavy weariness descends upon me. It seems this day will never
end. "And things are not great, is that it? Sit down. I'll wash out
some glasses."

He sits down on the bed while I take two glasses to the bathroom
and rinse them with hot water. I avoid looking at myself in the
bathroom mirror. I return to the room and hand the glasses to Paul.
He pours two fingers of scotch into each.

I say, "When Rob told me what a colourful person Susan was, and
what an off-beat wedding you had, I thought you were in for an
exciting life."

"It was wild at first. Drugs, orgies—you name it. And we considered going to live for a year or so in some far-off country—Malaysia, Australia, or maybe Brazil. But it turned out that what we both wanted was a quiet life. Sue took a series of odd jobs—teller, receptionist, courier—she never really had her heart in the hotel business, never finished the course—and we saved up and eventually got this house in Mississauga. At last we had a place to put all our junk. We had a swimming pool installed, and a driveway made of interlocking bricks, and a fireplace built with Tyndall stone from Eastern Manitoba. And we'd sit around the pool or by the fire and tell ourselves we were happy. But there was something missing."

"What was that?"

"Talk. We didn't talk. We *couldn't* talk. You know why? We couldn't reminisce! You know how you and I got talking about the good old days tonight? Wasn't that terrific?"

"I haven't had a good laugh like that for a long time."

"It was fantastic. But that never happens with Sue. You know why? Because Sue doesn't have any 'good old days'."

"That's because she's so young."

"She doesn't *care* about the past. For a long time now, all she's wanted to talk about is having a baby. We've had a nursery set up in the house for six years. She had two miscarriages but, Cath, since the day she knew she'd conceived for the third time, we have not made love."

"That's understandable."

"Is it?" He sips his scotch and leans forward to place one hand lightly on my knee. "Cath, it was so good going over the old times. Remember the play? Our one and only fling at the stage?"

"I had a second fling two years ago—at the same play. This time, I played Laura, for an amateur group in Montreal—"

"Good for you! I'll bet that brought back memories. 'We're soldiers, we are—willing to lay down our lives—' God!"

"The lines still make my heart flutter."

"Remember when you and I worked together at The Barbary? I ran the restaurants and you looked after the banquets?"

"The banquets made money and the restaurants didn't."

"Remember when you were on the front desk late one night and that guy came in and tried to hold you up and he didn't know I was there and I scared him away?"

"Your finest hour."

"Remember how we laughed?"

"Paul, do *you* remember the violent arguments we used to have? Do you remember the objections you had to my running the hotel? Do you remember my father getting you a job in another place so that he wouldn't have to fire you?"

"Cath . . ." He takes his hand away.

"The memories aren't all good, Paul. There are a lot of bad memories."

"We produced a great son, didn't we?"

"Yes, we did. I only hope he handles tonight properly."

"Funny the way things go . . ."

"You know, I'm very tired, aren't you?"

"I guess I am."

"We should get some sleep."

"Yeah, you're right." He downs his drink, stands, picks up the Iris Murdoch novel. "Is this good?"

"Excellent."

He puts the book back on the bed, takes a step toward the door and stops.

"Cath. That—that was very nice . . . in the elevator."

I say nothing.

"I always said you had the world's softest lips."

I look away from him.

"Cath?"

"Yes?"

"I hate to leave."

"But you should."

"Wouldn't it sort of put a capper on everything if—if you and I— you know—" He gestures toward the bed.

"Oh, Paul."

"For old times' sake?"

"I don't think so."

"It'd really improve my spirits."

"It might not."

"We have nothing to lose."

"I can't see what we could possibly gain."

"We've been getting along so well. Who would've guessed it? And that kiss in the elevator. That told me something, Cath."

"It was a goodnight kiss, that's all."

"I detected a little hunger. You and I could—"

"No, Paul."

"Can't we talk about it a little? Weigh the pro's and con's?"

"NO. Now, please—"

"Okay. All right. I'd better go." He walks toward the door, his shoulders drooping. He puts his hand on the doorknob.

"Wait," I say.

"Yes?"

"If you like . . . I could drive you and Susan to Wales."

"You could?"

"I was thinking of going, anyway, to look at a property."

"Do you think Susan can handle the trip?"

"We could make the back seat comfortable for her—let her have it all to herself."

"She'd love that."

"See you in the morning, then."

"Good night, Cath, and thank you."

"Good night, Paul."

As he opens the door, I go over to him and we kiss. This time, I pucker my lips and keep my mouth closed.

12

t w e l v e

"Shit, will you look at those cows!" Susan exclaims. "Are they bigger over here or *what*? They sure look bigger, don't they? Hey, you know what it is? These suckers are a lot closer to the road than ours are, right? Ours're always way off in the distance and, hell, that one back there could've hung her ass over the fence and *plop*! drop her load right on our car roof! Have you noticed—those hedges're right beside us. There aren't any shoulders on these roads. Oh, Catherine, can you make it past that bus . . . Christ! How do they get a bus that big around these curves! Look at those hills, will you? God, this stone wall must knock off a lot of side mirrors—I'm sure glad you're driving, Catherine—right, Paul? Hey, I've always liked cows. I wouldn't mind a cow for a pet—I'm serious. Do you have any pets, Catherine?"

I think of Mort and the way he loves to play. I finished the letter to James this morning and I sent it. I probably will never see Mort again. I also sent a card to Barry.

"No, I haven't," I answer. "I travel too much."

I must concentrate on the road. It's a narrow pavement that winds and winds through undulating countryside, dark forests and cramped little orange-brick villages. At times, our lane, which seems barely wider than my rented Cortina, takes us right up to the wall of a barn or a house that juts into the roadway.

"We've always had pets, haven't we Paul?" Susan carries on in her endearingly annoying stream-of-consciousness as I downshift around a corner. "First we had a cat named Eldridge. When we had to put him down, we got two more – Burton and Taylor. And of course our dog, Ziggy. He's a horny Lab, always looking for somebody's leg to hump. Male, female, it doesn't matter — just like David Bowie. Hey, can I have another chocolate bar?"

"Sure, honey," says Paul, who is sitting up front beside me,

202

navigating and dispensing the snacks. "And how about another Schweppes?"

The three of us had brunch with Rob and Fiona and the Brysons. Fiona seemed a little red-eyed, but as animated as I've seen her. Apparently, a night in the bathroom was all she needed.

Susan has bounced back remarkably. After her good sleep, she seems far more lively than Paul or I. When we stopped at a Staffordshire china factory, she came right in with us. We have arranged a bed of blankets and pillows for her in the back seat and she is comfortable and relaxed. Her appetite is amazing. The whole way from Nottingham, Paul has been passing her candies and cakes and chocolates and drinks and tasty leftovers from the Bryson tea.

Paul says, "You know you can drop us off anytime, don't you, Cath? Betws-Y-Coed's the next fairly big place—you could help us find a hotel and leave us there, if you like."

Of course, he doesn't mean this. He and Susan will accompany me to Ffestiniog and the Hovey Arms and they will take the big room with the view of the forest and the hamlet of Maentwrog. They will open up their casement window and let in the evening air. We will have a few pints with the tradesmen who come down every night from Blaenau, and, if the place cools off too much, the proprietor will start a fire and someone will tell a Welsh myth or sing a Welsh song. Somewhat tipsy, we shall retire to our separate rooms and, when the hotel has settled down for the night, someone who is a slate miner or a mason by day will walk down the hall singing a ballad.

"You know who's looking after Ziggy and the cats?" says Susan. "A great friend of ours named Shelly Goldfarb. Ever heard of her, Catherine? She practically runs Delta Hotels. Hers is the next wedding we've got to go to. She's latched onto the best-looking American lawyer you ever saw. She wants me to be Matron of Honour and the wedding's on the day I'm due, okay? Figures it'd be a real gas if I had the kid right there in the middle of the 'I do's'. Hey, look at that tiny goddam house. Who do you figure lives there, the Seven Dwarfs?"

203

part four

The Shark:
1986

1

Las Vegas, Nevada
Thursday, July 24, 1986

I open my eyes, put on my glasses, and there I am, spread-eagled on the ceiling. I look a little heavy around the gills, despite regular tennis. It's scary to see myself suspended up there, not moving.

I close my eyes and remember where I am. I open them again.

That's my mirror image up there. I'm lying naked on a heart-shaped bed, the covers tossed off to the side. Isn't that the way it goes: my first time on a heart-shaped bed with a mirror on the ceiling and I'm alone.

I crave a cigarette. Still haven't got over that early-morning craving even though I gave them up a year ago. I reach for a LifeSaver. Oh, good, a green one. I savour it while I look at myself in the mirror. (I always suck them right down to nothing. Poor Fran used to chew them a second after she put them into her mouth.)

On the night table is the paperback I've been reading, a new crime novel by Roman Danscy, *The Deadly Wedding Vows*, starring that all-Canadian private eye, Eric Engel. Dansey's the guy that wandered into the ridiculous wedding Paul and Sue had on the Glendon campus of York U back in 1972. Someone said there's a character just like me in the novel, but I haven't got to him yet.

I check my watch. Not quite eight o'clock. I'm meeting Dad for breakfast in an hour. Time to get up.

I haul myself out of bed. Ten o'clock in Toronto. I should call Kay to see if the Ralston deal went through. But I promised Dad I'd forget the company for a day.

Yesterday's *Las Vegas Review-Journal* lies on a chair. The front-page headline reads: "Prince Andrew marries Sarah". Sarah's eyes remind me of Fran's. I glance through the paper. Some Nevada prison inmates held a press conference to air their complaints; Rose Kennedy turned ninety-six; a doctor tried to clarify some things about a terrible new disease called AIDS. The world is a little crazier than it was last week.

I walk over to the round sunken bathtub, step into it, pull the curtain all around and start the shower.

"Hi, Dad. Are you up yet?"

"Jeez, I thought you'd never phone."

"Why didn't *you* call?"

"I didn't want to wake you. So I walked back and forth, just about wore a hole in the carpet."

"Are you ready for breakfast?"

"God, no. Would you give me ten minutes to get dressed?"

Dad puts a dollar coin in a one-armed bandit as we walk through the casino; he pulls the arm and there's an avalanche of coins into the metal dish. Fifty bucks! He's been having this kind of luck in Vegas for years. We have to stop while he collects his loot.

He skips ahead of me, a spry, wiry little guy with lots of white hair trimmed short. His sport jacket pockets bulge with the coins. We head out through the sliding doors into the bright morning. I take Dad's arm as we step onto the moving sidewalk. We've decided on Denny's for breakfast.

"Not bad out this morning," I say.

"Going up to ninety-five," Dad says. "I love it, but Marilyn thinks it might be stuffy in the chapel."

"I'm still amazed that everyone came. Las Vegas in July can be intimidating."

"Will we have enough limos?"

"We have nine. That should be enough, don't you think?"

"One limo is too many as far as I'm concerned. It's your idea to take everybody to the chapel."

"That way, they don't have to worry about finding it, and they all get there at the same time."

"Damn it, I wish I'd eloped."

The server brings our Grand Slams. Heaped on each plate are two eggs sunnyside up, three pancakes, two strips of bacon, two sausages, hash browns, a blob of butter, a cup of syrup. For a man of eighty,

Dad has a healthy appetite. Says all his plumbing still works perfectly, too. *Touch wood*, he'll say, rapping his knuckles on the side of his head.

"The do went well last night, Pop."

The bride hosted a small party in her hotel suite—drinks and hors d'oeuvres accompanied by the piano stylings of Mel Howard, who dressed in white to match his baby grand. Most of the wedding guests were there.

"Do you know," Dad says, "that danged woman wanted me to stay on after everyone had left?"

My mother died seven years ago and Dad's been a bit of a rascal ever since. When he still lived in Winnipeg, he'd come to visit us in Toronto and bring his latest lady friend with him. For a time, it was Molly Magnusson, a rolypoly little woman with thin red hair. From the first visit, I insisted Dad and Molly could not sleep in the same room. How would it look to our kids? So Molly got the guest room on the second floor and Dad slept on the hide-a-bed in the family room.

Same arrangement the next visit, but this time my son Sam was up late making himself a sandwich and he caught his grandfather sneaking up to Molly's room. Dad pretended to be on his way to the bathroom and Sam reminded him that there was a bathroom on the main floor. One night I swear I heard Molly giggling in her room. One of those obvious giggles.

Fran used to say, Wouldn't it be easier to let Dad and whoever sleep together? But I insisted the rules we'd set for our kids' behaviour when they were under our roof had to apply to everyone who wasn't married.

So Dad just stopped coming for visits.

Whenever Dad and Molly—or his next friend, Bobbie Finnegan—went off to Florida or somewhere together, I'd get a call from my sister, Reena. When was I going to put my foot down, she'd ask. The dirty old man's an embarrassment, she'd say. There must be something wrong with him, she'd say, the sex urge is supposed to fade after sixty. Who said they were having sex? I'd ask. Just because they go away together doesn't mean . . . Oh, Hugh, she'd say, where do you *live*?

And then, just when Reena thought she had Dad talked into an old folks' home, he started seeing Marilyn.

"So did you stay?" I ask him.

"Shhh! Here comes your old pal."

I turn and see Paul Hodges coming toward our booth with his two little girls, Jean and Judy.

"Hello, Max; hi, Shark," Paul says.

"Hello," I say. "Hi, girls, how are we today?"

"If I was any better, I be dange-us," says Judy.

Jean snickers and hits her sister.

"Care to join us?" I ask.

"No, no, we've had ours, thanks," Paul says.

"What did you have for breakfast, Jean?" I ask.

"She had Baby Ruth," says Judy.

"I don't see that on the menu," I say.

"No-o-o, it's a chocolate bar, silly," says Judy.

Dad lifts Jean onto his lap and she grabs the packets of sugar.

"Jeanie, don't!" says Judy, who has her arms crossed on the table and is leaning her chin on them. "She has a awful sweet tooth."

"Shark, Max," says Paul, "I didn't get a chance to tell either of you last night how happy we are that you included us in this. First time we've been to Vegas and we love it. We're truly grateful to you for—Max, don't let her drink your coffee!"

"She's okay," says Dad.

"We're glad you could come," I say.

"You work with old Sharkey, don't you?" says Dad.

"He used to, Dad. Used to."

"Susan wanted to try her hand at the business world," Paul tells Dad. "So I gave her $5,000 to start a lingerie shop and she's built it into three stores. I stay home with the girls."

"You mean you're the housewife?" says Dad.

"The househusband," says Paul.

"The world's gone crackers," says Dad. "Well, anyway, I don't blame you for wanting to stay home with these two beautiful young ladies. Identical twins, aren't they?"

"Yes," says Paul. "Even we have a hard time telling them apart sometimes. Just one distinguishing feature: Jean has a little beauty spot on her cheek and Judy doesn't."

"Really?" I say. "I've never noticed."

"It's not on her *face*," says Judy, beaming.

"On my *bum*," says Jean.

I'm not glad to see Paul at all. The guy's gone downhill since Susan talked me into giving him a job in the insurance company. Why did I let her talk me into it? I guess a shrink would say it's because I wanted to have an affair with Susan to get back at him for marrying Catherine. I don't know, shrinks can't always be wrong.

Let's face it, Paul screwed up. The company's Food Services got away from him and so I split that off and left him with Personnel. He did all right for a while, but I started to notice that his heart wasn't in it—he'd avoid meetings and he was drinking.

When Susan started *Teddies*, he resigned. She'd been itching to get out of the house ever since the day she came home with the twins. (Still claims she didn't know she was going to have twins until she went into the hospital.) Paul teaches a night class once a week but, other than that, he and Sue are happy to have him at home instead of some babysitter. The girls are a handful and he apparently manages them well.

I don't know, I think he could've done so much more with his life. Now, here he is, the failure, the househusband, with his young wife and his ex-wife and his two little kids. And here I am, the success, without a woman. Yeah, Sigmund, it pisses me off.

"Nice fella," Dad says, after Paul and the girls have left. "Used to be married to Marilyn's daughter, didn't he? I've never asked her what she thinks of him. Say, whatever happened to that other fella you chummed around with in school?"

"You mean Steve?"

"Steve, right. He was a little devil."

"He followed some woman to Australia. I keep meaning to track him down."

"Regular Three Stooges, the three of you."

I'd never thought of us that way. More like the Three Musketeers. Oh well.

"So, Dad," I say. "I gather you didn't stay last night."

"You're goddam right I didn't. As a matter of fact, if the truth be known, I've been thinking of calling this whole thing off."

"Oh, Pop, come on—"

"I'm serious. It's causing so many problems. Like, what do I do about—you know . . ."

"What?"
"You know—birth control—"
"Dad, you're both *eighty*, for God's sake—"
"But how do I know I won't catch something?"
"You mean you haven't—"
"After all, her last husband was a senator."

2

t w o

The guest list:

MARILYN BARBER FOSS, of Ottawa, the bride.

MAX GODFREY, from Winnipeg and now living in Ottawa, the groom.

HUGH GODFREY (me), the best man.

GERALDINE HENDERSON, of Ottawa and Brampton, matron of honour, about 75, close friend of the bride. Best known for the cross-country skiing parties she and her husband host at their home in the Gatineau hills. Was once an actress; had a successful run at Stratford as Queen Gertrude in *Hamlet*. Author of a cookbook called *What's Sauce for the Senator*.

CATHERINE BARBER, of Montreal, daughter of the bride.

SENATOR GARFIELD HENDERSON, of Ottawa and Brampton, husband of the matron of honour. Pushing 77. Good friend of Mrs. Foss's deceased husband, Senator Dudley Foss. Best known for his opposition to Senate reform and his crashingly boring speeches.

DOLORES McPHEE, of Montreal, Senator Foss's daughter from a previous marriage. 50-ish. Bilingual and active in anti-separatist movement. Said to have blamed Marilyn's cooking for her father's demise.

JACK McPHEE, Dolores's husband. In his 50s. Lawyer, rabid hockey fan and collector of memorabilia. Prized possessions: Jean Beliveau's last hockey stick and Jacques Plante's first mask.

SANDRA McPHEE, 23, daughter of Jack and Dolores. Flight attendant based in Vancouver. Says she's currently "between captains".

RICK GODFREY, my 25-year-old son, who had a brief stint in the NHL with Pittsburgh Penguins before suffering a severe knee injury. Now an insurance salesman in Toronto (with his old man's company).

DENISE GODFREY, Rick's 25-year-old wife, originally from Pittsburgh and a former model. Works part-time in Toronto Blue Jays promotions department.

JASON GODFREY, amazingly bright 3-year-old son of Rick and Denise.

FRANCES ANNE GODFREY, equally bright 2-year-old daughter of Rick and Denise. N.q.o.o.d. (Not quite out of diapers.)

BARBARA PASLOSKI, 24, my darling daughter. Toronto computer analyst/programmer and gymnastics coach. After six years, still finding it hard to adjust to life outside the gymnastics limelight.

JOE PASLOSKI, 28, Barbara's husband. Linebacker for Toronto Argonauts. Was separated from Barb but currently trying reconciliation. Finding it hard to adjust to being an adult.

TOD PASLOSKI, almost 3 and still n.q.o.o.d. at night. Son of Barb and Joe; suspected of being my favourite grandkid.

SAM GODFREY, of Toronto, 22, my ne'er-do-well son. This week, trying his hand at writing song lyrics and has sworn off drugs.

JANIE CHOY, 25, Sam's current live-in companion. Sometime model and TV personality. Rumours persist that her past conquests include both Joe Pasloski and Senator Dudley Foss.

KIM GODFREY, 17, my high-school-student daughter. Once overweight and now anorexic—some say out of grief over her mother's death.

KATE GODFREY, my youngest at 12, winner of several awards in junior-high Science and inventor of a way to quit smoking (dry leaves and dog turds) successfully used by me and Kim. Expected to baby-sit when required.

REENA FRAMINGHAM, 48, my sister and daughter of the groom. Part-time nurse and volunteer worker in several community projects in

Winnipeg. Avid curler and tennis player. To her, Dad is a nutcase and Sam should be locked up.

GEORGE FRAMINGHAM, 50, Reena's husband, owner of a top-notch Winnipeg courier service. Five-handicap in golf. Has a fine tenor singing voice and one of the world's great noses.

DAVID FRAMINGHAM, 18, son of George and Reena, entering Engineering at the University of Manitoba in the fall. Said to be the proud owner of an 8x10 photo of Janie Choy in the raw.

CY GODFREY, 75, brother of the groom. Almost as spry as Dad, Cy lost his right eye in World War II and refused to have an artificial one put in. Wears turquoise patch over the empty socket. Retired, in Winnipeg.

LORENA GODFREY, 60-ish, Cy's second wife. Display co-ordinator in a Winnipeg shopping mall. So fed up with Cy's snoring that she brought home a life-size mannequin to share his bed and installed herself in the guest room.

MILT GODFREY, 45, Cy's son, a professor of Philosophy at the University of Regina.

JOANNE TANANA, about 42, Cy's daughter. Phys Ed teacher in Winnipeg School Division #1. Health nut; jogs six miles every morning before work.

DON TANANA, 43, Joanne's handsome husband. Former service station lessee, now unemployed.

PORKY DRAPER, of Winnipeg, 76 years admitted to, old friend of the groom, tireless gambler. Played a role in assuring Dad that a Vegas wedding was a great idea. Known for the saying, "You know you've reached maturity when you realize you can't do a fucking thing about anything."

GORD BARBER, 45, of Vancouver, son of the bride. Changed careers in mid-life and is now a respected dentist. Sails his own boat in Vancouver harbour.

JILL BARBER, probably 45, Gord's wife, a Vancouver real estate executive.

WALLY BARBER, 47, son of the bride, now living in Thunder Bay. Has knocked around in a variety of jobs. The one bold move of his life was leaving his wife and kids.

DODIE ZAPORZAN, almost 40, Wally's housemate—the one he left his family for. Has a good job as an executive secretary with the railway.

MARNI JOSEPH, about 21, Wally's daughter, separated from her rock musician husband. Easy to spot because of her black lipstick and green hair.

DEEDIE CHARLESWORTH, of Halifax, supposedly 53, Fran's sister. Certified busy-body.

PAUL HODGES, of Toronto. Just turned 52.

SUSAN WALCHUK HODGES, Paul's free-spirited 34-year-old wife. Owner of spiffy chain of lingerie and stuffed animal stores called *Teddies*.

JUDY and JEAN HODGES, Paul and Susan's twin daughters, who'll celebrate their fifth birthday in a few weeks.

3

"Catherine. Anything I can do?"

She's been working closely with the hotel on tonight's reception. It's mid-morning and I'm on the phone to her.

"You can cancel the chapel," she says. "I just drove out there and it's the tackiest little dump I've ever seen."

"Cath, your mother and my father picked that place."

"I can't get over the change in my mother since she took up with your father. She's lost her good taste."

Some years ago, Dad was one of the top bagmen for Dudley Foss's political campaigns. He had a knack for getting rural Manitobans to make extremely generous contributions. Dudley had the best-financed machine of anybody in the west; only problem was, he never got elected. He ran for office twice in two different ridings—ran four times in total—and always met up with a charismatic opponent or a bad split in the votes. So he ran for leadership of the provincial party and got that, at a time when the people were in no mood to give his party any seats. When the election came and Dudley's gang was shut out, the Prime Minister figured it was time to reward Dudley and get him the hell out of politics. That's when he became Senator Foss.

I'm not sure how Catherine's mother got to meet Dudley. I think she was active in a few of the causes he was involved with—things like Children's Hospital and the "Save the Empire Hotel" campaign. When Marilyn Barber decided she'd like to re-marry, he was an eligible and eager widower.

Dad liked travelling around the country and, when he stopped coming to visit us, he started going to see the Senator in Ottawa. At first, he used to take Molly Magnusson or Bobbie Finnegan with him. I have no idea what sleeping arrangements Dudley and Marilyn offered, but Dad soon stopped going there and stopped seeing Molly and Bobby. I don't know if he'd already taken a liking to Marilyn and discretion kept him away or what. All I know is, when the Senator died, Dad helped organize the funeral.

A couple of months later, Catherine called me: "Shark, what is Max *doing?*"

She called me at work. I'd just heard that some major shareholders were talking about bumping me up to board chairman and bringing in a Harvard grad as president.

"Who is this?" I asked.

"Catherine Barber, whose voice you once said you'd never forget."

"Catherine, I'm sorry, I'm in a bit of a daze—"

"So is your father, it appears."

"Hold on, Cath. You're moving too fast for me. It's nice to hear from you."

I hadn't seen her or heard from her since Fran's funeral; that had been about five months before the Senator's. And that encounter hadn't gone as well as I would have liked. It seemed she was still upset about my behaviour at Rob's wedding in England. If I'd had the chance, I would have made some excuse about mid-life crisis or going with the sexual flow of the times or maybe even the truth, that I had been looking for some kind of replacement for her over the last thirty goddam years. But I never got the chance.

"Shark, Max is showing total disrespect for my mother's husband."

"I can't believe that, Cath. Dad thought very highly of Dudley Foss."

"Then why is he harassing my mother?"

"Harassing, Cath? *Harassing?*"

"He actually asked her out for a date."

"Did she accept?"

There was the rub. Marilyn Barber Foss was too healthy and too active to wait out a long period of mourning. After all, she'd nursed old Dudley for a couple of years before he packed it in. Besides that, she liked my father.

It appears that, after standing on ceremony for so many years with Barber and Foss, she was ready for a relaxing change. Dad, with his check shirts and corduroy jackets and plaid ties, seemed the right tonic for this time in her life. He put on no airs. He said whatever he felt like saying. He farted and burped after a good meal. And he still believed in chivalry.

Dad flew into Ottawa and took her to see a couple of Marx Brothers re-runs. The very next day, he took her someplace for "the best hotdogs on the Hill" and then to a high school production of *Oklahoma!* She told him she felt young again and he was sweeping her off her feet.

In a matter of weeks, he cancelled the booking Reena had made for him in Twilight Vistas and moved to Ottawa to take up residence down the hall from Marilyn in the Phoenix condominium complex.

"Why don't you accept the fact that your mother and my father are a couple of crazy kids head over heels in love with each other?"

"Shark, that chapel is awful. There are no trees and the sand and grit blow right through it."

"Cath, let's go for a swim."

"Didn't you hear what I said?"

"To quote my dad's friend, Porky, 'You know you've reached maturity when you realize you can't do a-a thing about anything.'"

4

f o u r

I'm lying on an air mattress, sipping a martini-on-the-rocks. The sun doesn't seem as strong out here on the water. There are all kinds of people, young and old, in and around this vast pool, sunning themselves and sipping drinks. White-clad waiters rove among the tropical plants and the people and the Roman columns. My son, Sam, a sometime musician and song-writer, is snoozing in a chaise while Janie Choy flirts with my professor cousin, Milt Godfrey. Janie makes a nice contrast with Milt, she in a string bikini that shows off her fine young buttocks and he covered from ribs to knees by the largest pair of boxer trunks I've ever seen.

Where's Catherine? She said she'd come for a swim.

I sip the icy cold gin and close my eyes behind my shades.

The memory returns: Catherine, Paul's bride of only a few hours, giving me a hug and kissing me on the cheek. "You have that lost-little-boy look. I wish Fran could see you." And: "Thank you for everything. We'll always remember this."

Always remember what? Their wedding, when all of us were so damned young and she and Paul so full of hope and I so jealous? The prank I played, bursting out of the closet? Our brief embrace?

I talked the motel operator into letting me hide in their room. I didn't know what the hell I was going to do there or how long I was going to stay. All I knew was I had to see Catherine again. For a wild moment or two, I thought, If I make my move dramatic enough, I'll convince her to run away with me and leave Paul in that crummy motel room.

When the critical time came, and Catherine looked so glad to see me and Paul so mad, I couldn't think of the right thing to say. I couldn't be the swashbuckling hero who swoops down and carries off the damsel. I was much better at playing the martyr, and I thought that would have an impact. *You have that lost-little-boy look.*

219

I got going with Fran because Catherine promoted it. *She took a shine to you at the rehearsal party; do call her, Shark.* Fran and Catherine were good friends, and seeing Fran brought me closer to Catherine. With Paul, we were a foursome in those early years.

When Paul and Catherine's marriage went sour, I thought what a cruel joke it was on me. If only I'd waited! I told myself. There I was, saddled with three or four kids, and poor Fran, who was so upbeat and supportive. Fran thought we should work hard to help Paul and Catherine hold things together, but I could see Catherine craved a career. She wasn't the homemaker Paul wanted back then, and, when her dad had them competing with each other in the hotels, it was unmanning for Paul. They split up, and I hated to see either of them, because it reminded me that I should've spoken up, there at the wedding, when Reverend Westlake asked if anyone had just cause to object to the marriage.

Best thing for me to do was try to forget them both and concentrate on my work. I moved up the ladder and got transferred to Toronto. I didn't know too many people there, so I looked up Paul, and that's when I met Susan and found out what a different life Paul was leading. He'd always been malleable, a quality I know Catherine never admired.

Fran and I still saw Catherine on occasion, and, when she moved to Montreal, I'd have lunch with her if I went there on business. She never said much about her personal life, and I couldn't make any kind of overtures because she was such a loyal friend of Fran's.

Through Paul and Susan, I met Dierdre. She was a mistake. Taking her to England that time was reckless, but she was getting nasty and threatening to go to Fran if I didn't take her. A month after we got back to Toronto, she ran off to Europe with a client.

And then, Fran got cancer. Fran who never asked for anything, never expected anything, who seemed almost grateful for what I did give her.

Meanwhile, in some perverse twist of fate, the company was booming. My personal life was falling apart but the company was on a buying spree, taking over other financial institutions at an amazing rate, and I was getting the credit. We had a big house in Willowdale and two Beemers. I drove my kids to their practices and nursed Fran and cheered on the Leafs and the Blue Jays from our corporate box and, two noon-hours a week, I'd run up to the Gerrard Street penthouse of our company lawyer, Robin Quinlan, for pizza in bed.

After Robin, there was Gloria. She worked in PR for the Blue Jays with my daughter-in-law, Denise. I was with her when the call came through on my beeper that Fran had taken a bad turn. By the time I got home, Fran was dead.

"Hey—what!" *Glug, glug, glug*—I'm floudering in the water. Capsized. Prescription glasses gone, martini gone. I grab the mattress, lift my head out of the water. It had to be Catherine. She sneaked up behind me and dunked me.

Through blurred vision I see her darting away, moving as smoothly through the water as a torpedo. Some kind soul hands me my sunglasses. I put them on. There's my assailant lifting herself up into a sitting position on the side of the pool. She looks over at me and laughs, her round little breasts jiggling and glinting in the sun.

It's Janie Choy.

5

My eldest son, Rick, the former hockey star, and his wife, Denise, the former model, are taking the kids to the pool as I come away. "Hi, Grampa!" says their bright three-year-old, Jason. We chat for a minute—Denise is trying out a new sun-block cream; Rick swears two-year-old Frances Anne can read a page of her Dr. Seuss book.

Grampa. How can I be a grampa and still feel so young? I look like a mature businessman; why don't I feel like one?

At the elevators, I show my key to the security guard. He nods. There's a shriek from a woman nearby—not terror but delight: another tourist who's hit the jackpot.

One elevator door opens and out steps Susan.

"Shark! Am I glad to see you!" She's wearing a snug-fitting cotton jumpsuit.

"Is there a problem, Sue?"

She looks this way and that. "We've got to tell Paul."

"Sue, I've got a lot on my plate. Pop's come down with a first class case of the jitters—"

"We'll play it by ear, okay? Pick our spot, maybe between the service and the reception. Just as long as you promise we can tell him today."

"I—yes, all right—"

"Good man."

She kisses my cheek and skips off toward the slot machines.

I was a mess at Fran's funeral. Blubbered at the grave site. A stupid time to feel guilty, but I did.

It was Susan who carried the burden that day. She insisted we have something of a wake. Fran wouldn't have wanted a bloodbath of grief, she said. She organized the food, hired the servers, got us all drinking and eventually laughing. It was Susan who remembered most

222

of the funny things about Fran—mostly things Paul must've told her. But I was impressed by how she carried off the event. She put everybody at ease and got us into the sauce without diminishing anybody's dignity.

We'd all been drinking quite a bit when she cornered me in the kitchen. We'd sent the help home and were stacking the last dishes in the dishwasher. She probably noticed a tear in my eye; she took me into her arms and gave me a hug.

"Squeeze," she said.

I did. It felt wonderful to hold her.

"Shark," she whispered. "If you need me for anything, call me. This is going to be a tough time. I mean it, Shark. Call me."

Over the next few weeks, I worked as hard and as long as I could. I took on extra projects and one was helping Susan get her account books in order. She'd been in business about eighteen months—had only the one store at the time—and she was struggling. I'd always applauded her initiative and her product mix of lingerie and teddy bears seemed to work. But the records were in disarray.

One night, she and I were in the cramped office of *Teddies*, next to the stockroom. We'd done a quick inventory and found shortages. Was she being shoplifted or was a staff member stealing money? Or was someone guilty of lousy arithmetic? Susan's approach to merchandising—buy it at this price and sell it at that and to hell with stock records—was admirable as long as everybody, customer and staff alike, could be trusted. The salespeople were likeable middle-aged women and all part-time. She'd been worried about not being able to make that month's lease payment, but I discovered a couple of calculation errors in her favour. She was on the verge of a profit. She'd be booming if her cash flow let her bring in large quantities of stock for the Christmas season. That was when I decided to become a silent partner in the business.

I change into casual clothes and go to check on Dad.

"I've got a real problem," he says, stepping back from the door. He's holding the waist of the dark blue trousers he's wearing. "Look!" He lets go and the trousers slide down.

"I thought that was a new suit, made to measure."

"It is!"

"You didn't try it on before—"

"I never have to try things on. I've been going to the same tailor for years. And my waist size hasn't changed in years, you know that. What the sam hill—"

"Put on a belt."

"The pants'll be all bunched up at the front—"

"Let's see."

"I didn't bring a belt."

"Will one of mine fit?"

"I don't know."

"Let's see." I whip off my belt. "It's brown, the wrong colour for you, but at least we'll see if a belt will do the trick."

"Marilyn's going to be unhappy. She helped pick the material."

He's so anxious, he has trouble threading the belt through the loops. I do it for him.

"All right, let's see," I say.

"God damn it, that's awful!"

"No, wait, it'll be okay if we just distribute the extra material . . . sure, there. Put the jacket on and no-one'll notice."

"Marilyn will notice!"

"I'll get you a black belt. In fact, I'll go out and buy you one."

"This wedding wasn't meant to be!"

A new and substantial injection of cash enabled Susan to go to Montreal on a buying trip. She asked me if there was any chance that I could meet her there. Spend some time going over plans for expansion. I had some business that needed to be done in Montreal, so why not combine things?

On my way there in the company jet, what she'd said at the funeral suddenly came back to me. With a jolt. "If you need me for anything, call me." I hadn't called her, but she'd called me, and she'd told me not to say anything to Paul. I wondered, Was this trip about business or something else? Did she feel sorry for me, or was she feeling a little needy herself?

She met me at the airport looking absolutely smashing.

6

We've got the limousines lined up at the entrance of the casino. All nine of them. I feel like Noah, marshalling the people two-by-two into their assigned places. Here's how we've planned this:

Car 1: The Groom and me.

Car 2: Reena and George Framingham, their son David, Lorena and Cy Godfrey.

Car 3: Denise and Rick Godfrey, their kids Jason and Frances Anne, my girls Kim and Kate.

Car 4: Barb and Joe Pasloski, their boy Tod, Joanne and Don Tanana.

Car 5: Sam Godfrey, Janie Choy, Milt Godfrey, Porky Draper.

Car 6: Susan and Paul Hodges, their girls Judy and Jean, Deedie Charlesworth.

Car 7: Jill and Gord Barber, Wally Barber, Dodie Zaporzan, Wally's daughter Marni Joseph.

Car 8: Dolores and Jack McPhee, their daughter Sandra, Garfield Henderson.

Car 9: Catherine Barber, Geraldine Henderson and The Bride.

So far, cars 2, 3, 4 and 6 are filled as planned and ready to go. Garfield Henderson is sitting alone in Car 8, chewing on a cigar that the driver made him put out when he got in. Jack McPhee comes rushing out of the casino, half in and half out of his suit jacket. His wife and daughter, virtual look-alikes with their auburn hair and light green dresses, hurry out behind him holding hands. The guy in charge of the limos directs them to Car 8.

We've got an argument going at Car 5. Marni Joseph wants to ride in that limo instead of the one she was assigned. I'm not sure what she wants most, to get away from her father and Dodie or to ride with Sam—she met him last night and thought he was cool. Porky Draper comes out carrying a giant manhattan-on-the-rocks, loving the fact that Las Vegas lets you carry a drink with you on the street. He says it's fine with him if Marni wants to ride in his limo. Despite the fact that there's lots of room, Janie chooses to sit in Milt's lap. Sam, in dark glasses, seems oblivious to everyone—he's tapping his foot to some rhythm in his head.

Cars 5, 7 and 8 are now ready to go.

Dad comes out wearing a white boutonniere in the lapel of his brand new suit. Not the suit he was having trouble with—we went to a mall and got him re-outfitted, right off the rack. It doesn't quite go with his pink shirt and purple tie, but what the hell. He waves to everyone as we walk to the front car.

"Is Marilyn ready?" I ask him.

"How should I know? I've been avoiding her. Bad luck to see her on the day, isn't it?"

"If you believe in those superstitions."

"Christ, it's probably bad luck to marry her! With her record for knocking off husbands." He keeps waving. "Hi, Jason. Hi, Kimmy. Hi, Francesca Angelica."

I look back to the end of the procession. Catherine and her mother and Mrs. Henderson are getting into their car.

"Okay," I say to the driver of the lead car. "Let's go."

We head down The Strip and turn onto Warm Springs Road. The wind blows clouds of dust and grit in from the southwest, blurring the sun with a sandy haze. The chapel sits out on the bald prairie like an oasis for Barbie dolls. We have to stop at the parking lot entrance to let another procession of limos come out.

"Can we all fit in there?" Dad asks.

"No problem," says the limo driver.

The last of the departing limos leaves and we drive in. Dad and I get out and there's a woman in blouse and slacks beckoning to us from the chapel door. I take Dad's arm and lead him to her, both of us shielding our eyes from the blowing dirt.

"Hiya," says the woman. "You the Godfrey-Foss party?"

"Right," I say.

"How're you paying?"

"American Express."

"Good. I'm Rosalyn Blaine."

We shake hands and she takes us into the chapel. It has about forty chairs set up in a few rows. That's about all there's room for. We go to the front of the chapel which is dominated by a huge bouquet of fake flowers. Beside that stands a tall, erect woman with short blond hair and glasses. She's wearing a business-like cotton dress.

"This is Reverend Mary Polk," says Rosalyn. "She'll be conducting the service."

"How do you do," I say, shaking Mary Polk's hand. "I'm Hugh Godfrey, the best man. And this is my father, Max Godfrey, the groom."

"It's never too late, huh?" says Mary, shaking Dad's hand.

"Just get us through this," says Dad.

Two guys in T-shirts and jeans emerge from an anteroom.

"These two will be handling the videotaping," says Rosalyn. "Okay, Godfreys, you stand right there. You could step a little further forward, Dad, and we'll get a nice shot—whoa, that's good." She hears the door slam and she looks up to see my sister and George and David coming in. "All right, folks—hi. You friends of the bride or the groom?"

"The groom," says Reena, looking around the cramped quarters with a critical eye.

"Fine. Take those seats right there by the window—that's it, move right on over to the window."

"Mr. Groom, sir," says the guy with the video camera. "You'll have to move a step to the left."

"We've got an X on the floor for guys like you, Dad," says Rosalyn. "See that X? Stand on it, okay?"

When I see Susan and Paul come in with their little girls, I think, How much does she want me to tell him? What does she want me to say?

That's what I worry about through the short and snappy service.

Mary Polk turns Dad and Marilyn around to face the assembled gathering. "Ladies and gentlemen," she says, "let me present Mr. and Mrs. Max Godfrey."

We all applaud. Even tiny Tod Pasloski claps his hands. Marilyn beams. She's wearing a lovely aquamarine dress and a matching hat. She looks handsome and radiant. I go to her and give her a hug and a kiss.

"Welcome to the family, Marilyn," I say.

"Thank you," says my new stepmother. "Oh, Hugh, didn't you

just love the service?"

"Did you notice how I got God into it?" says Mary Polk. "Not many do in Las Vegas, you know."

"Okay, everybody," says Rosalyn Blaine, "this way out."

7

s e v e n

"Sue's mother and dad offered to come to Toronto to look after Jean and Judy," says Paul, "but we thought we'd like them with us. We're glad we brought them; they're having a ball."

Paul, Susan and I have come to my room between the service and the reception. My daughter, Kate, is baby-sitting the kids in their room. I'm not at all happy about this—I should be with Dad—but it is time we told Paul. I can't believe he hasn't figured it out by now.

"How are your parents, Sue?" I ask. I hand both of them drinks.

"Oh, Dad's getting all set to retire and Mom's minding Nadia's two little ones—she married again, you know. Nobody knows what to do about Boris—they say he's knocked somebody up. Can you believe it, in this day and age?"

"You're telling me!" I say. "I swear kids are harder to bring up now than ever."

"Shark," says Susan, "shouldn't you—"

I hesitate, unwilling to engage Paul in anything other than polite banalities. Susan frowns fiercely.

"Right, yes. Paul . . . I think maybe you've been kept in the dark too long. I guess in some ways I wish . . . I mean, we're all mature adults here—"

There is a long moment of silence as Paul stares first at me, then at Susan.

"No!" he says suddenly, draining of colour. "No, you didn't!"

"Paul, let him finish."

Paul jumps to his feet. "All those times the two of you got together!"

"Paul, Paul," I say.

But there's no reasoning with him. He hits me, right in the face. I drop back into an armchair—not from the punch, more out of shock. Wow. It's something I wish *I'd* done. Why hadn't I punched his weak, pretty, long-suffering face years ago?

"Paul, for Christ's sake!" says Susan. She's as surprised as I am. She

229

grabs his arms as if she expects him to go after me again. "We didn't do anything."

"What?" He's standing there, posing like a boxer. Waiting for the referee to let me up so he can finish me off.

"Listen, Paul," says Susan. "We're trying to tell you The Shark invested in the stores. I never could've expanded without him. We were wrong not to tell you—"

"You haven't been—"

"No, Paul," I say, touching the tender place on my cheek. I look at my fingers: no blood.

"Shark, I'm sorry," says Paul. "Are you okay?"

"I'll live—"

"Paul, how *could* you? Your oldest and dearest friend—"

"It's all right," I say, as Paul helps me to my feet. Oldest and dearest? *Like hell.*

"Shark, you know I'll pay you whatever you—"

There's a knock at the door. The three of us are silent. We stare at the door for several moments.

"I'd better answer it," I say.

I open the door.

"Hugh, I can't go through with—" It's Dad. "Oh, blazes, I didn't know you had company."

What actually happened in Montreal:

She drove downtown from the airport and we talked about where we could go and she said we might as well go to her hotel and so we did and we were both giddy as we walked through the lobby and got on the elevator and when we got to the room we tossed off our coats and she was wearing a gorgeous sweater and these tight jeans and we called room service and had then bring us up a pot of steaming hot coffee and some nice plump muffins and butter and I took off my jacket and my tie and I opened my brief case and took out the rolled drawings I'd got from the architect and the photos and the spec sheets from the shopping centres and we spread everything out on the carpet and we knelt there like a couple of kids playing marbles and Christ we got excited visualizing the new storefronts and doodling some ideas for decor and displays and I was up and down getting things from my brief case and sips of coffee and bites of muffin and she was up and down with sheer exuberance and she had to go for a pee twice and we got all sweaty and breathing hard just talking and sketching and realizing that this dream was going to be—as she put it—"a fucking reality".

8

_e i g h t_

A good wedding reception depends on two things: lots of booze and great speeches. If the wedding is dry and the speeches are dull or amateurish, you have a disaster on your hands. If the booze flows freely, it doesn't matter what the speakers say or how they say it. If everyone's sober, the speakers better be damned entertaining. Good booze plus good speeches equal a memorable time.

Dad's reception was okay because there was lots of good booze. (The food was good, too; Catherine made sure of that.) But the speeches were lousy.

Senator Henderson gave the Toast to the Bride and he was terrible. He forgot Dad's name twice and called him Dudley. He tried to wing it with no notes and, when he couldn't remember what came next, he pretended that forgetting was cute, and he made fun of himself, which was all the more painful coming from a politician. When he finally pulled out his notes, he couldn't find his place and he dropped the pages. At last, he mercifully abandoned the speech and said, "Ladies and gentlemen, please raise your glasses and we'll all taste the bride."

Dad wasn't much better. While he spoke, he nervously played with one of the mauve match books that had "Max and Marilyn" printed on them in fluorescent ink. He tore matches out and nearly set himself on fire. That distracted people from his speech and lucky thing, too, because he got cruder and cruder until I reminded him that there were little kids present. Sam was the only one who laughed—he loves other people's discomfort.

Marilyn spoke longer than Dad did and told us again and again how delighted she was to have been married in a quaint little chapel and how fortunate she was to have met a grand fellow like Max whose love of gambling had led him to take this real gamble on _her_. What she said wasn't so bad, but she made it into one long sentence that went on and on and on and wore everybody out.

I was pathetic myself. Too much on my mind, I guess—Catherine's

232

complaints, looking out for Dad, the dunking by Janie, and that terrible episode with Paul and Susan. (I should've retaliated. I've always preached that violence doesn't settle anything, but, just this one time, I should've cleaned his clock.) I hardly knew what I was saying, and I forgot to read the telegram from Paul's son, Rob. (He and Fiona are off in Nicaragua with Farmers for Peace.)

All through dinner, people got into the habit of clinking glasses to have the bride and groom kiss. We decided to stop it by asking people to perform—a song, a recitation, a skit—if they wanted to see a kiss. This resulted in some corny lyrics like "Max and Marilyn, Max and Marilyn, go together like a church and carillon . . ."

Toward the end of dinner, Sam came to me and told me he was taking off for L.A.

"With Janie?"

"No. With Milt."

We're dancing to taped music. Dad seems to be overdoing it, waltzing, jiving and bopping with every woman but Marilyn. He's red in the face—too red. She's dancing, too, sometimes with her matron of honour. I'm so glad of the activity, I find myself dancing every dance.

My dance partners:

1. *Reena.*
   (At a sisterly distance.)
   "Hugh, have you looked at Dad's face? Do you think he's all right?"
   "Boiled lobster is his best colour."
   "What are you going to do if he drops dead on us?"

2. *Barbara.*
   (With a daughterly tendency to lead.)
   "Things seem to be going well between you and Joe, kid."
   "He's being a real doll, Daddy. He's taking us out to see the dam tomorrow."
   "Great."
   "But, Dad, why did you let Sam take off for Los Angeles?"
   "Have I ever had any influence on that boy? It's all right, he's

going with Uncle Milt."

"But, Dad, surely you know Uncle Milt is gay."

3. *Deedie.*

(She tries to dance too close, her large mouth invading my comfort zone.)

"It's a different kind of wedding, Shark. What would Frances think?"

"She'd be loving every minute of it."

"Don't get me wrong—I'm glad I came. But you wonder how two people their age could choose to come here."

"It's Dad's favourite city in all the world."

"I know. Well, it takes all kinds, doesn't it?"

4. *Frances Anne.*

(I carry her on one arm.)

"Don't you like it better up here? You don't have to do the dance steps and Grampa Shark doesn't have to bend way over."

"Shark. Sharkshark."

"Do you like being at a party with the grown-ups?"

"Shokshokshokshokshok."

"Oh oh. Did you do something in your pants?"

5. *Dodie.*

(We bop around to *Wasn't That a Party?*, our heads extended toward each other as we talk.)

"I'm here with Wally—you know, Catherine's brother?"

"Of course. You're Dodie."

"Right. The black sheep. I'm the siren that lured him away from his cute little wifey. You wouldn't believe the stress that caused the family. I don't think Catherine ever forgave him."

"Oh, I don't know. She thinks he's a lot happier."

"Yeah, *right.* If you believe that, then I'm a virgin and I've got a bridge I'd like to sell you."

"You don't think he's happy?"

"Let's forget about him for once in our lives. What about me?"

6. *Marni.*

(It's some kind of punk rock or acid rock or heavy metal and she's got her eyes closed and she's so into it, she can hardly stand it, and I try to keep up but I might as well not even be there.)

7. *Denise.*
(Overly conscious of her body and her scent, I hold her too far from me and botch several waltz steps.)
"Did you see the new ring Rick bought me?"
"No—oh—that's lovely."
"I think so."
"What's the occasion?"
"No occasion. He's just sweet. Do you notice anything different?"
"About Rick?"
"No, me."
"Your hair—you've—"
"No. Guess again."
"I can't guess."
"Don't you think I look thinner?"
"Denise, you've always been so trim—"
"I had fat deposits removed from my abdomen."
"You? Fat deposits?"
"Shark, don't tell me you don't see a difference. Come *on.*"

8. *Marilyn.*
(We ignore each other's clumsy moves and the two or three times we step on each other's feet.)
"At last I get to dance with the bride."
"Oh, Hugh, isn't this a marvellous evening, and isn't that father of yours the most gallant gentleman, the way he spreads himself around the room and makes sure all the ladies have a chance to dance with him? Do you know that I haven't danced with him since we started the whole thing off with the very first dance, the one you had us do at the very beginning after the speeches? Oh, Hugh, I'm so lucky to have him and we're so lucky that you organized this whole affair, it's so absolutely marvellous that we were all able to come here, and one of the nicest touches was taking everybody in all those limousines out to that little gingerbread chapel . . ."

9. *Susan.*
(Dancing close but seeming tense.)

"Are you avoiding me?"

"No! I'm sorry if I—"

"Let's run away together."

"Sue, really—"

"I don't know if Paul believes us yet, so why don't we get together later? Might as well be hung for a sheep as a goddam goat."

"Lamb."

"What?"

"A goddam lamb."

"Shit—we aren't getting anywhere with this dance, are we?"

"No—"

"Let's sit this one out. We obviously weren't meant for each other."

10. *Janie.*

(Dancing very close.)

"Are you avoiding me?"

"No! I'm sorry if I—"

"I like you, Shark. You're so much more—I don't know—so much more *suave* than your son."

"Thank you. He can be a bit of a fool sometimes."

"You're telling me. Imagine him taking off like that."

"Pretty inconsiderate."

"I didn't want to go with him."

"I don't blame you."

"Hold me closer, okay?"

"Like . . . ?"

"That's nice."

"Yes."

"Mmmmm."

"Mmhmm."

"You know, under this miniskirt, I'm not wearing a thing."

"Oh?"

"Think about it."

11. *Catherine.*

(Dancing at a discreet distance.)

"Poor mother. She's getting hopelessly dotty."

"She's happy, though."

"Is Max avoiding her?"

"Oh, I don't think so."

"He seems a little intimidated."

"He'll be okay. I think they're both doing amazingly well."

"Have you and I ever danced before?"

"We must have."

"You're light on your feet."

"So are you."

"I saw you dancing with that Janie person. She was stuck to you like Velcro."

"It's the way the young people like to dance. Isn't it?"

"Ohh!"

There's a thump. Dad's lying on the floor. I run over to him. Reena's there before me.

"I *knew* he'd overdo it!" she says.

"What happened?"

Lorena gasps, "We were just dancing—!"

"He was bopping it up," says Marni. "Then he just sort of slipped and whammo he's down."

"Dad! Dad, are you okay?"

"Huh?" He opens his eyes.

"Dad, can you move?"

"Sure I can." He sits up. "Oww! My hip. Hey, get back to your damn dancing, I'm okay. Ouch!"

9

Dad's missing. I had another dance with Catherine and for a few
seconds I took my eyes off him. When I looked around for him, he
was gone. Kim said he told her he was going to walk off the aches.

Everyone else is accounted for; no-one's gone with him. I check
the banquet room washroom, but he isn't there. I check a couple of
other washrooms. No sign of him. I tell people not to let Marilyn
know we're worried; for now, I'll do the looking alone.

I go upstairs to his room. I have a key and when he doesn't answer
my knock I let myself in. I call his name. I look in the bathtub and
under the bed, even behind doors and drapes. He isn't there.

I start to get frantic. Has he chickened out and flown the coop?

Then it comes to me—I could kick myself. What's the one place
where he feels at ease? The casino!

I find him at one of the blackjack tables. All the stools are occupied
and he has three or four piles of chips in front of him. He's just
beaten the dealer and collected a new pile.

"Dad!" I say into his good ear. "I've been looking for you."

"I've been right here."

"I think you'd better come with me. Some of our guests are getting
worried."

"Okay, okay. Spoil my fun when I'm on a roll." He collects his
chips and steps down from his stool. "Ouch."

"You told Kim you were just going to walk off the ache. Is it still
bothering you?"

"Naw. I'm fit as a marathon runner. Hold on while I cash these in."

As he makes his way over to the cashier, he hobbles.

When we get back to the reception, we learn that the bride has
"retired" and Dad is supposed to meet her in the Bridal Suite. Reena
looks from him to me with a frown, but I wave her off and accompany

him upstairs.

When we step off the elevator, he says, "I can't go in there yet. Could you pour me a drink?"

"Dad. Marilyn's going to be worried."

"Pour me a drink! What kind of a goddam best man are you?"

Reluctantly, I take him to my room on the floor below.

"What'll it be?"

"A good stiff rum and coke."

I pour him one and he takes a healthy swig of it.

"Ahhhh." He wipes his mouth with the back of his hand and belches. "Son, tell me. What in blazes did I do in that chapel?"

"Come on, Dad, you know exactly what you did. You married a handsome and charming woman."

"But *why*?"

"Why does anyone get married? Dad, we've been through this." I'm getting weary.

"I can still tie my own shoe laces. I have a very good battery-powered back-scratcher. I make a perfect poached egg. *Why do I need a wife?*"

"Marilyn's a good conversationalist and she'll keep track of your glasses and your pills."

"Like hell she will. Gimme another drink. Stronger!"

I refill his glass and glance at my watch.

"I don't think you should drink much more, Dad. You've got to get to the Bridal Suite."

"Son, Marilyn . . . well, she's an amazing woman . . ."

"You're lucky."

"But she's demanding."

"Dad—"

"I'm not sure what she's going to expect."

"Dad, this is embarrassing—"

"How do you think *I* feel!"

"Dad, she's an understanding woman. She won't just snap her fingers and expect you to—"

"Oh, no? You don't know Marilyn, and I don't know if . . ."

"I can't believe this. Surely you've slept together before."

"We've *slept*—"

"Good lord, you haven't!"

"It's not that I couldn't have, but . . ."

"Pop, have a nice cup of tea with her. You can have room service bring it to you. Play a little gin rummy. So what if you don't—"

"I told you, she expects things. Sometimes I think she's a little crazy—"

"Dad."

"Okay, okay." He downs the drink.

"Dad, you've got to go. This is ridiculous. Come on." I walk him to the door. "Go. Your bride awaits."

"Um—which way is it to the Bridal Suite again?"

"I'll take you there."

When I get back to my room, the phone is ringing.

"Hello?"

"Hi there."

"Hi, Susan."

"Paul's asleep and so are the girls. What're you up to?"

"I just delivered my father to his bride. Now I'm going to try to relax."

"I'll be right up there for a nightcap."

"Sue."

"Okay, then, I won't."

"It's a nice thought, though."

"Yeah."

"Good night, Sue."

"We both love ya, Shark."

I sit on the edge of my heart-shaped bed. I refuse to lie back and see myself up there in the mirror, alone. It's too depressing. I think of Susan all sweaty with excitement about the stores. I think of Janie Choy without underpants. I try not to think about what my father is doing.

What the hell. I'm going to call her.

I take a deep breath and dial.

"Hello?"

"Hello, it's The Shark."

"I hear you found him."

"And delivered him to the blushing bride."

"My poor mother."

"Would you like to go down to the lobby for a nightcap?"

"What a wonderful idea."

"I'll meet you in the lobby by the elevators."

We're in the lounge listening to a combo play Golden Oldies. Catherine's glittery evening outfit suits her perfectly. She's put on new lipstick and her perfume is intoxicating. She sits almost regally, her long neck erect. Her short grey hair glistens.

"Who would have thought, when you hid in the closet on my wedding night, that our parents would be getting married twenty-eight years later." She chuckles.

"Or that you and I would be having a drink together in Las Vegas."

"Do you think you'll ever marry again, Shark?"

"I don't know."

"You will. I know what a good wife and mother Fran was. You'll miss not being married."

I fumble for a reply. "I'm amazed that *you* never remarried."

"I like being on my own. I don't know if I could stand to have another person around now."

I wince slightly, but manage to cover it with a smile. "Listen, do you know that my father was worried that your mother was going to demand something he was unable to—"

"Shark, really!" She laughs, more heartily than I can ever remember. "Mother was worried that *he* was going to expect—oh, my god!"

"That's incredible."

"I hope she's not trying to phone me. Do you know that I phoned her on my—"

"Cath, excuse me for interrupting, but isn't that your mother and my dad coming into the bar?"

"What? Yes, of course, it is, but—"

We both sit in awe watching Dad and Marilyn head straight for the little stage where the combo is playing. Dad speaks briefly to the leader. The guy nods and hands Dad the mike. The combo breaks into fanfare music.

"Ladies and gentlemen! Can I have your attention!" My dad's voice booms through the loudspeakers. "I have an important announcement to make. The next round of drinks is on my bride and me. We are proud to tell you that we have just consummated our marriage!"

There is a smattering of laughter, and then applause, and then the people in the lounge stand up and clap and cheer and the bartender and the two servers stop what they're doing to clap and cheer and the guys in the combo clap and cheer and some people yell, "Bravo!" and some go up and shake the couple's hands, and the applause spreads to the casino and pretty soon the whole goddam hotel is giving my dad and his wife a standing ovation.

part five

Janie Choy Show:
1999

ANNOUNCER

For this special Valentine's Day edition of *The Janie Choy Show*, we go out to the Gatineau Hills in Quebec—across the river from the nation's capital—and the picturesque area called Sky Ridge. Our host, Janie Choy, is on location outside the home of the Honourable Hugh Godfrey.

(Cut to JANIE CHOY on Basswood Lane, with snow-covered hills and forest behind her, a flat-roofed two-storey residence visible up the hill, approached by a winding gravel driveway. We get a panoramic shot of the area; there are signs of downed trees from the ice storm of 1998. Camera zooms in slowly on JANIE, standing at the foot of the driveway. As camera draws in more closely, we see the names on the country-style mailbox beside JANIE: "Barber/Godfrey".)

JANIE

(Dressed in stylish parka and speaking into a cordless mike as camera moves in on her) Good afternoon. Just a short time from now, the home behind me will be the site of an incredibly romantic event. More about that in a minute, but first, I want to go back to another romantic happening that took place right here a few years ago. Not long after he was elected to Parliament, Hugh Godfrey moved into this house with one of the country's best-known catering consultants, Catherine Barber. *(Camera leaves JANIE and slowly zooms in on the house.)* This scenic district is only about a twenty-minute drive from downtown Ottawa, and Godfrey and Barber chose it to be their home away from home—they'd live here whenever Parliament was in session. They also maintain a home in Hugh's suburban Toronto constituency. It was right here, shortly after they moved in, that Godfrey and Barber threw a New Year's Eve house-warming party and invited a few hundred of their closest friends. *(Camera lingers on the house, panning slowly across the front, along the upper deck which is accessible from the*

244

second storey, settling for a moment on the sliding glass doors into the living-dining area. Despite reflection of the overcast sky on the glass, it is possible to see shadowy forms of people inside.) On that occasion, an hour before midnight, Catherine and Hugh had a surprise for everyone.

(Cut to footage of the New Year's Eve party.)

JANIE

(Voice-over) I happened to be one of the invited guests that evening and I took along a cameraman because the hosts were two of Ottawa's up-and-coming movers and shakers.

CATHERINE

(On tape, surrounded by people crowding the living-room area—a log fire crackling in the fireplace behind her—she rings a dinner bell for attention) Could I have your attention for a moment, please? *(HUGH emerges from the crowd and she takes his hand. Two servers bearing trays of champagne make sure everyone has a glass. The noise level drops to a few chuckles and remarks.)* We'd like to make an announcement. *(There is silence.)* Hugh and I are going to be married.

(Camera pans the room as everyone cheers loudly.)

HUGH

(On tape, calling for people to be quiet) Wait. Wait. There's more to the announcement. *(Sudden silence)*

CATHERINE

(On tape) Because so many of our friends are here, and because we want a minimum of fuss and bother, and because we don't want you to feel you have to go out and buy us gifts, we have decided to make things easy for everybody. We are going to hold the wedding right here and right now. *(Gasps and screams from the people, then applause)*

JANIE

(Voice over) Only one person besides Catherine and Hugh knew about the plan, and that was Judge Ozzie Mitchell, the man you see taking his book from his pocket and joining the newlyweds-to-be in front of the fireplace.

(Cut to JANIE live.)

JANIE
What made that evening even more romantic was the fact that Hugh Godfrey confessed to me he'd wanted Catherine Barber to be his bride for a very long time—since high school back in Winnipeg. Both were married once before, Hugh to Frances Drake, who died in 1985, and Catherine to Paul Hodges, whom she divorced in the late 1960s. *(She starts walking up the Barber/Godfrey driveway.)* Now, here, on Valentine's Day, 1999, we're anticipating another exciting event. We often hear people say there's too much cynicism and jadedness in our society, but I think, by what you'll see transpire here this afternoon, you're going to believe that romance is alive and well as we approach the Millennium. I want you to meet a young woman who is one of the key players in our real-life drama. *(As Janie reaches the crest of the hill, where the driveway curves into the garage, a young woman comes out of the front door of the house. She's wearing a stylish ski-jacket and pants and nothing covering her long blond hair.)* Let me introduce you to Hugh Godfrey's youngest daughter, who practises law in Toronto— Kate Godfrey. Hi, Kate.

KATE
Good afternoon, Janie.

JANIE
Kate, give our audience a little background on what is going to happen here today.

KATE
Well, I guess you could say I'm a bit of a computer nerd— or geek, is it?

JANIE
Either one.

KATE
I spend a lot of my time on the Internet. I've been meeting people that way for a while now, but, about six months ago, I started to exchange e-mail messages with a fellow in Australia. He lives in Port Douglas, which is north of Cairns in Queensland and he's connected with one of the companies that take tourists out to the Great Barrier Reef. I love exotic fish, have a number of different species in a tank at home in Toronto, and he told me about the many kinds you see in

the Coral Sea. He said he regularly went out on one of the company's large-scale catamarans to scuba-dive and see the fish first-hand.

JANIE
At some point, you started to be more interested in him than you were in the fish or the reef.

KATE
(Chuckling) He asked me if I was single and I said I was and he said I should come down there for a visit. It was tempting, but I couldn't take the time I'd need and, besides, I wasn't quite sure about him. You meet a lot of creeps on the 'Net and maybe he was telling me stories that weren't true, but somehow I believed what he told me. He said he was divorced. We discussed his background. We discussed everything under the sun—what kinds of things we liked to eat, what things bugged us, what sports we liked—well, you know, everything. One day, he phoned me. He sounded very nice.

JANIE
Then you exchanged photos.

KATE
There was a picture of him on his Website, but we thought we'd like to see real photographs and we sent some to each other. I was a little surprised that he was older than he sounded. But I told him I didn't care about age.

JANIE
What did your family say?

KATE
They didn't try to give me advice. They could see I was pretty enthralled with this fellow, moreso than with any man I'd met up to then. They've always said I was level-headed, so they didn't interfere. I've been living away from home for years, so this was my call. I think, deep down, they thought it was an infatuation that would go away.

JANIE
Then, one day, he proposed.

KATE

On Christmas Day. By e-mail.

JANIE

And you answered by e-mail.

KATE

Yes, but I didn't accept right away. I wanted some time to think about it. I accepted three days later.

JANIE

Without ever seeing him live.

KATE

That's right. I checked on a few things. I made sure he worked where he said he worked and I made sure he had bank accounts in the banks he said he had accounts in. I wasn't being mercenary; it was just a detail worth checking. My lawyer instinct. We exchanged medical records. He sent me gifts about every week—clothing, jewellery. I started sending him things. I had a good feeling about him.

JANIE

Tell us what's happening here today.

KATE

We thought it'd be fun to meet on Valentine's Day. He said it was possible for him to get away and come to Canada. Then he suggested we get married the same day we meet. Why wait? he said, but he wasn't pushy. The idea was so off-the-wall, I had to go along with it. So I suggested we get married right here, where Dad married Catherine. John's been on the way from Australia for two days now and he was scheduled to arrive in Ottawa this morning. He's coming out here with a friend of his from Toronto who's going to be the best man. By the way, did I tell you John is Canadian? He moved down under a few years ago.

(A tall, middle-aged man appears from the front door.)

JANIE

Here's your father, one of our newest cabinet ministers, the Honourable Hugh Godfrey. Hugh, your daughter, Kate, just mentioned that the prospective groom is a Canadian but I understand there is an unusual twist to this story.

HUGH

(Wry smile) Rather unusual, indeed. We found out early on that he was an old friend of mine from Winnipeg. I was astounded. I wondered if this was a coincidence or—

KATE

Dad thought it might be intended as some sort of elaborate joke on him. I told him John and I deserved more credit than that!

JANIE

The groom and the best man are on their way at this moment. Is the minister here?

KATE

They're bringing him with them.

JANIE

And the maid of honour?

KATE

My good friend, Darcia. I think she's coming out now.

(The front door opens and a distinguished-looking middle-aged woman comes out with a woman about KATE's age.)

JANIE

Here's Kate's stepmother, Catherine Barber, along with the maid of honour, Darcia—

KATE

McGeachie.

(JANIE and camera move over to CATHERINE and DARCIA.)

JANIE

Catherine, Darcia, don't you think this whole event is a little crazy?

DARCIA

Wild and crazy! Kate has a knack for doing stuff like this. In law school, she was completely unpredictable.

CATHERINE
I think this is the most exciting thing that's happened around here since Hugh was re-elected.

HUGH
(Off camera) I believe our groom is approaching.

(Camera pans to the road, where a car has turned into Basswood Lane. It is a dark blue Toyota Avalon with Ontario plates. A small crowd has begun to assemble near the driveway.)

JANIE
(Off camera) Here it is, folks, the moment we've been waiting for, and it's happening right on time. The groom, John Evets, from Port Douglas, Queensland, Australia, is not going to keep his bride waiting. He's about to meet Kate Godfrey for the first time after a six-month courtship carried out entirely on the Internet. The car is turning into the Godfrey driveway. It's a gorgeous winter day here in the Gatineau; the sun has come out, the snow-covered trees are still, and I know there's at least one woman whose heart is beating just a little faster right now.

(The car drives slowly up to the space in front of the house. Kate goes over to meet it. Two of the car doors open. Out of the back seat steps a young minister in a clerical collar and a black suit. Out of the driver's side steps a middle-aged man in a raincoat. He takes off his sunglasses and walks around the front of the car.)

JANIE
(Off camera) There's the best man, Paul Hodges, going to open the passenger door for the groom . . .

PAUL
Hi, Janie!

JANIE
(Off camera) He's opening the door . . . and Kate walks over—amazing how calm she seems under the circumstances—and out comes the groom . . . *(A swarthy man in a black leather jacket and sunglasses and holding an Australian bushman's hat steps out of the car; he has a receding hairline and gun-metal grey hair down to his shoulders.)* Look at that! He tossed his hat away and he's taking Kate into his arms and they're

kissing. *(Camera zooms in on the bride and groom. They pause to look at each other and then resume kissing.)*

PAUL

(Off camera) How are you, Shark?

HUGH

(Off camera) A little dazed by all this, frankly. When did Steve become John Evets?

PAUL

Well, as you know, he's always been Evets to me, and John's his middle name. He wasn't trying to trick anybody. He just wanted a new identity when he moved down there.

HUGH

Susan couldn't come— ?

PAUL

(Proudly) She's such a dynamo. She had to go to New York for a hush-hush meeting. It looks like she's found a corporation that's prepared to pay big money for her stores.

(STEVE and KATE break from their embrace and turn to face the camera and everyone.)

JANIE

Hugh and Catherine go to greet their prospective son-in-law. . . .

STEVE

(Shaking HUGH's hand and laughing) Hi, Dad! *(He gives HUGH a hug.)*

HUGH

(Holding STEVE at arm's length) You know, if you had a little patience, you could wait and marry my granddaughter.

CATHERINE

(Giving STEVE a quick hug) Steve, you old charmer. This is amazing.

JANIE

(Moving into their midst) John, Kate, can you describe the feeling of seeing each other in person for the first time?

251

STEVE

Oh, God, how to describe—it bloody well beats bungee jumping, let me tell you. My life was pretty much in the toilet when I left Canada—but it's taken a very sudden turn for the better.

KATE

Can I say this on TV—I can't wait to get him to bed—

JANIE

Well, I understand we have a few formalities first—

(STEVE and KATE laugh. Camera frames JANIE with STEVE and KATE arm-in-arm.)

JANIE

We're going to go inside the Godfrey-Barber residence now for the wedding ceremony . . .

(Fade to scene inside the house, near the fireplace, where other family members, like DENISE GODFREY and BARB PASLOSKY, are standing, awaiting the proceedings. In front of them, seated, is HUGH's father, MAX GODFREY, now in his 90s but still looking alert. MINISTER, smiling, stands with his back to the fireplace. As in the earlier video, there is a crackling log fire burning and there are servers dispatching refreshments. Camera picks up JANIE and STEVE and KATE et al as they enter the room. KATE quickly introduces her fiance around.)

JANIE

Here in the Godfrey-Barber home, you are about to witness, live, the wedding of these two cyber-space lovebirds. What a fitting way to celebrate Valentine's Day . . .

MINISTER

(Looking around, smiling, overly conscious of being on TV) Are we ready? Paul, over here . . . that's it. *(PAUL and STEVE and KATE and DARCIA take their places in front of MINISTER. Camera moves to side to pick up the five principals. The others are grouped in a semi-circle behind them)* Okay. We can start. Good afternoon, everybody. We are gathered here today . . .